If the Fates Allow

MARJA GRAHAM

If your first reaction to being taken care of is to panic, this one's for you.

Playlist

Have Yourself a Merry Little Christmas – Phoebe Bridgers

after the holidays – Faith Zapata

Nice To Each Other – Olivia Dean

Wish That You Were Here – Florence + The Machine

Let Me Love You – Amber Mark

There She Goes – The La's

Please Be Rude – Gigi Perez

FTSG – Emma Andersen

Someone New- Hozier

Author's Note

Though this is a lighter read, there are some topics that readers may choose to avoid due to preference or for their mental health.

Financial Trauma (and the stress, hypervigilance, and anxiety that comes from it)

Incarcerated Parent (White Collar Crime)

Discussions of food restrictions relating to athlete training

Sexual Harassment

Explicit Sexual Content (including elements of bondage)

1

Henri

W hat's your job again?" Porter asks as he fidgets at the table next to me. His blue eyes jump from my face to the heavy oak doors of Bide, a quaint restaurant with warm lighting and dark wood accents that *Spitfire Magazine* has labeled as *the perfect place to make your midwestern parents feel at home in the heart of Manhattan* on its iconic, yearly "Feast in The City" list.

My late-lunch date is handsome in the way he doesn't know that he is, with freshly-cut honey-brown hair, a crooked nose that his glasses insist on sliding off of, and persistent stubble hugging his square jaw. Not handsome enough to typically excuse forgetting basic facts about me before meeting his parents for Thanksgiving, but this isn't exactly a typical situation.

"I'm a freelance consultant," I say, flashing my practiced reassuring smile.

He flushes, nodding and dislodging his glasses yet again. "Oh, yeah."

"If they ask for more I'll answer, but usually parents don't. I've done this plenty, so if you feel like you're stuck just tap my foot with yours under the table twice and I'll take over." I tap his foot with mine to demonstrate the motion.

My clients tend to be anxious, which is understandable. I would be anxious too if this wasn't my hundredth time pretending to be in a committed relationship with someone I've come to know through a series of surveys and interviews.

The entry doors open, letting in a flurry of snow along with a brunette woman in a peacoat and a tall, blond man with fogged-up glasses that he pulls from his face.

Porter pushes back from the table abruptly, causing the pristine white plates to clatter against the glass table top. I rise with him to meet his parents as they're led to us by the hostess.

"This place is just like Nanette's, isn't it Jacob?" Audre McCabe asks her husband, who has finally gotten his wire-framed glasses to clear.

Both are real estate agents in Ohio, members of their local bowling league, and advocates for their only child to move closer to home and out of the city. All of which are facts I have written down on a stack of notecards tucked into the side pocket of my monstrously large purse, so they don't get lost in the extra changes of clothes I have stuffed inside.

My mission for the next hour? Not only help sidestep their pleas for him to return home, but also, with any luck, show them how much he belongs in Manhattan. If all goes well, the family will get through this late Thanksgiving lunch miraculously argument free.

"Yes, yes it does. The herbs," Jacob agrees.

"Rosemary," Audre asserts, then turns to her son with an expectant expression. "Porter, doesn't this make you miss home? I bet it's half the price and just as good, same as everything else."

"Well, I would miss him if he left," I say to disrupt the classic nostalgia angle she's employing. I grab Porter's sweaty hand and give it a quick squeeze. "I'm Juliet, his girlfriend."

Not my real name, of course. It's a fun part of the fantasy and I couldn't help but indulge. Maybe it would be different if I was a Sara or an Emily, but there aren't enough Henrietta's running around for me to just be handing out my actual name to folks.

And there's the added bonus that if you search Henrietta Elm you'll find about a thousand articles where my name is referenced alongside one Jeremy Elm, embezzler extraordinaire. I've got to give credit where credit's due, though, and the truth is, my dad knew how to steal money from his investors. He had a hundred million stowed away before the Feds started to sniff around. Call me crazy, but most people don't want their sons dating the daughter of one of the most infamous white collar criminals of the last decade.

"Oh my gosh, she's a stunner! You didn't tell us that," Audre gasps. I'm quickly learning she's the type of person who can make even a breath end in an exclamation point.

"I promise, I tried to," Porter says to me, a wince crinkling the corners of his eyes.

"They were just excited to see you! I mean, who wouldn't be?" I say, then turn to Audre. "You have to tell me where you got the coat from."

"Thrifted five years ago. They don't make clothes like this anymore, and there's no point buying something new every season if what you have already works," she says.

"I couldn't agree more; I've had this dress for years." I gesture to the simple, red knit dress that hits just above my knees. Guiding conversations. Slipping to the right clothes. Picking the appropriate restaurant. All of it is an art—how to be the perfect date. If I were to have worn something flashier, or invited them to a small plates restaurant instead, I would have set Porter up for failure. "That's why I think you'll love this place—classics, the way they should be. I'm so excited for you to try everything. Let's sit down and eat."

Porter wraps his arm around my waist as we wave to his parent's cab. He's relaxed considerably since the start of dinner, and a soft smile has found its way to his lips.

"Thanks for tonight," he says, stepping away now that their cab is out of sight, lost in the relentless stream of Manhattan traffic. "Really, I just wanted to get them off my back for the holidays, but they actually seem excited about coming back to visit again."

"Of course. You obviously love the city and they love you. I'm just helping bridge the gap," I explain.

Usually, that's how simple things are. Be the girlfriend, but more importantly, be the intermediary for people who care about each other, but need help communicating because they're scared to voice how they really feel. I'm the person at the dinner table my clients know is on their side no matter what.

If I'm there, they're not alone. Sometimes knowing you're not alone is all you need.

"Can I tip you?" He starts to reach for his pocket, his coat flapping wide in a gust of brisk late fall air.

"Please don't, you've already taken care of everything." My services during the holidays don't come cheap. "The rolls I snuck out in my bag are enough."

"I mean, damn, you really say all the right things. Is there a possibility . . ." His expression brightens with misplaced hope.

My stomach sinks. He had to go and ruin it, didn't he? God. I hate it when they get the wrong idea.

This happens plenty, which is why I stay as professional as possible—throw in as much business jargon as I can. I'm their perfect person for them for a few hours. I love doing it, helping in some small way that will hopefully support the relationships with those around them. But that's not the real me, and I need to remind them I'm not actually their perfect person.

I'm not saying the right things. The woman they're paying to play their partner is.

I'd blame the male loneliness epidemic, but that's probably the reason I have a semi-steady stream of income. I just wish men didn't mistake a moment of kindness for genuine interest.

"I'm glad I could help, but I should get going—Thanksgiving is busy for me. I'll send you the exit survey if you'd like to fill it out. Happy holidays, Porter," I say, and give a curt nod before striding away.

Stopping around the corner, I pull out my phone and text my roommate, Iris, to let her know I'm alive.

Me

The nice Midwesterners didn't serial kill me.

It's the nice ones who look like they'll make you pie who will get you.

Next up: Tech Moguls.

Iris

You should actually get with this one. Marry rich and get it over with.

"Fuck!" someone shouts from the sidewalk near me as a taxi zips by. Its tires squelch as they send a spray of gray slush onto the curb.

Returning my phone to my bag, I look up.

A tall man is standing on the curb, pinching the bridge of his slender nose, now muttering to himself. His brown hair is plastered to one side of his head, and freckles paint his skin, kissing their way along his nose and up his cheeks, dispersing over his neck and forehead.

"New to the city?" I ask, taking pity on him. And hey, it's the holiday season. It's not like I'm a festive person, but holidays mean work. And work means I'm not constantly stressing over my bank account, so I'm in a pretty good mood.

"Four years," he explains, giving a sheepish smile that causes his full bottom lip to pop into an accidental pout.

"Here, hop in with me." I step out onto the street, waving my hand over my head. If I wasn't working I'd take the subway, but I build taxis fare and other transportation costs into my contracts.

"Good luck getting one," he mutters.

A cab with its light on comes our way and it pulls to a stop next to me.

I'm halfway in when I look back out the open door. "Are you coming or what?" I can't help but sound a little smug.

He takes a moment to register the invitation then rushes over to join me as if I'll rescind my offer if he takes another second. I scoot the rest of the way in to make room for him, before giving the driver the address for *Pivoine*, a Michelin starred small plates restaurant listed in *Spitfire*.

This is my first Thanksgiving in New York, since I move every six months or so, and *Spitfire* has always been a pleasure read for me. Not a guilty pleasure—I don't believe in feeling guilty about one of the few things that makes me happy. Now that I have a chance to use their renowned "Feast in The City" list as a guide for my clients and not pay a dime for any of it, I sure as hell will.

"And you?" I ask my companion.

"I'm headed that way too."

"Great. Now look out the window until I tell you it's all clear." That's all the warning I give before stripping off my dress.

"Woah! What the hell are you doing?" he yelps as I lift my hips, skimming the cranberry knit fabric up over my thighs. He's turned a deep crimson, eyes plastered to the ceiling.

"Changing. I warned you." In one swift motion, I fling the dress over my head and to the floor. "It's not like I'm naked." Without my dress I'm still in a shapewear bodysuit and my fleece-lined leggings. Call me high maintenance, but I'd prefer not to freeze my ass off. "And you're the one who got into my taxi. This is less than I see on the L train most days."

Bending over, I pull out a vintage tweed Balmain dress, sticking with the same leather, knee-high Stuart Weitzman boots. It's one of three combinations I have for the five dates I have today, and I'm thankful that this next stop is known for its small portions so I won't explode. The dress is old—from my mother's closet—and can now be considered rare instead of last season.

It's a relic from a time when such luxuries were standard finds from mid-week shopping trips. Those types of things change when the SEC and FBI swoop in one day and change everything. But it's been six years since finding out my dad wasn't the person Mom or I thought he was, and there's no use in dwelling on it. I'm just one more girl with daddy issues, big whoop. Still, I've never been able to shake my affinity for high-end clothes, it's just that, now, I appreciate them more and have to buy them second-hand.

"I'm sorry if I'm not desensitized to pretty New Yorkers suddenly stripping next to me," he mumbles.

Poor guy. I might kill him with the mere suggestion of nudity.

"Ahh, you think I'm pretty? Not a New Yorker, though; I'm from Texas." I grunt a little as I work the unforgiving fabric over the modest swell of my chest and down my waist. I damaged my corduroy pants last week doing a similar quick change and would love to not need a repeat. "I promise you, this is not the worst thing that's happened in this backseat."

Our driver gives us a grunt of affirmation.

"You can look now," I say, adjusting the skirt to where it hits mid-thigh, "but you need to pay the price of taking advantage of my cab haling abilities."

"Wait, w-what?" he stammers, looking at me, still red. Actually, redder, if possible. This can't be healthy. He should probably get his blood pressure checked.

"Do you get laid often?"

He goes non-verbal, opening and closing his mouth, but nothing comes out. Sue me for having some fun after having to play it all prim and proper all day. And it's not like I'll see this guy again.

"I'm not offering. It's just you're having a very strong reaction to the sight of my shoulders. Honestly, you're attractive. Got that tall, nerdy, and bashful thing going for you." I scoot toward him. "All I was going to do was ask if you could zip me up. Can you manage that?"

"Yes," he says in a gust of relief. His fingers fumble with the zipper for a second, and when he attempts to pull it up, it's apparent that he's trying to touch me as little as possible.

"You have to hold the top bit together."

He does, fingers feather-light where they brush against the nape of my neck, ruffling the ends of my blunt cut blonde bob. Then with a tug, he secures me in, just as we pull to a stop. Shoving my discarded clothes into my bag and tossing my coat over my shoulders, I head out and toward *Pivoine,* with its floor to ceiling windows and lush interior shrouded by a wall of plants.

When I reach for the door, a hand darts forward, blocking my way and grasping the brushed brass handle.

I look up. There, next to me, is the scandalized man from the cab.

"You've got to be kidding me."

I don't realize I've said it outloud until Andrew, my final date for the day, asks, "I'm sorry, is everything okay?"

"Yes. I just need to head to the washroom." I give him a smile then nod toward his sister and her fiancé on the other side of the table. "So sorry to stall such a great conversation; I'll be right back," I say, already pushing out of my seat.

This is the easiest meal of the night, especially since I'm supposed to play the part of a woman he's already broken up with. Andrew just didn't want to disrupt the holidays and the plans he already had before the breakup. That's where I came in.

But Andrew and his personal drama aren't on my mind since Cab Guy has just walked in, being led past us by a hostess. This is the third time—well fourth, if I'm including the time I ran into him after I met with Porter, but that was pre-cab—he's shown up after me and each time he managed to look more disheveled.

I nearly run into the hostess trying to return to her station with how quickly I round the corner. There I discover a row of small secluded candle-lit booths. Cab Guy is in the one furthest down the line.

"Are you following me?" I demand as I slide in across from him.

His knee jumps, colliding with the underside of the table, causing the wax in the candle centerpiece to slosh and drip over the sides. "What the fuck? How do I know you're not following me?"

"You took *my* taxi and I was here first. Did you put a tracking tag in my bag?"

"Yes. I followed you to a restaurant where you have to get reservations months in advance, waltzed right in, and got a seat," he deadpans, cocking his head.

True. I booked all the spots I've gone to tonight over the summer, knowing I'd have the perfect client for each when the time came.

"Okay, then why are you here?"

"Probably the same reason you are. I mean, I haven't gone on dates with four men tonight, but I *am* following *Spitfire's* 'Feast in The City' list because I'm doing this year's write-up."

The majority of the restaurants on the list are the same each year, and someone would have to go and eat at each of them to give consistent reviews.

Still, for some reason, I'm hesitant to believe him. "Aren't you supposed to have a notebook or something?" The only thing on the table are the candles and the menu.

"In my bag? It's best to not broadcast to a restaurant you're reviewing them. Special treatment can lead to a biased review."

Okay, yeah, that checks out, and maybe I deserve the perplexed look he's giving me.

I fold my arms over my chest and lean back into the firm upholstery. "I'm impressed that you can form coherent sentences, since you were practically monosyllabic a few hours ago."

"Believe it or not, I'm fairly composed when someone doesn't suddenly rip their clothes off next to me." Still, the barest hint of pink blooms on his cheeks.

"Great." I slap the table. "If that's everything, I have someone I need to get back to."

Before I can go, Cab Guy leans forward placing an elbow on the table and rests his head on one hand as he looks at me through long lashes. "Just curious, is this your last date of the night, or should I expect to run into you again?"

"Well, I'm not a cheater, just so you know." I'd have to actually be in a relationship to be one, and I've had approximately zero since my junior year of college.

"Just dating four men?" Something about him shifts as he asks the questions—his gaze sharpens, eyes roving over me, inspecting, searching for a scrap of information. Yup, totally see him as a journalist now, picking people apart for the sake of an article.

"I liked you more when you couldn't stand the sight of me."

"I was trying to be respectful, but now that you have all your clothes on." He shrugs, gaze lazily trailing from my face to the dip of my dress that reveals the smallest bit of cleavage. "It's hard to turn away."

Annoyance zips up my spine. Is he flirting with me? Where do men find the audacity? "Five, and it's just for the night. It's not a sex thing, and wouldn't be wrong if it was. I'm just a holiday date and I'm great at it, by the way," I snap. "So don't think I'm going to add you as number six."

"Sounds fake," he challenges.

I don't have time for this. My bathroom excuse will only go so far. "Here. If you're a writer, you have a pen, right?"

He blinks once and then pulls out a pen and paper from a worn black leather messenger bag, sliding them across the table to me.

I scribble my website on the crumbled page. "If you don't believe me, check this out."

Without waiting for his response, I head back to Andrew.

If I'm going to talk to a man, he better be paying me for my time.

2

Henri

I know I'm late, but I have a caramel mousse with your name on it!" I call out to Jimmy, Fender's owner, who's working behind the bar that's dimly illuminated with tangled multi-colored Christmas lights as I rush to the break room that's at the back of the long room.

Fender caters to the nine-to-five happy hour crowd in FiDi and isn't packed today, but has a generous amount of people around tables sipping on drinks. It has a manufactured divey feel, with pool tables, wood paneling, and a collection of old neon signs, but our clientele would probably walk out of an actual dive bar with a broken nose they absolutely deserved for saying something stupid.

In the break room, I quickly change out of my dress and into the dark-wash jeans and black shirt I keep stashed in my locker for my shifts. I've been working all day, but the exhaustion has yet to catch up with me. Sure, I've spent that time sitting on my ass eating fancy food, but there's an emotional toll. It's like the moment I stop moving my bones start creaking, warping back into the shape that is uniquely *Henri,* the way werewolves do in movies, contorting and twisting until they're panting and tired.

And if I'm being honest, I prefer to put that transformation off as much as possible. It's easier to play pretend than to be myself. Though, if you asked, I'm not sure who Henri Elm is beyond a workaholic with champagne taste.

For the next thirty minutes, I help with a wave of customers, going through the automatic motions of grabbing sticky syrup bottles, smacking the shaker with the heel of my hand, and shaking until my arms are numb.

"Whatcha doing back there on a holiday?" asks a guy wearing a standard issue finance bro quarter zip. He's slurring slightly as he speaks.

I cut him a smile over my shoulder as I pour him the dark stout he ordered. "Making sure good people like you get to drink."

"Parents dead or something? Hot girls like you always have trauma and are great in bed," he drawls. Has this ever worked for him? Oh to be the broken girl coveted by a lackluster man, because when he inevitably ends it, he doesn't feel guilty because she's already busted up and it's not his fault.

Cute.

"Nah, my dad's in jail and my mom is spending the holiday on her six-month-long honeymoon." I slide the pint to him, smile firmly in place. I've found that seeming okay with my trauma tends to make people un-comfortable enough to shut the hell up.

The truth is, we never do Thanksgiving together. Mom knows this is my busiest season and she's supportive of what I do for work. After Dad left us high and dry we learned how to survive together. She went back to teaching high school history while I transferred to an online college to finish my degree while working as a bartender at our local Chili's.

Being a bartender is how I learned how to shift—be the person someone wants me to be. Usually, people just want someone to listen and really be heard, to validate the way they feel so they feel a little less lonely. The tips

I got from laughing at bad jokes and talking to divorcees are what paid for groceries.

The mass-produced finance clone smirks, grabbing his drink. "If you need company—"

"She has me," Iris interrupts as she takes the seat directly in front of me. "And based on the fact you're dressed like five other guys I walked by on my way in, I'm more interesting and won't give her an STD. Something about you screams pubic lice." Iris waves her hand over the lower half of the guy and it takes everything in me not to let loose a snort of laughter.

"There was that one time . . ." I say, raising my brows suggestively as I grab the copper mug for the Moscow mule she always loves after getting off a ten-hour shift as an ER nurse.

Even after what was guaranteed to be a grueling day—family time and alcohol make idiots of us all—her brown hair has stayed put in its slicked-back ponytail. With her height and fine bone structure, her hoodie and curve-hugging jeans make her more like a model than someone just trying to be comfortable after a long day.

"That was mono," she corrects with a dismissive flick of her fingers. "And you're the one who didn't want to get your ass up to get your own spoon. Technically mono isn't an STD, it's an STI."

"I'm going to go." The man takes a step back and hooks his thumb toward his friends.

"Good riddance," Iris says, then swivels in her stool to face me. "What would you do without me?"

I pluck mint from the julep cups we use to store garnishes and thwack it against my palm before tucking it along the edge of the drink. "Get better tips but have to put up with more assholes?"

"Fair trade-off." She shrugs and takes a sip, her blue eyes rolling back as she releases a low, satisfied moan.

I met Iris in Philadelphia three years and seven cities ago. She was a guest at one of the first weddings I was hired to plus one for. I hung out with my date until he left with a bridesmaid. Iris was the one who told me I was probably being cheated on and I explained the whole deal to her. We got to talking about how both of us move from city to city every few months, her as a travel nurse and me with my work because the longer I stay somewhere the riskier it is that my clients will overlap, and by the end of the night we were set to be roommates.

She is also the only person I can call my friend. I used to have more—people I'd known my entire life, Kurt and Laura. We went to the same schools from daycare, fed with silver spoons, through college, where we'd bailed each other out more times than I could count. But the moment the news about my dad went public, they wanted nothing to do with me.

Call me picky all you want, but you sure as hell can't tell me I don't have a reason to be. Trust is earned, and Iris is the only person who has managed to win me over.

Another customer bellies up to the bar, and I take care of their order of five tequila shots and a cosmo. When I get back to Iris, she's done with her first drink and I make her a second.

"Someone better be paying for those," Jimmy says as he walks behind me, carrying a bucket to get more ice. He's a stocky man with a dash of grey striking through his nearly-black hair, who, like me, is working tonight so the staff with family plans could have the evening off.

"How many burns did you have to treat tonight because of idiots deep frying turkeys?" Iris asks.

Jimmy cocks a thick brow. "Zero."

"Wow, what a coincidence! That's how much I plan on spending tonight." A hand flies to her face in faux shock. "If it makes you feel better, call it a health-care-worker discount."

"You're a menace, Iris." Jimmy shakes his head as he opens the ice machine and starts to fill his bucket.

"He says it like it's a bad thing," Iris says.

"You know, one day he's going to make you actually pay your tab," I tell her.

"If I keep flirting and you work the shifts no one else wants, I doubt that. It also helps that you bribe him with leftovers. Speaking of which . . ." She pauses and flutters her lashes. "Did you bring me rolls? I'm starving."

"Break room," I say.

Iris goes to retrieve them from my bag while I help a new batch of customers. By the time I get back to her, she's tearing off pieces of bread and popping them into her mouth.

"Which one is that?" I ask.

In answer, she holds out a piece for me to take a bite. Even hours old, the bread is soft and the piney taste of rosemary blooms on my tongue.

"Bide," I say. "Just wait until you get to the cheese rolls."

"So the *Spitfire* list lived up to expectations?" she asks, taking a sip of her drink which does nothing to conceal the smirk capturing her mouth.

"Come on, I haven't talked about it that much."

"If you say so," she chimes. "Are you going to compare notes when the updated list comes out tomorrow?"

And to think I had almost forgotten the freckled and flustered highlight of my day. "Yeah, probably not going to happen since I accused the guy writing this year's reviews of stalking me after I helped him get a cab and changed in front of him."

"Shut up." Her jaw unhinges for a moment before her eyes sparkle with excitement. "Do you think he could be L. Hughes? Did you flash your celebrity crush?"

"I didn't flash anyone. He saw me in a bodysuit and leggings." I groan. "God don't make me think that it could be him. Also, L. Hughes is not a celebrity."

I like his writing. It's refreshing to see a man engage in traditionally feminine topics without bashing them. Simple as that. And yes, maybe I've commented on a few articles, but that's normal.

"Please tell me he's hot because if it was L. Hughes and he wasn't, you'll have nothing to masturbate to anymore."

Heat crawls up my neck. "Oh my God. I tell you I accuse him of stalking me and you ask if he's hot?"

"So you do get off to the idea of him?" Her smile tips into a self-satisfied, almost feline, smirk. Okay, sure, she's right, I've thought about a man who could be L. Hughes. I think competence is hot. Why would I be into a loser? But it's not like I have a reference since, unlike the other writers, there's no picture of him to accompany his byline.

"Not the point."

"Being vigilant as a single woman is smart, though I think confronting him isn't great. But you hang out with strangers for a living; I can only expect so much from you."

"Your faith in me is always appreciated."

"So," she says, waving her hand in a circular motion, urging me to answer.

I pause, taking a moment to conjure up a memory of Cab Guy. "He looked like someone just woke him up after he fell asleep in a library. And he had all these freckles, like a billion. Not hot, but handsome." I shake my head. Why am I even entertaining this conversation? "But that doesn't matter. I ate good food. I got paid," I say firmly. I walk out from behind the bar and grab a few abandoned glasses off a hightop table. "And now I'm working."

"Working? You? Never. If you don't hear back from the admissions office soon, I'm going to go there in person. When you go back to school at least you'll be able to sit and make connections with people in your classes."

"It's the holidays; it's normal for there to be a delay." My eyes fix on the counter as I scrub at a red, sticky spot of dried Grenadine.

Truth is, I got the email notification that my admission status had been updated on Monday, but that would mean I'd have to log on and check it. Even after transferring from Brown to an online state college to save money, it took me four years of putting away every dollar I had to pay off my loans. I'd taken the privilege I'd grown up in for granted, and once my dad was arrested, I didn't know the basics of how to be a person. It was embarrassing.

The first time I tried to wash my own clothes I used bleach instead of detergent and ruined the entire load of laundry. I'm proud of the simple skills I've learned—the basics of checking cost per ounce on items at the grocery store, knowing exactly which gas station I could save a few cents at, using my local library's computer to submit a final exam when my laptop broke and I couldn't afford repairs.

Getting my master's in counseling will open doors, but it's the biggest financial risk I've taken. I initially wanted to start a new online program, but Iris encouraged me to apply for my dream program here in New York, and thus reclaiming a college experience I never fully had. I have nearly enough saved to completely cover the first two years of tuition and rent, but only if I get financial aid.

After years of building a new life, I'm not sure I'm ready to take the risk. And there's the fact that it will be the first time I've settled down anywhere. I've grown used to being unmoored.

A master's program means committing to one place. One topic. One cohort of people. It means committing to being the same person day in and day out, and I'm not even sure who that person is. Or worse, if I like that person.

Last time I was in school, I was lazy and stuck up, cheating my way through the entrance requirements. What if that part of me is still lurking beneath the surface just waiting to break free the moment I relax?

"You're going to get in and you're going to go. It's not like you can bartend and date people for money forever. Those are things you're going to age out of."

"I don't know, I think I could break into an older market," I joke.

A beat-up fuchsia leather purse thuds on the bartop next to Iris. Jasmine, one of Fender's afterwork regulars and Iris's current flirta-tionship, slips onto a barstool.

"I think I just set a record for how fast you can get the hell off Long Island," Jasmine says. "All the cousins have kids now and won't do edibles with me anymore, so I was there sober, while my aunt told us about all the wart removals she's had this year. And it's been nearly a decade since I've come out and my dad still thinks that if I 'give football a chance I'll really like it.'" She looks at me with wide, pleading green eyes. "Please help me not be sober anymore."

Coming to the rescue, I make her a Negroni while she and Iris chat.

"Here," I say, placing the deep amber cocktail in front of her.

"Iris is saying you might stay in New York a bit longer." Jasmine cocks a brow.

"Not you, too," I groan.

"All I'm saying is, I wouldn't be mad if you stayed," Jasmine says, coyly, as her eyes flick to Iris.

"I'll get to it faster if people stop reminding me. And there's nothing that says if I leave you have to go with me," I tell Iris.

I hate the feeling that I'm holding her back, but she never complains. I don't do relationships, but she does. Yet, she always cuts them a month or so before we move.

"Nope, you're not getting rid of me anytime soon. I worked my ass off to be your friend and I'm getting a return on my investment."

At first, I was determined to make sure she was just a normal roommate, but she made it her mission to get to know me. She's the only person I've opened up to about how I really feel about what happened the winter of my sophomore year of college with my dad and how everyone in my old life stopped talking to Mom and I the moment the news broke.

"God," Jasmine groans. "My roommate's the same way. He's planning on moving home after the holidays."

I point between them. "See if we both leave then you could live together. Now if you'll excuse me, I have drinks to make."

3

Liam

Once late November hits, pitch meetings at *Spitfire* become a competition for who can come up with the most inventive ways to use the company card for their personal gain.

It's the Monday after Thanksgiving, and all of the mid-level and senior staff writers are seated along a narrow gray conference table with their notebooks splayed in front of them. I stand with the three other junior writers to the side with our backs to the bay of windows, awkwardly cradling our notes in our arms.

"Jasmine, go ahead and start that piece on styling clothes from high school for the holidays," Fallon Saito, our editor in chief, directs. She's in her late thirties—young by industry standards—but was able to secure her position and the development of *Spitfire* through consistent viral success. Her black hair is tied back, out of her face, in a high ponytail. She commands the room as she writes down approved pieces on index cards before securing them with magnets to a whiteboard. "We'll be getting a shipment of pleasure accessories later today. I expect everyone who is comfortable to pick one up and submit their review by next week so we can finalize the listicle for the start of 'Horny for the Holidays.'"

A few people let out whoops at this. We continue to go around the table, throwing out gift guide themes and holiday excursions and pop-ups to try out in the city. We'll be putting out twice the content as usual, which also means a peak in ad dollars from the digital site with a push for material featuring sponsored items.

When I got my MFA, I didn't aspire to work at a fashion and pop culture magazine. There aren't exactly enough writing jobs out there to be picky about where you land, but I love it here. Sure, there's pressure surrounding deadlines or pushing past creative blocks, but it's an environment that embraces joy. *Spitfire* has a primarily female audience, but it's a space for anyone if they want to be a part of it.

Fallon directs her focus on me. "Liam, what do you have for us? Excellent work on the Thanksgiving list, even if I did have a heated call from Bide's owner this morning."

A few annoyed glances shoot my way. The person who writes the review list each year is selected at random so they aren't recognized by the restaurants and given preferential treatment. It's a coveted spot, partly because of the free meals and partly because if you succeed you're on Fallon's radar for the upcoming year, which means more freedom with the pieces you take on and the potential for promotions. Because I'm leaving *Spitfire*, following in the steps of three generations of Hughes men before me to move home to help run my family's ski hill in Dulcet Point, Colorado after the New Year, other staff members thought it was a waste to have me write the list.

"Christmas cards with friends or roommates, moving away from the traditional family card and moving toward something more aligned with the modern trajectory of people in their twenties and thirties," I say.

"Great!" Fallon says. "Touch base with whoever you want to bring along with you and talk to the fashion department about styling. I'm thinking ugly retro, but follow their suggestions. That's all I have for you all. Remember, look over the sex toys but do not fight over them. We *do not* need a repeat of the Valentines Day incident." Grabbing the rest of her note cards, she taps them into a neat stack and puts them into her bag.

The room fills with the swooshes of chair legs on thin pile carpet.

"You better pick me for the holiday card," Jasmine says, crossing the room to join me.

She and I started around the same time at *Spitfire,* both of us coming from MFA programs and working our way up from being interns. She moved up the ranks six months ago, being given her own column focused on sex and psychology, rooted in her personal mission to help people understand they aren't alone in what they feel or what they *think* they should feel. We live together in a cozy rent-controlled apartment in Tribeca that she lucked into when she first moved here.

"Why? Because you look great in tinsel trimmed polyester?" I ask. When we reach the door, I hold it open for her.

"Because if you don't, I'm revoking your best friend status and will be wildly offended."

"Sorry, I thought you knew that I was just using you for premium rent."

"Whatever. I need something I can send my parents. My tits are out in most of the pictures I have and I need ones that won't send them into cardiac arrest." Jasmine takes a seat at her desk and spins around in her chair.

I start to head toward mine, but Fallon says my name. "Liam, walk with me for a minute will you?"

"Sure," I say and fall into step with her as she rolls the white board to the concept wall where the rest of the details for the holiday issue are laid out. "Is this about the list?"

"I said it in the meeting, but I do want to reiterate, excellent work. If you were staying with us, I'd put you on more culinary pieces. But it is the reason I'm going to ask you for a favor," she says without looking my way. "Alara was planning to do a write up on Christmas tree farms, but she's put on bedrest for the remainder of her pregnancy and will be submitting a shorter version of the original article. It was supposed to be a huge piece for digital. All other senior staff members have their assignments, so I can't ask them to come up with another piece. I believe if you had stayed you'd be up for a promotion next year, so I'm asking you to do a holiday feature."

"Oh, wow. Thanks," I say, nearly tripping over my feet in shock. It's always a bit of a surprise when I'm praised for my work.

"Is there any specific angle you have in mind?"

Since I left Colorado and went to college, writing has been my passion. I pursued it despite knowing it would be something I'd have to put on the back burner once I turned twenty-eight. I feel like I'm putting parts of myself out in the world that I can't take back, even if they've been edited a thousand times.

Fallon continues as she adjusts the white board so it's flush to the wall. "I'm open to any pitches you generate but will need to approve the subject of the feature by end of day tomorrow," she explains. "I know it's short notice. You'll be home for the holidays, and I know you're hesitant, but a profile on an Olympic legacy family could be huge."

I force my lips to maintain a smile even as my stomach drops. Three generations of Hughes are winter Olympians, making us essentially royalty in the world of winter sports. My parents now own and operate Dulcet Point Ski Lodge in Colorado, where many elite winter athletes including my sisters, Penelope and Juniper, train. The only reason I'm not doing the same is because of an injury when I was sixteen, though that didn't change expectations. When I majored in journalism, the unspoken hope was that I would go into sports coverage. Obviously, I diverted from that plan. I like to keep these two halves of my life separate, letting myself pretend my time in New York isn't some temporary dream.

My life here is something I've claimed wholly for myself, and I do everything I can to separate it from the other parts of my life. It's mine, and will continue to be mine even when I'm stuck on the side of the mountain decades from now. I won't let the last thing I do here center around my unavoidable future.

"I'll take it under consideration and update you if I come up with something else." I give a quick nod. "If there's nothing else, I need to book the photoshoot for my roommate Christmas card pitch."

"That's all. Best of luck Liam, I can't wait to see what you come up with."

Dismissed, I stride back to my desk directly across from Jasmine's. Only our computers divide us, so I have a decent view of her avoiding my gaze.

"What did Fallon have to say?" she asks innocently as she picks at the skin around her thumb as if she wasn't eavesdropping the entire time.

"That she's giving me a holiday feature." I slump back in my chair searching my head for any ideas but my mind is blank. It's been a busy month. Between packing up my life here, working, and dodging calls from my dad who is excited enough for the both of us about my return, I'm worn the hell out.

"Of course she did. If you walked up to her and asked for a mid-level staffer job she'd give it to you in a heartbeat. Your articles have some of the best metrics, I mean besides mine," she says, humble as ever. Though she is one of the best known writers here, often asked to go on podcasts and give workshops on sexual health and empowerment. "Just stay and tell your dad to shove it. He can hire someone with an MBA and a suit to run everything."

"You know it's not that simple." I sigh as I log on to my computer, pulling up a browser that auto-populates with *Spitfire's* home page. "My dad and I have a deal."

"I'm so sick and tired of that deal. Just pay him back for college and stay. I don't want to find another roommate."

The arrangement I had with my dad was that he'd fund my college and any further education, as long as I agreed to come back to Dulcet Point, saying that it would be good for me to get out into the world and know how a company works. If Dulcet Point wasn't my home, maybe I'd be able to say yes to Jasmine's request. But even though I retired from skiing at a young age, I can't just walk away from the place I grew up and my obligations to it.

"Jas, you'll find a roommate just fine. I need to get to work on this pitch so my final article here isn't hot garbage," I tell her and pull on my over the ear headphones before she can protest.

I spend the afternoon searching for an open slot for a department store photoshoot, eventually selecting one for the end of day tomorrow. Once that's wrapped up, I scroll through past years' holiday features. Exposés on glitzy celebrity New Years parties. Emotional biographical pieces on how people have transformed over a year by dedicating themselves to a "yes" list. Visits to towns that seem like they're right out of Hallmark movies.

Due to my lack of non-family celebrity connections, limited timeline, and the fact that outright plagiarism won't get me anywhere, I might be fucked.

Five o'clock hits, and hoping to find some last minute inspiration, I reach into my bag to retrieve my notebook. When I pull it out, a loose piece of paper comes with it and tumbles onto the pale wood of my desk.

It's wrinkled, so I smooth it out to read the single line of writing.

A website. A long shot.

> *Dear Juliet,*
>
> *I'm not sure if you'd need me to go through a background check first (per your policy), but would you be interested in an interview.*

I sigh and hold down the delete button as words vanish. It's the next day and I'm starting the fifth version of the email that I couldn't get right yesterday, trying to sound professional instead of saying, *Hey, remember me? The guy who didn't stalk you the other day? We shared a cab and I called you pretty because you made me nervous and I didn't know how to shut the hell up? Yeah, that's me. Would you let me pay for your lunch, and forget all of that ever happened?*

Fuck.

"Why would someone need you to do a background check for an interview?" Jasmine says, looking over my shoulder. At this rate, I need one of those privacy screens.

She's dressed in a Christmas sweater that is covered in silver tinsel, bows, and hand-stitched trees. Every time she moves it crinkles. Mine isn't much better. I have about three dozen miniature bells attached to me that chime each time I move.

We're waiting on the sidelines as Rowan and Ava, the two fashion assistants joining us for the shoot, move into a series of purposefully awkward couples poses as the camera flashes.

"It's a smart move for her job," I say, turning off my phone and shoving it in my back pocket. "Have you ever heard of someone being a professional plus-one for holidays and weddings?"

"Shit. I have, actually. My cousin tried to book one but she was booked through spring. Classic men, planning at the last minute."

"Thanks."

"You're like ten percent better. You know the difference between a zucchini and a cucumber when I send you to the grocery store."

"I'm glad that common sense is enough to be in your good graces. But I might have ruined my chances with this girl." I groan, remembering how she came at me like a storm.

Short blonde hair that flicked out at the ends. Intelligent rich brown eyes that mercilessly cut right through me, yet held a barely restrained humor. The powerful confidence that emanated off her in waves and made my heart go off rhythm.

By some miracle I was composed—okay, not stammering through every word—the second time we spoke. Probably thanks to the three glasses of wine I'd had that day hitting my system.

"Why's that?"

"We didn't exactly have the best first encounter on Thanksgiving. She thought I was stalking her. But I think this is the right story to help me get the promotion."

"Give me your phone." Jasmine reaches out her hand, palm up.

"Why?"

"You don't want to sound like a creep, right?"

Resigned, I unlock my phone and hand it over. She types for a moment then rereads her work.

She shows me the screen, revealing an email far better than mine was. Finger hovering over the send button, she says, "You get this on one condition: we get drinks tonight. You still haven't celebrated killing the Thanksgiving piece even though it was fucking flawless. After your birthday, you have to let me have this."

How was I supposed to know that the last minute interview I was asked to take over was at the same time as the top secret surprise birthday party Jasmine had planned for me? And it's not like I'm the best people person.

Making the best of my time in New York has mostly focused on writing, which in turn has exposed me to more of the city than I could have dreamed of.

"Seriously? You're holding my email hostage?"

"Ready for you two whenever!" the photographer chimes, calling us over for the final set of photos next to the lopsided waist-high trees that had absolutely seen better days.

Jasmine cocks a brow as her finger shifts to the delete icon. "You've driven me to extreme measures. You can be a quirky shut-in when you're old and ugly."

"Fine," I acquiesce, accepting my fate.

4

Henri

Y our celebrity crush wants to buy you lunch and you didn't immediately reply yes?" Iris says, slamming her hands on the bar top in
exasperation.

"He's *not* a celebrity, he's just some writer. And I haven't decided yet."
I got the email just before I needed to head out for my shift at Fender. I've
barely processed, let alone decided what to do with it.

L. Hughes.

You know what they say about meeting people you idolize.

Don't.

Because if you're like me, you'll make the world's worst first impression
and lose one of the few things that bring you joy. I was happy to be in
denial that it was him, until this year's "Feast in the City" was released with
his name on it the day after Thanksgiving, and the unanswered email only
further confirmed my worst fears. This is what I get for helping a man. I
should have just left him on the slushy sidewalk.

"You're fucking joking, right?"

"I don't know if it's a smart move. This job is important, I don't want to ruin it."

"You're only going to be doing this for a few more months—this is the perfect way to commemorate it. Imagine in ten years, you're sitting around with all your new, less-interesting-than-me academic friends and you whip out this badass article about your cool life in your twenties." She gives me a wide-eyed expectant look. When I don't immediately respond, she softens her voice. "If you're worried about work, just make sure it's anonymous."

"Even if I do that, I'll screw it up."

I'm great behind the bar or on dates. I know exactly how to meet expectations. It's not exactly a high bar—let's be real, men aren't creative when it comes to the dream girl they want to take home to their parents.

But being the person who talks instead of listens? Being me? Fuck that.

The only reason I was starting to move on from the interaction with the man—who I now know was L. Hughes—in the cab and at the restaurant is that I have no plans on ever seeing him again.

"I think it's safe to say that if he still wants to talk to you after everything that happened, you'll be just fine. And this proves your celebrity crush isn't an asshole. Not all of us get to say that. You have to tell him yes. Go out with him."

"It wouldn't be a date. It would be an interview," I remind her, but I doubt my words will do any good to shatter her delusions.

"And it will go great. He'll fall in love with you, because how could he not, and you'll have yet another reason to stay in the city." Iris perks up, attention shifting from me, thank God. I follow her gaze to where Jasmine is weaving toward us wearing a comically ugly Christmas sweater trimmed with tinsel. She calls out, "Help me convince Henri to fuck her celebrity crush."

"I'm going to grab dishes and pretend you're not using my sex life to flirt." I head to the side room just off of the bar where we keep the dishwasher and extras of the liquor we tend to go through most of.

We're not too busy yet, but that will change now that it's four. I load up my arms with steaming, freshly-cleaned glassware. I let Iris do her thing as I put everything up at both well stations, hoping by the time I'm back they'll have already covered the meager details of my sad excuse for a romantic life.

I haven't actually dated anyone since college, and I was never actually in a relationship with anyone then. At first it was because I was too busy. Now that I have a more flexible schedule, it would be too complicated. I move too often for anything long-term and I don't know how well telling someone I date people for a living would go over.

Iris has tried to help get me laid over the last few years, and I always say no. That's the one area I'm not quite sure how to perform in—to be the person a partner would want. I'm not a virgin, but a handful of sloppy, fumbling frat party hook ups does not an expert make.

I can play at being sexy, but the idea of being with someone and disappointing them makes me feel vulnerable and anxious.

I like it this way. I have complete control over who I meet and when I leave.

"Jasmine, what can I—" I start, turning to face her but the rest of the sentence catches half way up my throat.

"Manhattan for me and whiskey sour for Liam," Jasmine says eagerly, apparently not noticing how I've turned to stone at the sight of the man next to her, also wearing a gaudy sweater with about a hundred tiny bells attached to it. "Thanks, Henri."

"Yeah, thanks, *Henri*." L. Hughes makes my name sound like a new inside joke he's testing the shape of—rolling it around on his tongue.

Keeping my eyes fixed on the bottles in front of me, and thankful for the bar between us, I make drinks as the conversation picks up again.

"Liam, you have a lot of freckles," Iris says loudly, making sure I can hear. "Don't see too many people with so many. I bet there's like a *billion*."

"I guess I haven't thought about that?" His voice tips up at the end in confusion.

"Well, now that you're both here, you have to help me convince Henri to go out with her celebrity crush. She got this email and she's thinking of saying no." Flames lick up my body. I won't have to worry about grad school or the future if I die right here from humiliation.

"It's not a date." I enunciate the best I can through gritted teeth. "Just a work thing. *If* I say yes."

"What exactly do you do for work? Sounds interesting if you're being given an opportunity like this?" Liam has the gall to sound innocently curious.

"This, and freelance consulting on the side," I say. Finishing the drinks, I hand them across the bar and give Iris an *SOS* glance.

"Jasmine, how do you feel about pool?" she asks. Traitor.

"That I'd love you to teach me how to play." Jasmine's mouth cracks into a wide smile as she scoots off her barstool. Iris guides her further into the bar where a pool table has opened up.

Iris looks back over her shoulder and I take the opportunity to mouth *"I hate you."*

She blows me a cheeky kiss. Just wait and see how she likes it when I don't bring her back leftovers anytime soon. That'll show her.

"Jas is really great at pool," Liam says.

"Well, Iris sucks at teaching people things. One of the few actual fights we've gotten in was when she tried to teach me a card game. And her only goal was to leave me with you, so I guess they're a perfect match."

"Yeah, I figured." His eyes flick down and he trails a finger over the rim of his glass. "Am I really your celebrity crush? Not that I'm complaining.

It's a pretty nice ego boost after being cornered and told off for stalking you."

Just when I was starting to think we'd spend the entire night talking about our friends, he had to ruin it.

"I *used* to like your articles." I shrug casually.

"Used to?"

"It might be a while before I see your name on a byline and don't die of shame."

"So . . ." he starts slowly, drawing out the word. It's like he's composing and rewriting his thoughts between sentences, causing him to speak in a jerky stilted sort of rhythm. "Would being a part of one of those articles be completely off the table then? I sent an email a few hours ago asking, but there's a chance you haven't seen it."

"No, I saw it, and I don't think it's a good idea."

"Because you realized you were desperately in love with me?" The way he says it is less cocky and more like he thinks it's ridiculous. Like it would be impossible for me to fall for someone like him. His eyes have gone wide and his bottom lip protrudes in a pout.

"Stop it." I laugh despite myself, holding up my hand to shield my gaze from his pitiful expression.

A customer comes up to the bar, giving me a moment to collect my thoughts as I take their order and make their drink.

When I get back to Liam, I say, "I'm not good at talking about myself. It took me months to write my personal statement for my grad program. A thousand words to convince a school to let me pay them a shit ton of money and it took months." And my essay was amazing—had to be since my grades were average at best even after relentless studying.

"Nice. What type of program? I did an MFA, so I get it on some level. But it was expensive as hell and I was lucky to have some assistance from my family."

"Mental health counseling."

"Is there a reason why?"

"Right now, I get to help people for a night or a few days, depending on what they need. I want to do more—I feel like I can do more if I have the chance to." I've always had more fun solving other people's problems than my own.

"So, you're a liar."

"How? I mean I am sometimes, but not right now." I throw my hands up and nearly knock a glass into my ice.

"You are good at talking about yourself."

"Oh." I can't help but smile. "Only because you tricked me."

"I think that's what they call being a good interviewer." His hand dips back as he grabs his phone from his pocket. He taps at it then sets it on the counter with the recording app up. "Since you're so vehemently opposed to having lunch with me, we could talk now."

"And you'll keep me anonymous?" Even though I plan on quitting the professional fake dating job I've invented for myself if I get into grad school, I don't want to risk the reputations of my clients. It would be nice to keep the business going and have some extra cash, but the last thing I want to do is run into someone I went on a date with only to find out they're a classmate.

"Of course, *Juliet*," he says. "I'll make sure not to include your name or your pseudonym."

His playful tone sparks something rebellious in me and I reach over and tap the record button. "Then ask away."

For the next two hours, I walk Liam through the basics of my process from background checks to picking the perfect outfit. Even as I'm hit with small rushes, the conversation never truly stops. In addition to using the recorder, he writes in a small spiral notebook with a tattered green cover that has seen better days. When he's not writing, he taps his pen on the bar top or shoves it behind his ear only to forget momentarily where he put it.

The next shift comes in, and I'm cut for the day, but have to take care of my closing tasks before I go home. I say a quick goodbye to Liam as I restock liquor and soda.

I'm tugging on my puffer over my work clothes as I step out of the break room.

Iris is there, waiting for me. I'm sure the reason she didn't ignore the employees only sign and join me has something to do with how her arm is slung low around Jasmine's waist. "We're going to head out back to Jas's place. You two all good here?"

"Yeah." I nod.

"Great, you can entertain Liam," Jasmine says, flashing a wicked smile before she steers my roommate toward the exit, leaving Liam and I alone to fend for ourselves.

"Take pity on me? The walls at our place are thin." Liam says, rocking back on his heels with hands shoved deep in his pockets. Standing so close to him I can tell he's tall, but he holds himself so his shoulders are curled in and he looks far shorter than he actually is.

"I guess I can show you where the magic happens." I slip my arm through his and nudge him forward. "Come on, let's get out of here."

5

Henri

Ten thousand steps around the city? Easy.

Five flights of stairs? I become the monster from the black lagoon—sweat drenched and heaving as I desperately suck air into my burning lungs. You'd think after five months it would get easier, but it never does.

When we reach the top I catch myself against the wall.

"Just give me a moment," I pant, my hand fumbling in the endless depths of my bag for my keys.

"Fuck. I swear I workout," Liam says, hands braced on his knees next to me, eyes pinched shut. "If my siblings saw me right now, I'd never hear the end of it."

"They wouldn't be with us, wondering if they also need an adult asthma diagnosis?"

"Athletes."

"Oh, those fuckers."

He huffs a laugh. "You've never met them."

"That doesn't mean I don't feel insulted by the mere suggestion of their superior lung capacity."

Managing to grab my keys, I finally open the door. I walk in, sweeping my arm wide to present the space. The apartment was a good deal and came pre-furnished, thanks to the support we received from Iris's travel nurse agency, but it's still small.

I shrug out of my coat and hang it up by the door.

"Is that . . . ?" Liam, cocks his head toward my office.

"Where I mastermind all of my schemes? I'll give you a look if you want," I say and his eyes catch with mine.

"For the interview," he says, as if reminding himself.

"Yeah, for that." Somewhere along the way, this started to feel natural. Like the two of us have done this before. I can't remember the last time something was so easy with someone. Even with Iris, it took work. But Liam with the silly pen tucked behind his ear and his genuine curiosity has snuck up on me.

"Each set of index cards has the basics of the people I'm still working with," I explain, tapping one for the tech mogul's son. "Names I need to remember, timelines of the relationship, who I need to be for them to get the most out of the experience. I was with this guy on Thanksgiving, but I'm going to be texting him a few times over the next week and call him while he's around his family once before I break it off."

"Why do you break it off? Why not them?"

"That way I'm the villain." I shrug. "Juliet isn't the star of some rom-com, she's part of a tragedy. She kills Romeo in her own roundabout way, so that's what I do. I kill the relationship and my clients are in the clear."

Clean cut. I leave exactly when I plan to. I'm never the one people walk away from. Not anymore.

"After that, what do you do? They get to go on with their lives, but what about you? It must be draining to constantly be carrying such large emotional loads."

I'm so taken aback by the question that I just blink at him for a moment. "I have to keep going. So I do." Work and keep working because if I don't, the emotional exhaustion sweeps me under like a riptide and threatens to drown me. I force the corners of my lips up and push past the melancholy starting to take hold. "Want to see something cool?"

"Don't tell me, someone asked you to impersonate a lounge singer," Liam says from where he's perched on the edge of the full-sized bed, the only surface in my sparse room that's not covered in clothing. He lifts his phone to take a picture of me that he swears he's only using for reference and won't include any in the actual article.

With my hands draped one over the other, I lean dramatically against one of the four clothing racks that line the perimeter of the space. The low-cut, floor-length red dress pools at my feet since I've neglected to wear heels. I designed it myself and it fits me like a glove.

"Oh, come on, this is obviously an *I need to make my ex jealous and prove to her I won't die alone because I have a hot girlfriend* dress." My voice tips up into a perky infomercial pitch. "Perfect for occasions such as weddings, high school reunions, or upscale outings with mutual friends. You work at a women's magazine; you're supposed to know these things."

The dress is the fifth outfit I've tried on after showing him my bedroom and he's taken this fashion show in stride. I don't ever get the chance to show off this passion and he's intent rather than dismissive, making me want to keep going.

"What high school reunion are you going to in that?" he asks.

"You'd be surprised." I walk over to the bed and sit next to him. "It's mostly weddings though. No one wants to run into their happily-coupled-up ex at a wedding when they're still single, especially if the ex is the one getting married. I made this just for those occasions that need an extra wow factor."

Liam's brows shoot up in disbelief at this and I stifle a laugh. "You made that. Fuck that's incredible."

"It's just something I learned to do when I realized I couldn't afford some of the things I wanted to buy. It's not perfect but it does the job."

"I'll say. Why do you put so much into the details of something you could probably throw any dress on for and then make small talk?"

"I get to charge more for my expertise, of course," I joke, then flop back onto the bed. My gaze traces over the ceiling texture that, from my first day at the apartment, has reminded me of a breakout of splotchy hives. "It's quite simple, really. We like to think we're all so different and that's why we're special. If everyone was special, my job would be a lot harder. But most of us just want the same thing."

"You call this easy?"

I laugh. "Okay, yes, I get what you mean. I put a lot into my work, because it's what my clients deserve and expect."

The bed shifts, fabric rustling as Liam lies down next to me. His hair brushes against mine as he adjusts.

"So, what is it that we all want?" he asks, and I can feel his eyes on me.

I nearly look his way, but this, the core of it all, makes me feel naked. Like, over the last few hours, I've stripped down. Losing my armor, but I don't feel unsafe. If anything, it's the opposite. Somehow that's more terrifying. "We want to be people who are worthy of love, and we want the people we care about to see us that way. Yeah there are plenty of smaller reasons, promotions, convincing parents to drop arguments, feuds, but to be loved is to be seen, and all that."

"Henri," Liam says. Finally, I roll and look at him. Up close, I can tell his brown eyes are hazel—brown blooming from his irises to be swallowed up by rings of gold streaked green at the edges.

"Yeah?" I swallow hard, willing my racing heart to settle before Liam can hear it pounding. There's a part of me that wants to reach out and touch him, just to make sure he's real.

A phone chimes with a text notification, and he sits up, pulling away from me before grabbing his phone where he's set it on my nightstand.

"It's Jasmine." He rises to his feet, teeth toying at his bottom lip as he reads. There's something about him, the way all of his feelings live unrestrained on his face, that makes him easy to talk to. It's easy to see why people feel safe opening up to him.

"Headed out?" I prop myself up on an elbow and ask as disappointment creeps in.

"I should," he says, almost hesitantly. "Thanks. I think I have everything I need. The article is going to be a hit."

"Of course it will. The great L. Hughes is writing it."

"You give me too much credit."

"I don't think you give yourself enough credit." I don't want this to end, this resonant humming between us.

"I should . . . Umm."

"I guess."

I stand up too quickly, forgetting I'm in a dress. My feet tangle in the fabric causing me to stumble before catching myself on a wall.

It hits me all at once. I'm just a girl in a dress. A story.

A girl who is so starved for genuine attention that I let him in a little too much. This is exactly why I don't do this. I keep work and myself separate, otherwise I'm too eager to give all of myself a scrap of belonging.

I take a moment to get myself together and walk him to the door.

"I can send it to you when it's out," he says, lingering halfway into the hall with his hand on the doorknob.

"No, it's fine. You don't need to go out of your way to do that." My practiced smile is back in place as I remember who I am to him. No one.

When he goes, I lock the door behind me and I slump onto the floor. Left alone, again.

6

Henri

Yes, I completely understand. I'll process the refund of your initial deposit as soon as we're done with this call," I say, massaging my temples as I try my best not to lose my shit.

It's been a week since Liam came over and two days since the article went live. It was an instant hit, and had been reposted everywhere within twenty-four hours. When I went to get coffee, the girls in line in front of me had it pulled up on their phone. Mom sent me an essay in the form of five separate texts about how well he captured what I do. I've been tempted to read the piece myself, but after the other night, it's for the best if I avoid anything that will draw me closer to Liam.

Everyone else though? They've read the piece spawning a tidal wave of online commentary. Millions of hits. Great for him.

For me? Well, the article's widespread success is the reason I'm currently lying on the slightly warped hardwood floor of our living room, legs pressed up against the wall in a pose that promises to be relaxing and restorative, dealing with my third cancellation of the day.

"Thank you for understanding. My sister, she's the type to dig—swears she could be in the FBI—and I don't want to risk her finding out we're not actually together," Terrence explains, sounding genuinely apologetic.

This is a concern I've had to deal with in the past, but have managed to work through it by making sure my clients have a few pictures with me as well as a text history. My personal social media is private, has my real name, and the profile picture is a stupid hand-drawn cat on a wine bar napkin, courtesy of Iris.

"Of course. No problem," I reassure him even as I cringe, mentally deducting money from my bank account.

Terrence was going to be my big holiday client. Four days over Christmas with his family at their lake house in Michigan. For the last three years, I've been saving so I can cover all the costs for grad school, and though I was guaranteed to freeze my ass off during this job, the money from it was exactly what I needed to reach my goal. I was so close and now I'm three steps behind.

Refusing to let myself waste the day wallowing, I finish my call with Terrence and check my waitlist and incoming emails. In my personal email, there's yet another notice that my admission status has been updated, which I promptly ignore the same way I do every day when the automated message pops up.

Even if I am accepted for my master's program, at this rate I might as well defer another semester to make sure I have enough saved.

Work wise, I find yet another cancellation. A majority of the dates on the waitlist requests have passed, but I send out a few follow-ups for late December and New Years.

Once cleared, the top email is from Liam. Or more precisely, L. Hughes at *Spitfire.*

> *Dear Juliet,*
>
> *Thank you for spending the evening with me. I feel like I didn't end the night properly. My words tend to come out best in black and white. I'm better edited. I wanted to let you know, if I could always have nights like that, I'd leave my apartment more often.*
>
> *I've attached the version of the article going to print tomorrow. Read it, or don't, since I know you're avoiding pieces with my name in the byline.*
>
> *L. Hughes (your not-so-celebrity crush)*

I open it again, my cursor hovering over the delete icon. I'm going to do it—delete the evidence. Maybe I'll see him again with Jasmine, but I don't need to keep this like some text thread to pine over and misinterpret.

Here I go.

My computer pings as a new message pops up on the top of my screen, indicating I have a hit on my intake form. I close Liam's email—a problem for another day.

The new request is for a holiday work party tomorrow night. Usually, I'd outright reject it. But Jasper, the potential client, has given plenty of information that boils down to wanting to impress his boss and show he's committed to staying in NYC. He explains the reason for this is because in the past he's sought out new work positions every two years, but now he's hoping for a promotion.

At the bottom, he's filled out the optional portion saying he has a referral from someone I've previously worked with. I don't get many, because giving one requires essentially admitting you've hired a fake girlfriend. Still, I'm not sure how comfortable I am with this. Iris and I have a system in place for whenever I feel unsafe and nearly every date or event I go to is with plenty of people and never anywhere secluded. But I need the money.

I decide to get out of the apartment and think about it while I walk. I bundle up in a sweater and coat, popping in a headphone as I head downstairs. It's been steadily snowing all morning, but the sidewalks outside have already reached that slushy state that makes the world look forlorn and gray.

In my hand, my phone rings with an incoming call. With gloves on, I have to tap the screen multiple times to pick up.

"Hey, Mom, where are you guys today?" I ask. She and Daniel have been honeymooning for two months now. My new stepdad is an actuary who's never taken a vacation in his life. So after they got married, he decided to use all his accrued vacation time and now they're globe trotting.

"Verona. There's this Christmas market here that's to die for. They have these Italian holiday cakes—God, so good. But Daniel and I ended up walking with this other couple, cute as hell. The wife was wearing this sweater I got the link to. I'm sending it to you now." She pauses, and my phone chimes with the incoming message.

"That's great. Did you just want to tell me about the sweater?" I ask.

"The sweater is just a fun little treat. While we were at this stall with all these mittens, I overheard them talking about your article. Isn't that crazy? People in Italy know about you!" she gushes. "I mean they're American, but they've been here for a few weeks so I think it counts."

I huff a laugh, sending a cloud from my lips. "It sounds like you're having the time of your life. What's next on the itinerary?"

She launches into explaining their route through Italy before heading to Vienna where they'll be spending Christmas. I've heard it before, but I can't get enough of her sounding so excited.

We weren't close when I was younger. I was embarrassed by her eccentricities when the rest of my friends had normal parents, which usually meant stuck up and hands off, but I couldn't see that at the time. My mom was a free-spirit who married into money where the rest of those around us had been born into it. After Dad was arrested, she tried to make our new life seem like a grand adventure. But I was twenty by then and resented her optimism before I could come to appreciate it.

She taught me to work hard. To scream into pillows after shitty shifts. The best brand of cheap wine. She taught me that surviving is hard but it's more bearable when you're in it with someone you care about.

Now, she's found a man who's embraced her love of putting knicknacks on every flat surface of their new home and is traveling to a dozen Christmas markets with her. I know I could talk to her about going to school again and the financial blow I've taken over the last few days, but I want her to enjoy this new life of hers without having to worry about me when I'm capable of taking care of myself.

"Have to go! We found mulled wine!" she chimes. "Love you."

"Love you."

I walk another block before I reach Trove, my favorite, and completely out of my price range, vintage store. Its large glass windows display mannequins in vibrant ensembles. Rich brocade Valentino. Metallic futuristic 90s Alexander McQueen. Vibrant Emilio Pucci dresses straight out of a romcom. I love museums as much as the next gal, but point me toward the nearest vintage store and I'll be lost for hours, or until I'm asked multiple times if I intend to buy anything.

"Henrietta, darling, we just got in this haul from an estate sale—Galliano era Dior. Very Sarah Jessica Parker," Marty says from behind the front desk as I walk into the bright curated space. Marty is in his fifties, arms adorned with American traditional tattoos, and has the best salt and pepper hair you'll ever see. He runs the store front while his partner, Alexi, travels the east coast sourcing items. Iris and I met them at Pride when we first moved here in June, and I've visited ever since.

Usually, I avoid putting down any firm roots in new cities, but with the potential of staying here for school on the horizon, I've allowed myself this one exception. And after the morning of doom and gloom, it's nice to escape to somewhere familiar.

"Don't tempt me. I'm about to be on a sodium rich ramen diet. I just stopped in to see beautiful things," I lament.

"All that sodium might be worth it. Good clothes feed the soul, and you know what else does?"

I flutter my lashes. "I bet you're going to tell me."

"Helping an old man rearrange furniture. Someone bought the Herman Miller lounge chair and a side table. It's thrown this entire place out of wack."

"No, not the therapist chair." I pout, mourning the loss of the black leather vintage chair that cost as much as three months of my rent.

"Just wait until you see its replacement." Marty's green eyes light up and I can't help but get excited.

I follow him to the functional display with the hole where the chair used to be. Removing lamps with stained glass shades, we shift side tables to make more space then grunt as we lift the tandem sofa with avocado vinyl seats. Once everything is in place, he guides me to the processing room, a treasure trove of all of the inventory that's yet to make it onto the floor.

"Isn't she something?" Marty says, sitting at the heart of the wine red anemone chair.

Delicately, I run my hand over the plush velvet. "Can you tell me who ends up buying this so I can steal it?"

"You and me both," he says, pushing up and out of the chair and toward one of the work tables. "That reminds me. Alexi found this and snagged it for you. Apparently he had to fight off a Real Housewife of somewhere for it. Real bloodbath, the way he tells it."

He grabs a red velvet dress with a bow on the bust that is undeniably breathtaking and sets it on the work table for me to inspect. My mouth goes dry. Vivian Westwood Red Label.

It's a bit big in the waist and has a tear in the hem, but even after everything that happened, the one thing I've never been able to completely let go of is my expensive taste. So I learned how to hand sew, my Singer sewing machine being one of the first things I bought with money I earned. I'd scour local thrift stores for hidden gems, quiet luxury items from brands people rarely flaunt and tailor them. I've made my own clothes too, and I love them, but I'm a far cry from the greats.

When I was looking at masters' programs, I also glanced at FIT and Parsons. But fashion isn't a career I could comfortably rely on, so I keep it as a passion.

"No. I can't accept this." I put my hands behind my back even as I yearn to touch it.

"You're taking it. A Christmas gift. I see you staring at all of those dresses out there." He looks down his nose at me. "Holding them up to see if they're your size—always the best stuff, might I add."

I shake my head even as I run my fingers over one sheer sleeve. "This really is too much."

"Think of it as payment for all your free labor if that makes you feel better. Take it and make sure to wear it somewhere glamorous." Marty grabs a garment bag, sealing the dress inside.

And it does. His words cause my shoulders to relax. I don't like feeling like I owe people anything—that they have some sort of power over me.

We chat a bit longer before I head home for a lunch of leftovers. After eating, I try on the dress, practically moaning as the high quality fabric slips over my skin. I twirl in the mirror, the hem swishing flirtatiously over my thighs.

Still wearing the dress, I reply to Jasper, sending him my contract.

I want to stay. I want this life. I've worked hard for it, and will continue to.

7

Liam

How's Iris?" I ask Jasmine, handing her an iced latte from the office building's lobby cafe.

She looks up from the document on her computer screen outlining an article. "Iris is great. We're going out again tonight. I do love it when you ask about my life without any ulterior motives. It makes me feel loved, cared for, and not used at all." She swivels in her chair to face me and smirks, taking a long sip of the coffee, draining it a quarter of the way in one go. "The bribe is a nice touch, though."

"I just haven't heard back from Henri about the article," I say. "And I'm worried that I messed up. The only reason she'd ignore me is that she's mad, right?"

I've played back that night a thousand times, both in my head and relistening to the recording. She has a sultry scratchiness to her voice that seems to come from constant use, and I can't get enough of it. As someone who listens to a lot of recordings, I'd like to think I know a thing or two about a good voice.

But my favorite part?

About halfway through, she changed, just relaxed. Juliet is put together with clean-cut professionalism. Henri? Oh, Henri is just a touch weird—the best type that draws you in and entices you to be yourself. Laughing and saying whatever's on her mind. Dancing around her room barefoot in an evening gown at two in the morning.

So why haven't I heard back from her yet? It's been three days since the article, but a week since I sent her the pre-print.

"The article? That's the only thing you want to talk to her about?" Jasmine cocks a brow.

"I—"

"Liam, would you come meet me in my office?" Fallon asks as she strides by us, heading toward her glass-walled office.

"What do you think that's about?" Iris asks. "Cause the article about Henri? Whoo." She fans herself with a copy of last month's issue.

"I guess I'm about to find out."

I shrug, then follow Fallon, not wanting to keep her waiting.

The response to the article has been great. It's the most traction I've gotten on anything really. It feels like a punch in the gut that my career seems to be taking off just before it ends. At least I'll have this high note to reflect back on.

I close the door behind me as I enter Fallon's office. The space is chic with mid century modern leather furniture, warm wood finishes, and a few strategically placed plants that provide pops of color.

"Go ahead and take a seat," Fallon says from behind her desk as she flicks open her silver laptop.

I do as she instructs. "What did you need to talk about?"

"You're single, right?" she asks so casually that it takes me a moment to register her words.

She can't mean . . .

"Um . . . I . . . I'm sorry, but I think I'm missing something?" I stammer.

Fallon types something quickly then lowers the screen most of the way. "Just making sure there wouldn't be any complications for a follow-up piece. We have the opportunity to push your initial article further. Instead of just an interview about what it's like to be a professional plus-one, why not go out with her and get the real experience. You've had a viral moment and we need to capitalize on it. I know I'm asking even more of you but our site traffic doubled and those numbers will really help us close the quarter on a high note and help me justify increasing our budget to the board."

"I can reach out, but I'm not sure if I'll be able to book something—she's a busy person," I rush to say. A week, that's an appropriate amount of time for a follow-up email, right? There's always a chance my first one got buried in her inbox.

Yeah, Liam, stay delusional. This is the girl who only invited you over because you got sexiled.

She didn't even want to be around me when I offered to buy her food. Still . . . By the end of the night there was something between us. Time felt like it had stood still. I could have watched her try on clothes until the sun came up. I can't make myself delete the pictures of her on my phone even though I don't need them anymore.

I could have just read the whole thing wrong; I'm not exactly great with people. Growing up, kids my age were always my competitors and I was encouraged to never get too friendly with them. I was trained to distrust and be sceptical of people's motives. In some ways, the mentality has helped me during interviews, allowing me to understand that people are often hiding something that's worth finding, not to use against them as my father would urge us to do, but to understand.

But Henri, she's a master of shapeshifting. She gave me scraps, answers that she knew I'd want to hear, but there were moments of more when she'd accidentally let something real slip out. I can't quite nail her down, no matter how much I want to.

"Make sure she knows we'll pay for her services. Ideally, we can do something for Christmas or New Years." Fallon cocks her head as she weighs the possibilities. "If you can't do it, I could see if someone else would be available."

"No," I say a bit too loudly, prompting Fallon to raise a brow. "I've got it, and she took a while to open up so I wouldn't want anyone else to have to repeat that process now that I have a connection." *Really smooth, Liam. Not suspicious or desperate at all.*

At least I now have an official excuse to send a second email, and I'll be damned if she goes out with someone else.

"Great." Fallon nods. "Thank you for stepping up. Know you'll always have a place here with us, if what you have back home doesn't work out."

She opens her laptop again, and taking her dismissal, I head back to my desk.

That afternoon, I send Henri a follow up email with Fallon's proposal. I find myself clicking between my inbox and the tabs I have open for various top-selling colognes and men's self-care items for a piece I've been asked to consult on. From what Henri explained, she works evenings and does admin during the day. She has to have seen my email. Is she ignoring me? Did she read the article and hate it?

When an argument breaks out about the sexiest Christmas movies, the entire office starts a voting poll and I welcome the distraction. The top contenders are *Eyes Wide Shut* and *The Holiday*—a battle between raw sensuality and Jude Law in glasses showing emotional vulnerability.

After work, I head back with Iris to our apartment, but she only sticks around long enough to change and touch up her lipstick.

I get food delivered and try to keep busy so I won't check my email.

Around seven my phone lights up, pinging with a rapid influx of notifications.

Mom

Starting to build a list of snacks to have in the house when you visit. Send me ideas!

Pen

I don't know what I want to eat tonight. How will I know what I want to eat in three weeks?

Me

Just make Pen get it when she comes back from Chamonix

June

Yeah, great idea if you want her to get crushed tomatoes instead of salsa

Pen

That was one time!

June

And there was a blizzard so we had nothing else.

Mom

Liam?

Me

I'm fine with whatever.

I hesitate for a moment, before typing.

Me

What if I brought someone home with me this year?

I'm just testing the water, laying the groundwork. I'm not saying I will bring someone home—if Henri says no, or I can't get ahold of her, then I'll just say plans have changed.

Mom messages me separately and there's no avoiding answering her.

I barely have time to press send before a Pen's contact photo floods my screen with a FaceTime call. In her contact picture, she's asleep in one of the lodge's overstuffed chairs, hot chocolate staining her mouth, her honey-brown hair plastered to her head from wearing her helmet all day.

"You're dating someone! Please tell me she's cool and really into galleries or something so I can visit and do something interesting," she chimes. "And why is this the first I've heard of this?

It's late in Chamonix, but Pen is one of those people who sleeps at odd hours, crashing for naps between incredible bursts of high energy. I think part of it is that she's never in the same time zone for long. She's sponsored by the energy drink company BLITZ, and is in a constant cycle of being the subject of their high octane extreme sports content. She also competes at national and international levels, but her one true love is adrenaline.

"It's new. I'm only bringing it up to help with planning." And if by some miracle Henri replies, I want to start hinting at the relationship now. It's one of the things she mentioned during the interview, creating some sort of believable history to sell the date. I also like talking about her with someone other than Jasmine.

"Have you told June already?" Pen hates being left out, always has. When we were younger, she always insisted on coming with us to the more challenging runs, which has led to Mom now blaming us for Pen's extreme sports career.

June and I always have been the closest because we both specialized in Alpine Skiing and are only a year apart in age. And with Pen being five years younger than me and primarily snowboarding, I rarely trained with her before I quit entirely. Plus, there's something about going through life with someone, experiencing nearly the same things as them, that creates an undeniable bond. Still, after I quit skiing and moved away for college, that bond has been tested constantly.

"This is the first time I'm talking about it with any of you."

"Good. Send me a picture. I want to see what she looks like."

"Fine. Just don't be weird about it. She's private. Doesn't have social media or anything," I say.

Scrolling back through the photos from the other night, I select one of Henri in the red formal dress, draping limbs dramatically over a clothing rack. From a technical standpoint, the lighting is terrible, all coming from dim floor lamps that cast diffuse shadows. But Henri makes the photo phenomenal. Her blonde bob is messy from a long day, chocolate brown eyes rimmed with smudged mascara locked on me, and a casual smile teases her lips as she talks.

It's the type of photo you find in a shoe box decades later and remember what it was like to be young.

Pen lets out a whistle of appreciation. "Shit. She's hot. Does she smoke? She looks like she smokes skinny cigarettes and tells people they're pretty in bar bathrooms."

"She doesn't smoke." I have no idea but it's a safe bet after not seeing any evidence of it. But the question tugs at a part of me that wants to know. Wants to see if after a night out she'll take a cigarette if offered. "And she's nice. She really likes to understand people—cares about strangers more than most people do." This I know for sure.

"You have to bring her. I'm going to teach her to snowboard, since you're out of practice and June is too uptight to teach her how to ski without scaring her off."

I wince at the reminder. I haven't been on the slopes much since my ACL tear at sixteen, only going out once or twice each time I visit to scratch an itch. Before then I was on track with June to go pro, I practically lived in the snow. Sportscasters ate it up—siblings destined for greatness to keep your eye on. Rising stars.

A new call from Jasmine comes onto my phone and I release a sigh of relief. "I bet she'd love that. Pen, I have to go. My roommate is trying to get a hold of me."

I hang up and switch calls.

"Everything okay?" I ask.

But it's not Jasmine who answers. Instead, Iris's voice comes through the speaker. "I need you to go get Henri. She's with a client right now and texted me she needs help."

"Are you sure I should?" I ask, but I'm already on my feet, heading to the door.

"You're closer than we are. Jas said the address is a block away from your place. And don't you dare say no. It's your fault she took this last minute job in the first place."

Shoving my feet into my shoes, I balance my phone, pressing it between my cheek and shoulder. "Don't worry, I'm almost out the door. What do you mean it's my fault?"

Iris sighs. "She doesn't like talking about money, so she won't tell me outright. But after the article dropped she keeps getting these calls that I'm pretty sure are cancellations. She told me about her date tonight at the last minute, which she never does. So I'm assuming she's only doing it because she needs to."

Shit. Well, at least I know why she's not talking to me. I hate the idea that I might have pressured her into something that ended up hurting her.

"All right, send me the address."

8

Henri

"C an you stop checking your phone," Jasper demands as we stand next to the thoroughly picked over remnants of the office party's buffet that's been set up in the open reception area of the law firm where he works. A cheap move, but I don't work here so I don't exactly have a right to complain about the thrown together affair.

Can you stop trying to touch my ass, I want to say. Instead, I put my phone away, plaster a smile on my face, and tell him, "Sorry, I have a friend who's been in the hospital a lot lately." Not exactly a lie, just an omission about why said friend is there.

"You promised me your full attention tonight. Isn't that what I'm paying you for? You look good and help make me look good." His hand slides down my waist to my hip, again. "You look great by the way."

Pinching his hand between my thumb and forefinger I remove it and step away so there's a foot between us. "Thank you. I'm a *professional*." I shouldn't have taken this job. He's the exact type of guy I'd reject after an initial meeting. Slimy and entitled. *Iris, if you could hurry up with the getaway car or emergency call that would be great.*

"So you have a lot of experience then?" Suggestion drenches his words.

"If you read your contract, then you'd know if you continue this behavior I'll leave without processing a refund."

"C'mon, all that legal shit is just to cover your ass—make what you do seem legit."

Sex work is work, hard work, but it's not what I do.

I'm not above kneeing this guy in the balls in front of all his coworkers, but I'd prefer not to. Angry customers are dangerous. Not just physically, but they could also leak my information. It doesn't matter if they've signed an ironclad NDA. Angry men are unpredictable and their unpredictability ruins lives while they get to walk away with a slap on the wrist.

Stupid. I was so stupid.

Wanting and wishing for a dream life made me reckless.

"I'm leaving," I say, ducking away from him. I take a step and a hand wraps around my wrist. As I tug, his grip tightens, making my eyes water with the shock of pain that radiates from the pressure.

"Bitch," he hisses. "I want what I paid for."

No one around us notices. The party has been going for two hours, moving past the point of casual chats and into drunken-mistakes-turned-HR-violation territory.

Bunching the skirt of my dress in my free hand, I stomp firmly on his instep, grinding my foot into his shiny leather loafer. It's painful, or startling enough, for him to let go. I don't look back to see the damage as I weave through swaying bodies. Men with their ties undone, dangling loose around their necks. Women dancing with their heels in one hand and drink in the other. My gaze remains fixed on the glow of the exit sign; the only stop I make is to grab my coat.

I shove through the door and slam into what feels like a wall. One that wasn't there when I came through these exact same doors earlier.

"Fuck," I yelp and stumble away from the structural anomaly.

Firm hands land on my shoulders, steadying me. "Henri, are you okay?"

I flinch at the sudden contact. "Liam, what are you doing here?" As I register the familiar voice, I tilt my head back to see him looking down at me, his unkempt brown hair hanging over wild, searching eyes. His face is the picture of unbridled concern.

"Iris," he explains, his voice is thin and breathy as if he ran here. "But it seems like you were just leaving."

I take his hand at the reminder that I need to get the hell out and start guiding him down the hall toward the elevator bay. "Yes, the princess saves herself in this one. But let's not wait around and see if I actually need reinforcements."

I jam my finger into the down button. The elevator chimes and doors swing open. We slip inside and I press the first floor and close door buttons in quick succession, my pulse still pounding in my ears.

"You didn't answer my question yet. Are you okay?" Liam squeezes my hand, causing me to realize I've forgotten to let it go.

I do now, bracing myself with both hands against the rails lining the elevator car. "I got out."

"Still not an answer."

"This has only happened twice before. I do the prep work to make sure it doesn't. It's my fault; I shouldn't have been so impulsive." My breath quickens, and I fix my gaze on the ceiling. This is so embarrassing. I'm good at this, but every time Liam's around, I slip up. Confronting him at the restaurant, reading too much into the interview the other night, and now this?

He must think I'm some sort of joke.

"From what I heard, this is my fault, not yours. And even if I didn't contribute to why you were in that room, no one has the right to demand anything from you that makes you uncomfortable." His voice is soft and coaxing. My job is to be concerned about other people, not myself. His worry for my well-being causes something to tighten in my chest.

"Why do you think this is your fault?"

"You've been getting cancellations since the article dropped, right?"

"Thanks for the reminder."

"See, my fault." He raises his brows. Touché.

"But at least it's a sign the article was good, which is expected since you wrote it."

"I've written a hundred pieces. None of them have taken off like this. I owe that success to you." There's a seriousness in his tone that causes me to finally look at him. When I do, my gaze latches with his and my breath catches at the firm intensity of his stare, leaving me no room to argue.

The elevator releases us into the lobby and we head out past the security desk and into the bitter cold of the night.

"So, where's the car waiting? Or did you take the subway?" I ask, walking toward the edge of the sidewalk, eyes on the cars parked on the curb. I'm ready for this night to be over with.

"I kind of ran here?"

I look behind me. Liam's flushed from the cold or embarrassment, I don't know. He's scraping a hand through his hair, and for the first time, I notice his clothes. Flannel pajama bottoms, boots, and a half-zipped parka.

"You rolled out of bed and ran here? It's freezing out."

"Technically, I was on the couch. Any other way would have taken too long. I live nearby—that's why Iris called, since I could get here faster than she could."

A smile teases the corners of my lips. "You look ridiculous."

"Excuse me if fashion took a back seat to your safety." Even with his anxious movements, his eyes are firm as they catalog every detail of my face. Snow starts to fall, clinging to his long dark lashes.

I fidget, uncomfortable. No one's ever shown up for me like this. My first instinct is to run hard and fast, it's the same gut feeling that's convinced me to ignore his email. But when was the last time I felt like I didn't need to be in complete control?

Easy, the other night with him at my place when I fought the urge to graze my fingers across the galaxy of freckles on his skin. But before that? I don't know.

"Thanks for showing up. I guess I should get a car." I hesitate, before reaching for my phone. "Unless you're hungry. I haven't eaten yet. I'll buy."

I wasn't all that hungry at the party, but now my nerves have settled and I feel like I'm running on empty.

"No way I'm letting you do that."

I argue with Liam about who should pay, until he lets it slip that he already started eating and has food back at his place. He insists that he has enough for the both of us, which is how I end up sitting on his floor, ravenously stabbing at re-heated sesame chicken.

"Maybe I should order more," Liam says, watching me as I dig in. He's let me borrow sweatpants and a worn Beach Boys shirt that has that fresh, almost powdery, scent of laundry detergent.

"I'll be fine," I reassure him, even as I try to remember if I finished off the bag of Doritos last night. I'm in no mood to cook, especially now that the adrenaline has drained from me and I feel boneless with exhaustion.

"Why is it that I'm the only person who's not allowed to buy you food? Lunch and now this?"

"I guess this means we have to find a way for me to turn down breakfast," I say as I mix sauce into my rice.

"Do you hate me so much that you won't even take free food from me?"

"It's not just you—don't go thinking you're special. The only men who buy me food are the ones who are paying me." I huff a laugh. "You don't think I actually hate you, do you?"

"I mean I'm going zero for three on emails. You tell me." He picks at his food, as if pretending not to care, but the divot between his brows gives away how much my answer must matter to him.

"I don't hate you, I'm just—" *Scared how much I wanted to be close to you the other night? Terrified that this life I'm building will fall apart and I won't be able to stay in the city I'm slowly falling in love with.* "I'm not the best with people."

He scoffs. "C'mon you're great at first dates. That's one of the hardest things when it comes to people."

I pick up my fork and point at him with it. "Keyword: *First*. And then there's the fact that I'm not actually me, I'm a character. People like me because they literally made up a version of me that they wanted. I'm not good at making friends when it comes to the real me." I try my best not to think of the past, of Kurt and Laura. Of how they knew me, yet found me so easy to leave when I needed them the most. The only person I can guarantee will show up for me is me.

"You have Iris," he points out, and he looks like he's holding himself back from saying more.

"I have Iris," I agree, "and we move every five or six months, land in a new city, make some money, and then we rinse and repeat. It's not exactly a lifestyle that lends itself to anything long-term." As I tell him this, there's a part of me that seems to scream, *See, there's no point in knowing me. No point in buying me food and asking me questions. Don't care about me. Stick around long enough and you'll learn who I really am and be disappointed.*

"But you're done with that now. You'll be here for grad school for three years? That's how long your program is, right?"

"If I can afford it." I push a limp steamed green bean across the plate, my appetite shrinking as my stomach churns with anxiety. "I've been saving for a long time since I don't want to go into debt. The clients who canceled were supposed to push me past the finish line with a small cushion. I thought the article wouldn't be a big deal since I had planned on this being my last year being a date for hire."

"Shit," he says softly, as if reprimanding himself. "Sorry, I keep bringing it up."

"It's fine. Not talking about it isn't going to make the problem disappear."

"What are you doing for Christmas?"

"Seriously, you don't have to change the topic . . . but, nothing. My client for that week canceled." This will be my first Christmas not working in years. It would be nice to get a bottle of wine and watch all the shows I keep swearing I'll get to. There will be plenty to do in the city. I'll be off for a whole week. I can't think of the last time I had so much time for myself.

Nope. Just like that I'm hit with a new muscle-tensing wave of anxiety. How fucked up am I that the idea of having time for fun makes my body feel like I've just been threatened at knife point?

His brows pinch. "And you're not doing anything with your family?"

"My mom's in Europe with my stepdad for their honeymoon. And Christmas isn't really a big thing for us, so I don't feel like I'm missing out on anything," I explain, then brace for the pitying look.

I don't mind not having Christmas traditions. At this point, work is my tradition. What I do mind are the looks from people that then make me feel like I *should* feel like shit. And then they make a big deal about it, and I have to make them feel better. This is my normal. Sure, I'd love to have a Christmas full of light and warmth, but that's just a dream.

"For the record, I'm not trying to change the subject. My boss wants a follow-up to our interview. I've been cleared to pay your fee to go out with you. I'm assuming taking you with me for the holidays will help cover a good chunk of your losses."

"Wouldn't that be redundant? If your family has read the article, don't you think they'd ask questions if you suddenly brought home a girl out of nowhere." I should just say, *Yes, please solve all my issues,* but for some reason I feel the need to talk him out of this—talk him out of me.

Like we've already crossed some invisible line in the sand that will make it impossible to uphold the professional boundaries that I cling to. But all we've done is talk, and yet, there's an intimacy between us I'd be a fool to deny.

"They don't read my stuff. I don't think they know where I work." He flushes as his eyes travel to the books stashed on a shelf in the TV stand. "I'm just their son who writes puff pieces when he could be doing something better with his life."

"Liam—" I start.

"It's fine. You have Christmas; I have this."

"I get it," I say.

"So is that a yes?" Hope shines in his eyes.

"Take me home for Christmas, Liam."

9

Liam

Two days after Henri came to my apartment, Fallon calls me into her office.

"I can't approve your budget proposal for the article." There's no hesitation as she hurls a wrecking ball into my plans.

Her words send a heavy rush of dread straight to my stomach and I'm grateful that I'm seated because I might topple over. "It's her standard rate plus travel expenses. Didn't you say that advertisers are already eager for that space?"

"Yes, but the point of this is to make money, not breakeven. The maximum we can do is seventy percent, in addition to the increased costs of last minute holiday travel expenses for her. I understand that because of the unique nature of her work we can't offer exposure the same way we do with most products, so this is the best we can do."

"But—"

"If that doesn't work we'll just have to axe the follow-up and come up with something else for that slot. This is a last minute addition, so this is stretching the budget as is." Her tone leaves no room for negotiation. *Spitfire* isn't the type of publication that could be considered a household name, and Fallon is a smart business woman. She won't risk going into the red over one piece, no matter how much potential it has.

"I'll send her our offer and negotiate." I rise shakily to my feet bracing my hands on the armrests of my seat.

There's no point in telling Fallon that Henri needs that money, or that our initial article is the reason why. Even if we pull it, the damage is done to Henri's career. I also have a feeling that if I voice this, Fallon will get as far as she can from the entire project to avoid any potential legal issues.

But Henri isn't like that. From what I witnessed the other night, she's the type of person who would rather work harder to make up for her losses than enter into a legal battle.

"Fallon?" I say. "What if I can get her to agree to covering travel expenses and we cover her standard fee. That way we wouldn't have to go through the hassle of collecting itemized receipts. And she travels a lot, so maybe she has miles?"

"If you can get her to agree to that, let me know and I'll issue an official approval."

Back at my desk I settle in and navigate to my email.

> *Juliet,*
> *Your rate has been approved and we'll move forward as planned*
> *for the project. As for travel expenses please send me whatever you*
> *need and I will book them directly for you.*
> *L. Hughes.*

> *Mr. Hughes.*
> *Sounds good to me.*
> *J*

> *I see how it is. I offer to pay for an all-expenses-paid vacation*
> *and now you respond.*
> *L.*

> *I'm a simple woman. I know my worth.*
> *If you're ready to get started, meet me at Moxy Cafe tomorrow*
> *at 10.*
> *xoxo*
> *J*

"You take all of your clients here?" I ask. The table wobbles as I set up
my notebook and phone to record. Moxy is tucked into the corner of
a line of shops in Brooklyn, with tall windows with yellow swooping
lettering complemented by emerald green paint on the exterior.

"Or places like it," Henri says from where she's seated across from me. "Go ahead, try the coffee. Let me know what you think." She tips her mug to her lips and waits.

I mirror her, interested to see what's so special about this shop. The latte hits my tongue and it takes everything in me not to recoil and cough. It's bitter and earthy. A film clings to my mouth even after I've swallowed.

"It's umm . . . different than I expected." I inspect my cup. Brown flecks pepper the liquid. Are those coffee grounds?

"Explain." Her lips twitch in barely-contained amusement.

"Well, it's . . . I . . ." I try to string something good together before slumping against the back of my chair. "Please tell me you don't bring people here."

"Why wouldn't I?" She smiles innocently.

I lean in so my elbows rest on the table. Lowering my voice, not wanting the teenage barista to hear, I say, "Do you want me to tell you this is terrible? I don't know how you're drinking yours."

"My *tea* is fine." She shrugs. "But that *is* the point. I take people here before I agree to work with them. I'm a service provider; I want to see how people act when something doesn't meet their expectations—if they're rude to the barista when they order, how they tip, and how they react to their bad coffee."

"I see." Nodding, I reach for my notebook and start to write, but as I write the final word and lift my pen, the notebook is torn away from me. When I attempt to grab it back, Henri takes the opportunity to snag the pen from my loosened grip.

"'Performs a social experiment on her clients to see if they can stand up to torture'?" she reads aloud. Then tuts, scratching out my words and writing under it. "Here, updated it for you." The table legs rattle as she plops down her updates in front of me.

Smart woman doesn't believe what men tell her, so she takes them to coffee.

"Okay. Fine. But what if someone looks up the ratings for the place?"

"We go somewhere else. This isn't just a test to figure out someone is an asshole. There are plenty of people who won't say a thing about the coffee and drink all of it because they are massive people pleasers. No matter what, coffee shops are neutral territory. Here people are more likely to show more of their true selves than they would on a survey."

I start writing again and Henri cranes her neck as I add one word before the word smart. *Really.* "You bring people here for your little experiment to see if they'll throw hot coffee in the face of a service worker and then what?"

"I get to know what I'm up against, what prep work I'll need to do. Sometimes there are certain skills I need to learn to become the ideal person. I've learned sports, read books, watched YouTube deep dives on movies. There was a wedding I attended that had a tennis tournament for the members of the wedding party. After a month of training, I had a pretty wicked backhand."

"I'm not going to ask you to learn a new skill, but my family has a tendency to make everything a competition." Gingerbread house making, tree decorating, even seeing who can make it into town the fastest—everything is fair game, and my dad has always encouraged it.

"Tell me about your family. What should I expect?" Henri leans back in her chair, arms falling to the side. A noticeably open posture. I wonder if it's unconscious how she seems to settle into this version of herself who seems ready to absorb something new.

My fingers trap my mug, enjoying the lingering warmth of the drink, if not the taste. I hesitate a moment, I try to avoid talking about these details, but I know they're necessary to share to fully immerse myself in the experience. "They're all Olympians and international title holders. All of them, except me." I pause for a second, watching to see if Henri reacts. She doesn't, but chances are she already knows. I bet she did her homework on me the same way I've done for her. "They're hard workers. My youngest sister, Pen, is a ball of energy. June is more reserved, but one of the most competent and capable people I know, even if she can come off a bit harsh."

There are only a few people out there I'd say I'm truly close to and my sisters are at the top of the list. When I still competed we trained together for endless hours, if one of us was worn out or needed an excuse to just be normal and hang out with friends we'd cover for each other.

Henri lifts her cup to her lips and a small hum escapes her as she takes a sip. I can't help myself. I grab my pen and write: *Hums when she likes the taste of something.* Putting her cup back down she continues, "What about your parents?"

"They met when they were both competing. My dad still coaches my sisters when they're home and runs the training facility and ski lodge—he takes it really seriously. Mom helps too, but has taken a pretty big step back recently," I explain.

Where Mom was able to soften and let go of her competition years, Dad has clung on, blurring the line between coach and father, even at home, comparing my siblings and I constantly. To him, what I do now, though not said outright, must be a disappointment—all my potential gone to waste. It's part of the reason he's so eager for me to come home.

I check Henri's face for a spark of surprise, but her features remain serene and impassive. "But you aren't necessarily the biggest fan of all of it, are you?"

"What gave that away?" It's not that I hide it, but there's something in my chest that seems to reach for her at this acknowledgement.

"For one, there's the fact that if you squeeze your mug any harder, you'll shatter it and ruin that notebook of yours." Her eyes rove over me. I think if it were anyone else, the pressure of their attention would make me uncomfortable, make me want to jump up and create an excuse before

I would head to the bathroom. "It's also the way you said it, like you don't feel the same way as most people, but feel like your experience is wrong."

"It's the truth. Pretty much everyone loves them." They're fun and so full of energy, constantly pushing for greatness or some new adventure. Electric. But that electricity can be draining.

"But I'm not working with most people. I'm working with *you*. I'm on your side in this."

"You're good at your job," I say. If she's like this with everyone no wonder she's as successful as she is. Or at least *was* before I ruined it for her.

Her lips split into a wide grin. "I am until you crack the illusion. I'm not used to doing this with people I know." There she is, tilting toward me, into my space.

It's like there's two Henris. The one right here, in front of me, full of joy and determination, and the other version that's muted and moldable, ready to take on any shape she needs. I wonder how many people get to see this part of her? Unfiltered.

"Speaking of that. I can't call you Juliet or whatever else you go by. I'll mess up and screw over the whole operation."

"Yeah, that's a fair point. It's best to go with as close to the truth as possible, less room for error. Now let's hammer out the basics. It will be your parents and siblings, so four people besides us?"

"Yeah, I don't think they're having anyone else over this year."

"Four people. Challenging, but not terrible. The more people who are there, the more likely something will slip, but we have the next few weeks to really solidify our story. That's where the planning comes in."

Now she's the one pulling things out and putting them on the table. Her purse is massive, which is probably intentional since the first time I saw it she was pulling out a whole wardrobe. With a stack of flashcards in front of her, she dedicates one for the info I've given her on each family member.

She's still writing when she asks, "So, have we had sex?"

I choke on air, having to pound my chest to take in a breath. "Not that I remember?"

"Your family, would they think we have? Sleeping arrangement wise, what do you think is expected?" She talks like that was obviously her meaning, but I have the feeling she likes toying with me, not that I mind.

"Separate rooms," I say almost immediately. Sleeping in the same bed as her? Yeah, I doubt I'd survive that. Even the thought of her body pressed against mine has me hot all over.

"Great. They think you're a virgin loser." She nods and writes it down word for word.

"Are you this mean to all your clients?"

"Just you." A wicked grin captures her mouth.

"Thanks for the special treatment."

"I think it's smartest to ground our story in facts. We met because our roommates kicked you out of your apartment while I was working at the bar and I was generous enough to take you in for the night. The only difference is the timeline, I'm thinking we say it was in September instead, though. Thoughts?"

"I don't see any problems with it. And you're good with being there for the full week?"

"Yeah, any particular plans I should be aware of?"

"There's a winter sports competition and party after on Christmas Day, but nothing else that I can think of." It's a fundraiser the resort is known for and tends to go over well, but the build up to it can be a touch chaotic.

Henri and I continue to talk about our plans up until the barista starts to pointedly wipe the tables around us. Looking at the clock on my phone, I find that hours have slipped by and the shop is about to close. We head outside, but neither of us walks away.

As the wind cuts by, Henri shivers and I note how her nose and the tips of her ears almost immediately turn pink against the cold. I have the sudden urge to pull her to my chest and warm her up, but of course I don't because like most of my thoughts about her, that would be wildly unprofessional.

She shifts her weight back and forth. "I should get going, but could you send me the flight info whenever you get it? And if I have any incidentals, should I email receipts to you or someone else?"

"Send it to me. I'll make sure it gets through the right channels." Those channels being my credit card, because at this point, that's the only way I can get this to work.

I want to take care of this for her. I fucked up, now I'm fixing it.

10

Henri

"Another date with Liam?" Iris asks as I fuss with the buttons of my cream, strawberry-spotted cardigan in the mirror. Usually I don't wear the clothes I really love out with clients. Knitwear with little fruits on them don't exactly scream *I'm a professional liar and can be trusted with all your insecurities*. But after how Liam and I initially met, I doubt it will make him see me any differently.

Now I have to decide, one button undone or two?

"It's not a date," I say. "Well, it's not a *real* date."

"Last time I checked, you usually only go on two or three with them. Seems disingenuous to lie for his article."

Over the last two weeks, Liam and I have seen each other four times.

Beyond the initial coffee shop meeting where we discussed our initial plans and accidentally ended up staying until closing, we went shopping for his family, because I refused to show up empty-handed. He came and sat at Fender to talk about scheduling, but we ended up talking until close.

Then there was three days ago at Rockefeller Center, where he pretended he wasn't good at ice skating before I called him on his bullshit for trying to make me feel better about falling every ten feet. And once he actually let himself skate, I couldn't look away. Usually he's curled in on himself, but on the ice, he was nothing short of graceful.

Afterward, hot chocolate in hand, he told me about the frozen lake by a cabin his family sometimes uses. The way that he'd skate until his legs gave out and then just lay on the cold slab of ice ringed by trees that stood watch over him like ancient noble guardians.

"It's not just about the article," I say. "And one of those times was because he came by with Jasmine, so those don't count."

"So there *is* another reason?"

Heat floods my cheeks as I settle on one button. "Yes. After the first article, I'm scared people will be hypervigilant about last minute holiday dates. So I'm spending extra time covering my bases."

"Oooh." Iris drops her voice into her best ghost impression and wiggles the fingers of her free hand at me. "The family's worst fear is a woman who won't eventually become their in-law and is only there because she's being paid to tolerate their bullshit."

I roll my eyes. "I just want to get this right."

"I know. But would it be the end of the world if you did enjoy spending time with him?"

"I can't date him. He's paying to spend time with me. That's not a dynamic I'm comfortable with turning into a real relationship." I repeat what I've been telling myself non-stop these last few weeks.

Distractions lead to mistakes and I literally can't afford to make any with so much on the line. I have a plan.

Help with this article. Get the money. Pay for my master's. Get a job that pays enough for me to not constantly stress.

It's already been put at risk once; I won't let it happen again.

She gasps, a hand flying to her chest. "Relationship. Have I ever heard you say such a dirty word?"

"I'm not that bad."

"I'm not going to justify that with a response. But I will point out that he's not paying you—*Spitfire* is. Plus, he knows what you do for work and wouldn't get all weird and judgy about it." Her mouth curls into a grin, proud of herself for finding a loophole. "And you can't say you're leaving soon, because you aren't."

"Iris," I start, but her phone chimes, interrupting me. Her face lights up with a smile. "You really like Jasmine, don't you?" I ask. A hand squeezes my heart, because, really, I want what she has. Not just someone in her life that makes her light up from the inside, but the ability to let herself be swept away. To fall without fear.

When I think about falling, what occupies my mind is the inevitable brutal landing. Maybe that's because the few times I've trusted people to catch me, they didn't.

"Yeah, she's been sending all of these updates for her big holiday shoot. But she's stressed as hell."

"So, are we officially in girlfriend territory?"

"Soon. I think part of it is that we're finally putting down roots."

The words are as close as she ever gets to admitting she's been purposefully holding off on pursuing long term relationships. I hate feeling like she's limiting herself because of me.

"If I don't get into the program and move you could stay here with her—if that would make you happy."

Iris props a hand on her hip and levels me with a stern expression that I know she must use on her difficult patients. "Henrietta Elm, you're not talking that way. You're smart and hard working and aced the stupid fucking standardized test to get in."

"Fine. Just promise me that you'll also take care of you. Don't put your life on hold because of me. Okay?"

"Okay." She reaches out and wraps me in a hug. "But remember, you're part of my life too, you hyper-independent idiot."

An hour later, I meet Liam at The Attic, a used book store along Union Square. It's on the second story of a diner, up a set of rickety stairs with steps that I'm scared to put my full weight on. Music hums through a small speaker on a stool and the muted chatter from the patrons rises up through the floorboards like smoke.

The spot was Liam's pick. Usually, I plan everything, but he suggested that we come here for the day. And it was nice not having to be the one in charge of every detail for a change. Most of the time, I like the element of control, but there was something exciting about being invited deeper into his world.

"Why this place?" I ask. It's small, as far as bookstores go, especially for New York with some shops spanning multiple stories.

"It's never crowded, which is nice. And kind of makes me feel like if I go anywhere else I'm cheating on this place because it doesn't have too many customers. It's also one of the first places I found when I moved here." We walk through the historical fiction section, arms brushing as I step aside to let an older man pass by us. His fingers hover over the dented and cracked spines.

"Have you brought anyone here before?" I ask and immediately wish I could take it back. I blame Iris for putting thoughts in my head. I'm not important to him and starting to act like I am is a bad idea. Maybe I shouldn't have agreed to this.

"No. But I don't really have anyone to bring here. There's Jasmine, but she wouldn't appreciate it and I wouldn't put either of us through that," he says, selecting a Hudson Sloane title. Does that mean he thinks I would appreciate this place? "Sorry if I just made it sound less special."

"I'm honored to be your first. Are books how you got into writing?"

He hesitates. "I had an accident when I was younger—ACL tear. The ligament was completely severed. My family lives on the ski hill pretty far away from anything else and I couldn't exactly be on the slopes while I recovered, so I hung out in the library and read."

"Do you miss it?"

"The mountain? Plenty. Competing? No, not really. I was always more concerned with what other people wanted than what I wanted. Honestly, I could have gone back, but I pretended the injury was worse than it was. Because of it, for the first time in my life I could pick my own path instead of having everything down to what I ate for breakfast planned out for me." His grip on the book tightens.

"Well, I'm happy with the path you chose because it means I got to meet you."

"Thanks. I still feel like I'm bumbling around, trying to figure things out." He laughs half-heartedly, scraping a hand through his hair.

"You're great—you know I think that. Not just anyone reaches celebrity crush status based on their writing alone."

"At the very least, this piece we're doing will make sure I end the year with a bang."

"I love a good bang," I purr in an attempt to lighten the mood.

Liam fumbles, the book in his hand falling, the pages flapping like butterfly wings before smooshing against the floor. "Shit," he hisses.

We both dive to the ground to retrieve it, each grabbing one corner of the cover. "Sorry," we say over each other. We're crouched, faces inches apart, in an odd type of tug-of-war, neither of us showing any sign of moving.

Liam's Adam's apple bobs as his eyes go wide and dilate. My own heart races, blood thundering through my ears.

"Excuse me, but could I pass by?" a rasping voice asks. I turn to my right to find the same old man from earlier.

"I've got it," Liam says and I release my end of the book and step away to clear a path. I pretend to inspect the titles on the shelf until I'm breathing like normal and won't feel like I'll combust just by looking at Liam.

When I do look at him, I find him smoothing the now-bent pages then pushes back up to his feet, offering me a hand as he does. "Let me show you something. It might be my favorite part of the shop."

I nearly refuse to take it, but that would mean acknowledging what just happened. We're supposed to be on a pretend date after all.

At the end of the stack is a reading nook with a faded cushion and an arching window that overlooks Union Square. A crowd snakes through the green-roofed wooden stalls of the winter market, arranged in a triangle to look like a tree.

I must stare because after a minute, Liam asks, "We could go if you want?"

"I don't want to take up too much of your time, and we should probably take a picture here before we go," I say, even though part of me wants to go down there with him. It's the same part of me that is jealous of Mom and Daniel's easy camaraderie as she reclaims her life.

I've never had a typical Christmas, full of family bonding and bickering. I swung from two extremes. Walking into a home with a tree professionally done up without having to lift a finger, and then working through every holiday. Mom still made those special with movies and a few useful gifts like socks or fabric for me to practice sewing with, but we were too tired and broke to do much.

Now that I typically go home with people for the holidays, I step into their lives for a moment, getting glimpses of what I never had. It's always so tempting to get swept up in the homemade ornaments and slightly burnt cookies, but I know the closer I get the more it will hurt when I walk away, to be left out in the cold once more.

Does it make me a fool for wanting it anyway?

"It's no problem. I always make extra room on my schedule for when we meet up."

"Because I'm long-winded and traffic is terrible?" I muse.

"Because I like spending time with you, Henri." His expression softens and something in me threatens to melt. He's so blunt and upfront that no matter how hard I try to come up with an alternative meaning to his words, I can't.

"Well, I like spending time with you, Liam. But that might just be the money I'm making off you. Money makes everyone more tolerable." Usually, that's true. This time, the money has nothing to do with it. But damn it's nice to have it as an excuse.

I expect my humor to crack his sincere expression, but it remains firmly in place.

He takes my hand. A laugh bubbles up out of my throat as he pulls me back through the store with fierce determination. "Come on. We're going to that market."

"I like living on the edge, walking out here with a hardened criminal," I tease as Liam and I walk side by side through the lanes of the market. The green tin roofs of the stalls are trimmed with garland and lights. The aroma of cinnamon and rich spice wafting from those with fresh baked goods. Glittering ornaments and decorations catch my attention every few steps and I have to remind myself to keep moving so as to not cause a traffic jam.

"Say it louder why don't you," Liam mutters. His cheeks are nipped pink with cold but grow a shade darker at my remark. "It was an accident and I paid in the end."

"But only after that poor bookseller chased you down the stairs."

It really was a great moment. Mostly, because I wasn't the one being chastised for trying to steal a book that cost less than five dollars. In his eagerness to leave, both Liam and I forgot about the book clutched in his arm and were stopped by the shop attendant.

"Don't blame me for being in a rush. I had somewhere important to be," he says and the sentiment causes my chest to warm.

I swallow hard and ask, "Where should we go first?"

His gaze wanders for a moment before he starts walking toward a stall with colorful thick knit hats and scarves. We each inspect the goods, fingers rubbing the soft cozy yarn. A hat would be nice. I keep meaning to get one, but I usually use part of my scarf to wrap my head. I wish I could justify buying something. Even though *Spitfire* has agreed to my fee, I'm still stressed about money.

I'm not sure I'll ever not be stressed about money, even if I have thousands tucked away. After the trauma of experiencing such a sudden, unforgiving change in circumstances once, I think there will always be a corner of my mind bracing for it to happen again. But at least I can window shop.

"I wish I could make a bed of this stuff and lay in it forever," I say. Though when I turn Liam is already checking out, his purchase is tucked into a stamped brown paper bag.

"What'd you get?" I ask as he walks over.

In answer, he pulls out the hat the same color as my coat and pulls it onto my head, causing my short hair to flip out around my ears.

I yelp, tearing it off and almost send it to the ground to be trampled. Instead, I leap up and attempt to put it on Liam, but he catches my wrists, holding me in place so my body is pressed against his. Even through my layers, my atoms seem to vibrate—on high alert.

Heat swells in my belly. *Danger. Danger. Danger.*

"Take the hat, Henri," he orders and fuck me it's kind of hot.

"It's too expensive. I saw the prices in that store."

"It's a gift." His hands slide up to work the cap from my grip. The scrape of his fingers against my palms sends a shiver through me and he must feel it because he says, "You're cold, and the tips of your ears always seem like they're on the verge of getting frostbite and falling off."

"I do like having my ears." Arguably the most intelligent response I could make.

"Of course you do, smart girl." This time he lightly pulls the hat over my head, smoothing my hair. "When you're done with me, you'll have something to remember me by. You'll be running out the door to class, and when you grab your favorite hat, you'll think of me keeping you warm."

"My favorite hat?"

"It has to be your favorite if it's your only one."

I know that even if I had a hundred hats, it would still be my favorite.

A phone rings and Liam pulls away, patting at his pockets until he retrieves his phone. "Hey."

"The daddy kink Santa chair is late." Jasmine's frantic voice is loud enough that I can hear her clearly, even if I have no idea what she's talking about. And so can a family walking by who give us nasty looks. Which is fair. I personally wouldn't want to explain that specific sequence of words to a curious child.

Liam flushes. The more I get to know him, the more I like watching his face, how he displays exactly how he feels without bottling it up. I never feel like I need to be scared of him hiding things from me. "Umm, could you say that again, but actually tell me what's going on?"

He and I step to the side and out of the way, brushing up against a cluster of trees with branches weighed down by ornate ornaments and snow. I stand close enough that I can continue to listen to Jasmine. "The chair for the Sexy Santa shoot was originally delayed by three days, so it was supposed to be here now for the shoot this afternoon. But I just got the update from the antique guy I'm loaning it from and he said there's a snowstorm, so who knows when it will be here, and the shoot is in an hour."

"What type of chair do you need exactly?" I ask and Liam tilts the phone to pick up my voice.

"Something old timey, throne like? Santa overlooking his domain in a broody yet sexy sternness. The more gold and red velvet the better. Please tell me your connections to the wealthy and hopelessly single can do something for me."

"I think I have someone I can ask."

11

Henri

I've consumed *Spitfire* for years. There are few constants in my life, but the writers followed me wherever I went. Familiar names on bylines and words that, after reading their work for years, felt like they came from friends. Giving me advice about everything from cleaning period stains to why I should finally watch every Nora Ephron film ever made.

Now, seeing the production for the magazine live, feels like I've stepped into my own personal Santa's workshop.

Though the Santa here has a very chiseled silver fox thing going for him—shirtless, with leather suspenders holding up his fur-trimmed red trousers. A hat sits jauntily to the side of his quaffed hair as he poses in front of the camera.

"I can make sure to text you when they're done here if you need to head back to the shop," I tell Marty, who came through with the replacement throne—a high back chair with hand-carved swirls and leather cushioning that he agreed to loan them for the shoot in return for crediting the shop.

Not the same as Jasmine's original vision, but when it arrived, she insisted that it leaned more into the topic of the article: why so many people have the hots for sexy Santa.

"I think I'll stick around to make sure the merchandise is taken care of."

"*Sure.* That's why."

"Maybe I'll buy Alexi one of those costumes. You know, for a party."

I laugh. "As long as you find one that's real velvet and not polyester or he won't wear it."

"You know I haven't heard anything about that velvet number we gave you. How are the alterations going?"

"None yet; I've been a bit busy."

"I see . . . I can't blame you. I'd be too preoccupied counting all those freckles." Marty's eyes find Liam, who's giving Jasmine a coffee from the full cardboard carrier. In the process, he nearly drops the whole thing and stumbles to catch it. His nervous laugh chimes through the room and causes me to smile. Once he regains his balance, he shoves a hand through his hair and says something to Jasmine I can't make out.

"It's not like that. He's a client—well, *Spitfire* is a client, and we're . . . friends?" After spending so much time together it feels wrong to act like he's a stranger. And unlike my clients, Liam is also getting to know me.

"You don't sound too sure about that."

"We work together."

"If you need to come up with excuses other than *you're not into him,* there's something there."

To which, I say, "No. There isn't." Only further digging my grave.

"There isn't what?" Liam says, heading toward us.

"We don't think there's enough fake snow," I blurt.

"Oh, I guess you could float that by Jasmine. She really wants this to be perfect." With some effort, Liam wrestles a cup free and hands it to me. "Mint tea. I think that's what you had at Moxy?"

Without looking, I can feel Marty's eyes on me. "Thanks. I also drink coffee, by the way." I don't know why I feel the need to tell him this.

"Just not from Moxy. Got it." Liam nods then pulls out another cup, offering it to Marty. "I guessed, but this is a gingerbread latte and really popular."

"Thank you. How considerate. Most people wouldn't go out of their way to do this for strangers," Marty gushes, eyes darting to me at the end. Not suspicious at all.

"Well." Liam's brows pinch. "It's no problem. And you're doing us a favor with the chair."

"Yes, the chair. I should talk to Jasmine about the snow. If my business is going to be tied to this article it needs to be perfection."

I hate you, I mouth to Marty as he walks away. But he either doesn't see or ignores me.

"Is he okay?" Liam asks.

"Just Marty being Marty. Thanks for the tea."

"It's no problem. This was a big deal for Jasmine and I'm glad I was with you when she called."

"Just returning the favor for the hat."

"That wasn't a favor, it was a gift. If you're unfamiliar with the concept, it isn't transactional," he says, though my brain doesn't want to accept that.

"Well, then this was my gift to you."

"I'm not going to let you act like it was some trade. I bought you a hat because I wanted to, and you can't change that no matter how much you try to."

"No. What is this?" Jasmine's voice echoes through the room.

"It's tartan," a man dressed in all black, who I assume works in the fashion department based on how Jasmine is talking to him, says as he props a fist on his hip. "It's Christmas-y. Red. Green. The works."

"It's giving school girl," Jasmine says. "And a sexy school girl sitting on Santa's lap is *not* what I'm going for. The complete opposite of the narrative we're unpacking. No infantilization or Lolita ass shit here."

And yes the sweater and skirt do lean toward a school uniform look, especially with the preppy headband the model has been styled with.

"I don't know what you want me to say. This is what Harman left before going to happy hour."

"You're in fashion. Do something fashion-y." Jasmine flails her arms in the direction of the model, who seems unphased by the chaos.

"And risk my job by redoing one of Harman's looks? I'm good. I busted my ass for this internship."

Jasmine looks like she's about to bite his head off, jaw clenching and fists balled at her sides. But she lets out a long-sustained breath and calls out to the room, "Can anyone help me get this girl into something else?"

My first instinct is to look for Marty. He'll be able to help put together a new look. I spot him off to one side, sipping his latte, just as Liam says, "Henri can do it."

"This is a bad idea," I say as Liam holds my hand, guiding me through the main floor of the *Spitfire* office. "I'm not qualified to help Jasmine find a new outfit for the model."

I really should tell him he doesn't have to grab onto me every time I need to go somewhere; I'm plenty capable of following him on my own. Though, maybe I can bring that up later. After he takes me wherever we're going.

And it's probably for the best because I'm completely distracted by our surroundings. I keep looking back over my shoulder at the central wall covered with material that is probably top secret.

"You style yourself for dates, have the biggest closet out of anyone I know, and sew your own clothes," he says with a firm certainty as we turn the corner into a hall. "Those sound like great qualifications to me."

I can't believe he still remembers all of that from the two hours we spent together weeks ago.

"You could get . . ." *In trouble* is what I was trying to say, but the words die on my tongue when Liam pushes open the door to heaven. Or at least my version of it.

Because, yes, a room full of hundreds of thousands of dollars of designer clothes is exactly where I hope to go when I die.

Liam lets go of my hand and I float inside. Hangers clink as I run my hand over the clothes. I only pause when my fingers land on a dramatic floor-length, pure-white fur coat that looks like it could have been stolen from an old Hollywood starlet. Mink, from the looks of it. I slide it off the hanger and check the label details. Faux fur, but an impressive imitation.

"This," I say. "Vintage glamour would be perfect." My gaze snags on a pair of iconic Kate Veau Velours Louboutins and grab them from the rack. "And these with some thigh highs attached to a garter belt? Almost a pin-up vibe."

I pause, finally catching myself. I shouldn't be doing this. The burden of the heavy coat is lifted from my arms as Liam grabs it from me. When I meet his eyes, the look on his face is nothing short of proud.

"What else do we need?" he asks.

"You're sure?"

"I wouldn't have brought you here if I didn't believe in you." There's not even the barest hint of doubt in his words.

"I guess Jasmine is in a rush," I say and give in to the need to finish selecting items for the look I've conjured up in my head.

Continuing to pull items, I put together two more looks for Jasmine to choose from so she can also choose between red or black. Still, I keep with the classic theme, imagining the model as Vera-Ellen or Rosemary Clooney in *White Christmas.*

When I exit my velvet-and-silk-induced fugue state, Liam is still watching me, now armed with a sturdy clothes rack to carry the clothes.

"What?" I ask, noting the soft smile on his mouth. He's seated on a circular stool at the center of the room, arms propped at his sides to keep him upright. "Don't tell me this is interesting for you." Iris refuses to go shopping with me because I can take up to an hour deciding on a single item of clothing, before getting to the register only to change my mind again.

"Oh, I'm irrefutably enthralled."

"Fancy words."

"Don't you know, I get paid to use fancy words," he counters. "Have you ever considered doing this professionally? I mean you're in New York, this is the place to pursue fashion."

I shake my head, adding a shawl to the rack. "I don't want to make money off it. Commodifying the one of the only things I can say I enjoy is a one-way trip to start hating it or getting burnt out. This is fun and all, but it's too important to turn into a job." I've thought it through. The lack of stability. The stress that would come with it, how it would warp my passions into something I resented. Money has a way of doing that, and I refuse to let that happen. "If I can get licensed as a counselor, then I can clock in and clock out, but also feel like I'm making a difference. What I do now is help for a day or two. I want to do more. I know what it's like to feel alone and helpless and if I can help others through that, I want to." I slam my mouth shut, surprised by my own candor.

"Smart girl," he says, voice low and gravelly, scraping over me before settling in my stomach. "Are you ready?" He cocks his head to the door.

"Could you take it down?" I ask, hesitantly.

"Don't you want to see what Jasmine chooses?"

"I will when it's posted, but watching her pick over it would be like listening to my voice in a recording, in front of an audience." I shiver at the thought. "I'll just wait up here for you to get back.

He rises and I step back from the rack for him to take it. He grasps one side then pauses. "Thank you for helping today. You probably had better things to do."

"No, I'm exactly where I need to be."

Our eyes snag for a moment, catching and threatening to rip the moment in two. But then he moves, pushing the rack through the door. I slump onto the stool, breathless.

12

Liam

I was planning on showing Henri the main office anyway, remembering how she was a *Spitfire* reader before we met, and now that we're here, I seize the chance to show her around.

"Correct me if I'm wrong, but I could take a picture of this and sell it for thousands?" Henri asks, stepping back to take in the concept wall for our December digital articles and print issue.

When it was first put together, the wall was organized and easy to read, but now it looks a bit like a murder board from a crime show. Fallon's scribbled notes mark what pieces have priority or need to be pushed to give them time to be reworked, now that we're in the thick of it.

There isn't much to see. There are other magazines in the building under the same publisher and ours is one of the smallest. Beyond the fashion closet, there are a few conference rooms, the main glass-walled offices, breakroom/kitchen with the busted coffee machine and promotional mugs, and here, the main bullpen, with our islands of desks for non-senior staff members.

"Probably not. I think every publication has about the same variety of gift lists and movie recommendations this time of year." I lean against my desk, taking in the view and sipping on my coffee. She's enraptured. The same way she looked when she spotted the Christmas market in Union Square. Unfiltered Henri. My favorite.

While she's occupied, I take a moment to pull out my notebook that lives in my back pocket—I'm not joking when I say I have an imprint of the rectangular shape in a majority of my jeans—and write new details about her down.

Drinks coffee (if it's good). Need to find out what kind she prefers.
Hates gifts. Or maybe just uncomfortable?
Fashion.

At the sound of her voice, I snap the notebook closed. "Why is your name next to Jasmine's on a card that says Santa Sutra?" She taps a card just above her head.

I cough and pull at the collar of my sweater which has suddenly become suffocating. "Before the sex positions go out for publication we, umm, have to make sure they're physically possible. Jasmine and I check a lot of them since I have the most upper body strength of the writing staff. So, we try them—fully clothed. In a completely platonic way." And have felt like a mundane part of my job up until this moment.

"Says the guy who was panting with me after climbing three flights of stairs."

"That's completely different and you know it."

"I think I'll need a visual. Is there a picture somewhere of how to do this one?"

"You're terrible," I grumble.

Her eyes go wide and a hand flies to her heart as she feigns innocence. "I just have a thorough interest in your work. This way I can talk about it with your family."

"If there is one thing you shouldn't do, it's talk about how I help with sex positions at work." I don't even want to imagine what they'd say if they knew.

"I promise I won't talk to them *if* you give me a demonstration."

"It's like this." I kick my feet out so my knees are at a ninety degree angle and prop my hands behind me, gripping the edge of my desk the way I would if I were prepping for a tricep dip. I lower myself once. "But you know, someone is on top and the movement is supposed to add, umm, stimulation." Just a regular exercise. I try to remind my body of that while trying my hardest to not picture Henri as a partner in this scenario.

"It just looks like you're working out."

"That's probably because I'm one half of the equation and these positions are supposed to be possible but not necessarily recommended."

She walks over to me and examines me for a second as I freeze. I'm about to quit this stupid thing when she takes another step then swings her leg over my hips, landing so she's rubbing against me, which would be good if we were actually having sex, but due to the circumstances, it is an absolute test of my control. Control that is threatening to snap at any moment. I suck in a sharp breath, my eyes darting up to the wall trying to read anything to distract me.

Mistake because when my gaze lands on the words *All Wrapped Up* on one of the cards all I can picture is Henri naked on my bed, secured into place with ribbon. Fuck. I'd give anything for that.

"Like this?" Her hand lands on my chest. "Or is it facing the other way?" She twists, unconsciously working her hips, creating even more friction between us. Is she trying to kill me?

"I don't think it matters," I grit out.

"Have you considered pushing a desk on the other side then maybe the person on top could bend over?" She moves again.

"Henri," I rasp.

"What?"

"Could you get off of me? I get what you're doing, but my body doesn't know the difference."

"I thought you did this with Jasmine? Why would it be different with me?" she cocks a brow, daring me to tell the truth. I just might to see what would happen.

"He does what with me?" Jasmine asks as she turns the corner, seemingly unfazed by the scene before her. "Oh, Unnamed Position three-fifty-four. Henri, put him out of his misery. What he's trying to say, while praying not to get a boner, is that I don't rub my ass on him like that."

"Oh shit." My arms give out and I fall on my ass, Henri landing on top of me.

"Fuck." Henri's eyes flare wide and she scrambles off me now that we have an audience.

"Just don't bring it up at Christmas," I mutter.

"Yeah. I don't think I will." The pink flooding her cheeks lets me know that at least I'm not alone in my mortification. My back thuds against the side of the desk.

"I think we need a drink!" Jasmine chimes.

"Yes, that would be great," Henri says.

"Oh, not for whatever the hell I just walked in on. We're celebrating my shoot being done. Despite being thwarted at every turn, Henri came through. Liam, can you come help me grab cups?"

I clamber to my feet and follow Jasmine to the kitchen. "I'm pretty sure it was an honest shipping mistake."

"And I'm pretty sure what I saw wasn't an innocent moment between you and the woman you're interviewing for a career-making article."

"She asked me to show her."

And you do anything she asks? Or is that just for sex positions no one should perform in a real-life circumstance if they value their dignity and pleasure?" Jasmine quirks a brow as she lowers herself to the floor and opens one of the cabinets. Tins clink and plasticware tumbles as she searches.

"So, yeah, if she asks me to do something, I'll do it." I say, knowing it's true.

Jasmine rocks back on her heels to look at me. "You've been here for years and the first girl you show any interest in is one being paid to spend time with you? Please tell me you know this."

"It's easy spending time with her."

"Is it easy, or is she someone who has experience becoming anyone's dream girl?"

"She's different with me," I snap, growing defensive. Lowering my voice and checking my temper I continue. "I've seen her on those dates—we were at the same restaurants remember? She's so composed when she's with her clients. Professional."

"Not sitting on their dicks?" Jasmine supplies and I shoot her a glare. "Point taken, but still, be careful. She's a runner. Iris talks about how she's never seen her really date. Commitment scares people like that. She's the absolute last person you want to start a long distance relationship with."

My jaw ticks at the reminder that soon I'll be across the country. "I'm not gunning for a relationship. I just like being around her."

I barely have any time left in the city and I'm happy to share it with Henri; she makes it feel like magic. It's the same magic I know she shared with her clients, pushing them to become the versions of themselves she knows they're capable of being, but I get another version of her. I know I do. One that's brighter and will say whatever's on her mind.

"Oh, the sweet strains of denial," she sings before returning to the cabinet. "Here it is." She pulls out a large cookie tin and pops off the lid, revealing a selection of canned cocktails I recognize from three months back.

"I thought you said we were out of the Bellinis?" I demand.

"I lied. But because of that, you can have more than you would have. Now, get some wine glasses and let's hope someone remembered to refill the ice tray."

I find a single ice cube that Jasmine claims because it's her celebration and her (stolen) drinks.

Jasmine pauses, cocking her head. "Is that?"

It takes me a second to pick up on the chatter she's hearing but when I do, my blood runs cold.

"Shit."

We rush around the corner and back to the bullpen. Henri is standing where we left her, but that isn't the problem. Fallon is there too. Henri has a visitor badge and is allowed in the building, but that doesn't make this interaction any less awkward.

"Liam, your girlfriend was just telling me how she helped out with the photoshoot. You didn't say you knew Marty and Alexi? Their shop is one of my favorites in Brooklyn," Fallon says. There's a twinkle in her eye that tells me she knows exactly who Henri is, and also means Henri is playing the part perfectly. She really does have a gift for it. Could Jasmine be right afterall? Am I just another guy mesmerized by the attention Henri gives?

"I don't really. I'm just lucky to be with someone so connected. She's a big fan of the magazine so I offered to show her around as a thank you," I say.

"And what do you think of our little publication?" Fallon asks Henri.

Henri beams. "It's a dream. I feel like I'm living out a scene from *The Devil Wears Prada.*"

"That's too kind; our fashion closet is nowhere close." Fallon cocks her head toward me. "Has Liam invited you to our holiday party? Significant others are invited."

"We've talked about it. My schedule fluctuates a lot so it's a bit up in the air." Henri doesn't miss a beat. For a second, I wonder if I did actually bring it up and somehow forgot.

"You have to come!" Jasmine chirps. "Liam never attends staff parties."

"Hopefully we'll see you there. It was great meeting you, Henri, but I do have to get going. I have a dinner reservation and I was halfway there when I realized I left the purse I pair with these shoes here." Fallon excuses herself and heads toward her office. I set down the empty glasses on a desk and follow after her, catching up just as she is through the door.

"I'm sorry. We didn't know you'd be in," I say.

"If you did, I'm assuming you wouldn't have brought your fake girlfriend with you?" she says, unperturbed as she retrieves a quilted handbag from a shelf. "I like her—quick on her feet. Didn't even hesitate to jump in as the girlfriend. Believable."

"About the holiday party—"

Fallon holds up a hand to keep me from finishing my sentence. "I think it would be smart to bring her. Call it a trial run, low stakes. Most of the people don't know she's a fake girlfriend, but if they find out, then it's no big deal."

"I'll try to convince her."

"You don't have to come to the party," I say as I hand Henri a freshly-cleaned wine glass for her to dry. I told her that I'd take care of them and that she should catch a ride with Jasmine who was on the way to visit Iris. But because this is Henri, she said no.

She takes the glass and wipes it with a drying cloth. "Do you not want me to?"

"No!" I rush to say, plunging my hands into the sudsy sink and sending a flurry of small soap bubbles into the air. "I just know that you go to office parties all the time for work and you're probably sick of them. I don't want you to feel obligated to do this when you didn't originally plan on it."

"I want to. I haven't ever been given the opportunity to choose to come to one with people I already know. It's a nice change. It could be fun."

"From what I hear, it's some lethal punch, makeshift karaoke, and basic holiday food."

"Is it true you haven't attended any?"

I shrug, working at a lip gloss smear on the lip of a glass. "Not really my thing."

"Why is that? It's not like you're an asshole. And the first time I met you, you were eating out alone, so don't tell me it's the fear of being perceived."

"I guess it's more self-imposed isolation than anxiety." I grab the final glass and start cleaning. "Or more that I'm anxious about making things into a competition. The way I grew up, my friends were also the people I was trying to beat. I was always told to be suspicious of people who got too close. During the first week of my MFA program, this girl asked if I wanted to trade writing assignments and get coffee." Heat flames up my neck. "I couldn't shake the idea that she was trying to steal my ideas."

"It just sounds like she was asking you on a date." Henri laughs, a light chiming sound that makes the entire room seem brighter.

"Yeah, I guess maybe." I've dated a few times, had quick flings with girls visiting the resort, but when it comes to it, when things started to look serious, I broke things off. The fear of failure, of disappointing others, clinging to me in so many facets of my life.

I move to brush my hair off my brow, but forget about the soap clinging to my hands and end up swiping it over my face.

"Here." Henri steps close to me with a rag in hand, her thigh pressing against mine as she angles herself to wipe the bubbles off my face. The tips of her fingers graze my cheek and I have to bite back a hum of satisfaction. "Were you really on track to go pro?"

Her question snaps me back to reality. Talking is good. This way, I have something to focus on beyond how she's so close that I'm hit with the spicy scent of her perfume.

"You've read the articles." I know she's thorough. I can picture it easily—her hunched over at her desk, forgetting to turn on the floor lamp so she's only lit by the screen, probably sitting in a way guaranteed to make her legs fall asleep because she's the most undone when she doesn't feel observed, or has to perform.

"I have. But the news has a way of exaggerating things. Painting the story in the most devastating way possible." Her eyes turn down and she bites at her lower lip.

I have a feeling that she's speaking from experience. "Are you talking about the piece I did on you?"

Her gaze snaps to me. "No. I still haven't read it."

"Ouch."

"Maybe I will someday. After this is done."

I wonder who will become her favorite writer after I'm gone? I hate thinking about it, but I can't help myself. I want to be that person and I don't want anyone else to take my spot.

"Come but, just don't tell me if you hate it." I hand her the glass. "I don't think my ego will survive."

"I promise if we go to this party, I'll have a good time and make sure to jump in before you challenge someone to a typing speed battle."

"It's a date."

13

Henri

For the three days leading up to the office party, I furiously work on alterations for the velvet Vivian Westwood dress Marty and Alexi gifted me.

Now, I'm standing in front of my phone showing off my handiwork to my mom while Daniel sleeps. It's past midnight in Vienna. I wouldn't have bothered Mom, but she's the one who called me.

"Do you think the red lip is too much? Like a red dress with a red lip, that's classic, right?" I ask, checking my image in the small square above hers.

In addition to the dress and makeup, I've curled my hair so it has a wave to it, and put pearl stud earrings in.

Mom has on her wire-framed glasses and is curled up under a blanket, sipping a sparkling white wine. Her lips tip up into a smile. "No, it's perfect."

"But is it the right shade of red? I can't tell if it has the right undertones in this lighting."

"I've never seen you so anxious about going out," she notes. "Is everything okay?"

She's right; I'm never this nervous. I never second guess any outfits for my dates, even for parties that are far dressier than this. But the difference is that for those, I'm going as Juliet—poised and proper. For the first time, I'm going as myself, and I don't want to mess this up. I want the people to like me.

"There will be fashion and makeup people there who will notice."

"You've gone to fashion events before and you never once second guessed yourself so much. It's okay to admit that you care about this. It's nice to see you nervous, it means you're excited. I haven't seen you excited to go out in a long time."

"I guess I am excited," I admit.

"Be honest. Is this a date?"

Liam's words from the other day ring through my mind. *It's a date.* But that's just something people say.

"No, but it's not exactly a work thing either. You know that magazine I like?"

"*Spitfire*!" she says a bit too loudly before looking over her shoulder to make sure she didn't wake up Daniel. "Yes. I still have all the old ones you bought in a box somewhere."

"That's where I'm going. With a friend who works there."

"That's amazing. It's nice to see you acting your age and having fun for a change."

"I'm always doing something fun."

I collect experiences on most people's bucket lists with some of the jobs I take on, eating at Michelin starred restaurants, or being flown to destination weddings, but I don't ever feel like myself there. I'm playing a perfectly-planned role that I know I can shrug out of when all is said and done.

This. Knowing Liam, Liam knowing me. It takes away that cloak of protection, but also allows me to feel closer to the action. From the start, he saw a version of me in that cab that was raw and uncontained. And I'm trying to wrap my head around if I love it, or if it terrifies me.

An almost sad smile claims her mouth as her eyes glisten. "You're such a hard worker that I worry about you putting too much pressure on yourself. After what happened with your father, you took on so much responsibility and you've built such a wonderful life, and you're just getting started."

My chest aches. I try my best to hide any of my exhaustion from her, but she knows me too well.

A text notification pops up on the top of my screen and I bite down on a smile.

"He's outside. I should go," I say.

"Have *fun*; you look great. If any of the fashion people give you shit, send them to me."

I nearly roll my eyes. "Yes, I will book them a one-way trip to Europe for you to set the record straight."

She hangs up mid-laugh.

It takes another minute to wrestle my foot into my knee-high boots. A knock comes from the door and I hobble through the living room to answer it as I attempt to pull the zipper up my calf.

Opening it, I find Liam. Under his gray wool coat he's wearing a black turtleneck that only serves to accentuate the sharp cut of his jaw, paired with burgundy trousers.

"Umm your neighbor let me in the building, I hope that's okay?" he says, a bit breathless.

"Stairs get to you again?"

"Yeah. The stairs." He nods, but his focus seems somewhere else—on me. "Wow. You look great."

"Same to you."

"Just . . ." He scrapes a hand through his styled hair, sending it into its usual state of disarray. I think I prefer him this way—just a little undone. "Wow."

Just. Wow.

The two words burrow somewhere deep in me. Swirling in my veins and taking a trip through the chambers of my heart.

"Let me grab my coat and I'll be ready to go." I swallow and wait a second before moving, inviting the moment to stretch.

I dip back inside with the door still hanging wide and I select a long tan wool coat that I tug around my shoulders. The key sticks in the lock as I jimmy it shut.

When I turn around, Liam's eyes are still on me.

"May I?" he asks, lifting a hand.

"Sure." Though I'm not particularly certain what I'm agreeing too.

He reaches out, fingers slipping under my collar, as he flicks my hair free so it brushes over the tops of my shoulders. His hand lingers for a moment longer than needed, fingertips grazing over the exposed ridge of my collarbone.

"Thanks." I step back as I'm flushed with heat. I forgot how hot this coat can be when I'm not outside. "Let's get going; I wouldn't want to be late."

On the way there, Liam explains that Fallon asks the staff each year if they'd rather have the annual party at an upscale venue, or for her to put the funds toward staff bonuses and host it at the office. Because the staff of *Spitfire* has basic common sense, as the elevator chimes, we walk out and past a familiar reception desk.

Still, the office has transformed. The islands of desks and computers have been pushed aside, and a karaoke corner has been set up, as well as a fully-stocked bar.

I grab a loaded plate from the catering dishes and start to look for a place to sit. Beside me, Liam stands, stuck in place, eyes darting around. Someone comes up to him and they exchange quick hellos. Liam visibly stiffens at the exchange.

I lightly touch his arm to get his attention. "Hey, let's go eat in one of the conference rooms; the party will still be here when we're done."

Relief washes over Liam's face. "You're sure?"

"As sure as I am that I'll be able to get you to do karaoke by the end of the night."

"Not a chance."

"Oh, I have my ways." I grin up at him and shimmy my shoulders. "What use are these feminine wiles of mine if I don't put them to work? Come on." I cock my head toward the hall entrance.

The conference room is two doors down. Neither of us flick on the lights as we go in, but there's a light glow from a Christmas tree in one corner. Liam perches on the windowsill, balancing his plate on his lap. I pull up a chair next to him and look out the window. A lazy snowfall has started to swirl and whiz through the air.

We fall into a comfortable silence as we eat, and there's something about the food I can't put my finger on.

"What's with the face?" Liam asks, a knowing smile tugging at his mouth.

"I swear I've had this before. I'm having this fuzzy, déjà vu feeling. But maybe it's just how you get when you walk next to someone with the same cologne as your college ex, and have a visceral flashback to when you watched them scramble for the ball while playing beer pong and realized you don't find them attractive anymore." I shudder at the thought.

He attempts to stifle a laugh, which only causes it to come out as a snort. "I'm happy to say I never had that experience. It probably has to do with the fact it's from Bide."

"Ahh the scene of the crime of my near public indecency. I remember it fondly. But isn't that a bit pricey for a full catering spread?"

"It would be without the discount Fallon was given." He pushes a clump of mashed potatoes into a pool of gravy. "Fallon got a discount on it—barely paid anything. I rated them lower than last year and they're trying to compensate."

"Maybe I should become a food critic if it means I get bribed like that." I take a bite and consider the flavors. "Now that you've said it, this is similar, but definitely tastes richer and more balanced."

"Really earning that spot as your celebrity crush."

I groan. "I was starting to think you'd forgotten about that."

"Never. I'm carrying it with me to my grave." He stops and holds up his fork. "Better yet, I'm putting it *on* my grave."

"The commitment is impressive."

"Why *Spitfire*? The Thanksgiving list? My articles? There must be hundreds of other things to choose from."

I hesitate for a moment. The truth feels like too much, and there's a tender part of me that is haunted by the last time people learned about my dad. How they left without a second thought. "I was nineteen, just halfway through my second year of college when my family was hit pretty hard financially. It's kind of embarrassing, but I didn't have any real world skills. I'd never worked, or budgeted, or thought too hard about anything because, before, if I wanted something, I just had to ask for it." My eyes turn down to my plate and I shove around a stray macaroni noodle coated in silk bechamel. "My mom was busy all the time, so I didn't want to ask her how to do things, and I didn't have anyone else. I was at the grocery store and saw a *Spitfire* magazine—-*A Broke Girl's Guide to Money* issue—and I picked it up." I remember how I ended up having to put back a bag of salt and vinegar chips to afford it, the kettle cooked kind that I'd been craving but couldn't justify buying because *God* why did they cost so much. "I read it and got my shit together. It felt like I was getting a no-nonsense pep talk from a best friend. It sounds silly, but it's the truth."

"I don't think it's silly," Liam says, and I know he means it. I look up and find that he's focused intently on me.

"Well, thanks." I shrug, my skin feeling tight under the full force of his gaze. The room seems to have shrunken too. "After that, I kept buying issues and looking online, especially when I started reading articles by a certain L. Hughes." Heat floods my cheeks. "Is it weird to say that it's like I knew you before we ran into each other. Maybe that's the reason it's so easy to be around each other?" That has to be it, right?

"I didn't know you before this. Maybe it's just easy to be around each other for some other reason."

"Yeah you're right." I shake my head, dislodging the thought. Okay, delusionally-hopeful hypothesis disproven. "If you're done eating, we could rejoin the group. It's hard for this to be a trial run of our fake relationship if we're alone."

"I prefer being alone with you than putting on a show." A flash of disappointment crosses his face as he rises to his feet, rolling his shoulders in a stretch. "But you're the expert—exposure therapy and all."

He grabs my plate and stacks it with his. When we are back out in the hall, the sounds of the party welcome us. Someone is singing a break-up song so intensely I'm genuinely worried if they're okay. Liam stiffens but walks with me. A few feet before the end of the hall, he pauses.

"Wait. Can I hold your hand? That would be a couple-y thing to do," he says.

"If you want," I tell him, pretending not to care even as my fingers twitch, eager to tangle with his.

"But wouldn't that help make it look like we're together?"

"Yeah, but only if you're comfortable with it. Sometimes I don't do any PDA, other times a kiss or two is appropriate for the situation, but only if agreed upon beforehand." I'd usually have already established these boundaries, but I've been putting it off when it comes to Liam.

"Just hand-holding."

I thrust out my hand and he takes it—stiffly at first, then his palm molds against mine.

A hush falls when we reach the doorway, then a few tipsy giggles leak from sealed lips.

Jasmine is standing nearby, a Cheshire grin stretched across her face.

"KISS!" someone yells from the crowd, but I'm not sure who.

I turn to Liam, but his neck is craned to look up, sounding angrier than I've ever heard him before as he bites out, "Who the fuck put mistletoe here?"

14

Liam

"Why is there mistletoe here?" I demand, again. My coworkers' cheers fade as they avert their eyes. It sure as hell wasn't there earlier.

"Chill. I put it up after you both went down the hall," Jasmine says as she holds up her hands in a calming gesture. "I thought it was going to be fun."

Fun. Some cheap entertainment for their enjoyment. A kiss for them to cheer for.

My boiling anger isn't just for them. I think about how many spectacles Henri has been expected to participate in for the sake of others. She deserves better than this. What's worse is that Jasmine knows that Henri will go to any lengths needed to sell our relationship and leveraged that for a practical joke.

"It's not a big deal," Henri says at my side as she holds my hand.

"It is to me. I think I'm done with this party."

Henri doesn't argue, but she does drop my hand as we head through the party, grabbing our coats before we take an elevator down. The silence between us is charged and nothing like it was when we were eating.

When we step outside onto the empty sidewalk, Henri pulls me aside, gripping the sleeve of my coat. "Why are you so upset? It's just mistletoe; we haven't talked much about it but I'm assuming we'll have to kiss eventually." Her eyes dart over my face, searching for an answer. The falling snow starts to dust her hair, forming a white crown.

I shake my head. "I don't want it to happen like that—in front of so many people."

"But that's the point. It's not for us, it's for them."

"Why does it have to be for them?" I rasp. "Why can't we have some of this for ourselves."

"Liam, what are you saying? I don't understand." I think she does and maybe she's just too scared to say it.

But I'm not. "If I'm going to kiss you, I want to do it right, not for some crowd. Maybe the rest of this is for the article, but would it be so bad to want something for ourselves."

She drags her plush lower lip through her teeth. "And what is the right way?"

I take a step closer, my hand finding her lower back and pressing her closer to me. I'm practically vibrating with need.

"I take you out on a real date. You wear this ridiculous red dress again, even though it's hard to breathe when I look at you in it. I pay when you're not looking so you don't insist on splitting the bill." I cup her cold cheek in my palm and tilt her face up to mine. Her lips are a few inches from mine. "And after, I kiss you in the snow because I can't wait any longer."

"Liam, we can't. We're working together." She's right and I hate it. I wish there wasn't so much depending on this article. If it was just about the article, I'd find another way, but she needs this more than me.

"Can we pretend for a second that I've just done all of that. And now we're standing here?"

Her shoulders shake on a shuddering breath even as she leans closer, the tip of her nose brushing against my cheek. I can count the snowflakes on her lashes, and I think I'd give anything to stay here to count each and every one.

"One second?"

"Just one." *And then another and another after that, until the seconds extend into infinity.*

"Fuck it."

And then she's kissing me. She's fucking *kissing* me. Her hand snakes around my neck, pulling me in, mouth soft and hesitant against mine. Like there's something she's scared of breaking. Something precious at risk of shattering in the moment.

I pull away, but only barely, my lips brushing against hers as I say, "Let's go somewhere. Anywhere. Give me one more second." *And then another and another.* "We can go to my place and just be there, together."

She stiffens and pushes away from me, already shaking her head. "We can't do that. This was already too far. I'm sorry. I shouldn't have said yes."

"Henri." Her name crawls up my throat as a plea.

"I need to go." Her eyes remain on me as she steps up to the curb and hails a cab. The yellow car slots neatly into place, ready to whisk her away.

I'm frozen, as if the slush under my feet has crawled up over my shoes and solidified into blocks of ice.

Gripping the top of the door, she pauses, and for a moment I think she'll turn back. But she doesn't, disappearing into the back seat, leaving me out in the cold.

She's gone. Just when I thought I had her.

But she was never mine to have.

15

Liam

Saturday and Sunday move by the same. I get up, check my phone for any evidence Henri will ever talk to me again, find none, and then wait until Jasmine leaves so I can go to the living room, turn on *Criminal Minds,* and finish the packing I've been putting off. Ever since the party I've been avoiding Jas, since I don't want to fight with her and I'd also have to admit she was right.

Henri ran.

I'll forgive Jasmine, eventually, but right now the wound is fresh.

I follow the same routine Monday morning, although there are texts on my phone, but not from Henri.

Pen

Dibs on picking Liam up from the airport tonight!

Mom

Just bring him back in one piece.

June

You just want to grill him and his girlfriend.

Pen

Excuse me for giving a damn.

I groan and type out a response before things can spiral further out of control.

Me

I'm getting a rental. See you when I get there.

The last time Pen agreed to drive me anywhere I found myself stranded for hours because she lost track of time on the slopes.

The text chain reminds me of what I should have been doing this weekend: packing. But the idea of the trip makes me sick to my stomach. We're supposed to leave from JFK at 2 p.m., but I still haven't heard back from Henri, and I'm only fifty percent sure she's still coming. So that will be a fun thing to explain—being ghosted by my not-girlfriend before Christmas.

Why couldn't I just leave it? Or not have made a big deal and kissed her at the party. I was just so angry at the thought of all her kisses being for show, and felt that she deserved romance and real fucking dates, as if I can give that to her when I'm planning on moving across the country.

I flop back against my pillows and consider smothering myself. Jasmine's bedroom door creaks open, and a few seconds later it's followed by the front door. At least I won't have to face her until I get to work.

I've been at work for thirty minutes, and frankly, I wish I wasn't here at all. Only half the staff is in today, since it's remote-optional this close to the holidays. On my way in, I walked as fast as I could, rushing past the spot on the sidewalk where I kissed Henri. I'm in a hell of my own making.

At my desk, I checked to see what I needed to get started on, but all my other articles were submitted. So, for ten minutes, I stared at my notes. When that didn't work, I plugged in my headphones to listen to our conversation at Moxy. I got to a part where she laughed at something I said and then played that back five times. Eventually, I pulled up a blank document and . . . Nothing.

A crinkled paper bag plops down next to where I'm resting my head on my desk, followed by a coffee. "Seems like you need this."

I shift to see Jasmine standing over me, worry painted on every line of her face. She wasn't here when I arrived, even though she left before I did. For a minute, I thought she had left to see Iris, or her family.

"Yeah. I do." I open the bag and am hit with a mouth-watering savory aroma. "Shit, this is—"

"From the deli in the East Village, yeah. This is an *I'd-get-up-early-to-get-you-your-favorite-bagel* type of apology."

"You're late."

"I still got up before you, and it's the thought that counts," she says as she walks to her desk across from mine and slumps into her chair. "I was a presumptuous dick. I just thought that if I put up the mistletoe you'd get an excuse to kiss her, because I was pretty sure you wanted to."

"I did."

"Did want to?"

"No. I kissed her for real and then she went silent. I fucked it up." I groan and drop my head into my hands.

"And you haven't heard from her yet?"

"Nothing."

I was never supposed to care this much. I felt my feelings for Henri creep up on me and didn't bother to keep them in check.

"I can ask Iris," she offers.

I shake my head. "I appreciate it, but please don't complicate your relationship because of my—" I nearly say *mistake*, but it wasn't, and I won't pretend it was. "Choice. The best thing I can do is work and get my mind off this."

"We're doing the New Year's affordable champagne tasting today, so at least there's that to look forward to!" Her voice carries a level of enthusiasm I know neither of us feel.

"Yay! I'll get to pre-game my flight, and arrive with a hangover," I mutter while booting up my computer and opening my email.

I think Jasmine keeps talking, trying to take my mind off Henri, but it's not fair to expect her to succeed when I have an email from her at the top of my inbox.

Liam,

I'll see you at the airport. Sorry for the limited contact. I've been busy.

Juliet

She's still coming.

Now to figure out what the hell I'm going to tell her when I see her again that doesn't involve falling to my knees, begging, in the security line.

16

Henri

I can't remember the last time I missed someone. Like aching to see them again, bones weary from the effort of it.

Even when my father was arrested, I didn't miss him. He was a busy guy, the type to work eighty-hour weeks and we didn't have the strongest relationship. Back then I was so sure it was because he cared about us, that he was absent to make sure we had everything we could ever want. What a nice delusion. Which really should have been an early indication about where I sat on his list of priorities.

But I never really missed him. Even Kurt and Laura, people I used to consider my closest friends—I didn't really miss them after they stopped responding to my texts. I just missed the feeling of having someone on the other end of the message.

Of not being alone.

And I guess I've never broken out of that—hopping from one stranger's life to the next, with the exception of Iris, who has texted me consistently since I left the apartment, scuffed suitcase in hand.

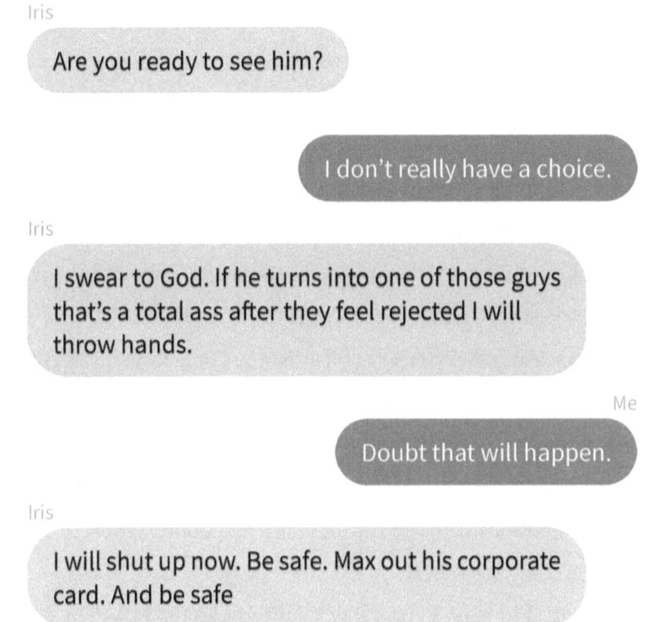

She's had my back from the moment I walked through the door, lipstick smeared from my kiss with Liam and mascara running from the subsequent crying session in the cab. I had to tell her it was ridiculous to cut off Jasmine, but the fact she was willing to go to such lengths for me was so incredibly special.

All that and I couldn't tell her that I missed Liam because it makes me feel pathetic and weak.

He's just some guy.

I don't cry over guys. They pay me to be emotionally detached. It's what I'm good at—walking away and never looking back. And I tried SO hard. I sent a damn email instead of texting him. Okay, so maybe not that hard, but this is uncharted territory for me, and I should be given some grace.

But here I am, vibrating as I sit at the bar nearest our terminal, head on a swivel to see what way he might be coming from, and keep the seat next to me free just in case.

I've splurged on a martini and fries. Instead of soothing my nerves, the briny concoction has only served to send me into a spiral. Does Liam hate me for kissing him and then running away? Will he be able to trust me during the rest of the trip, or is what's between us broken?

If I had just stuck to my own damn protocol, then he and I could've at least gotten out of this as friends. He just makes me feel seen, like the parts of me that I doubt are worth showing to the world. I want that for more than just the holidays, and I went too far.

My phone nearly flies out of my hands when someone's duffle knocks squarely into my shoulder as they run by me.

The screen lights up with a call—a call from him.

Shit shit shit.

How am I supposed to get through our first conversation in nearly a week without any facial cues?

"Uh, Henri. I'm here. I guess that's a bit vague. I'm by—" he says and relief washes over me like a cold shower in the middle of August. Shocking, yet refreshing. His nerves are palpable. Liam with his emotions out there for me to see, or I guess in this case, hear.

Thank you for not being stoic and broody, I nearly say, but don't because that makes no sense, and because I also spot him. He's in a faded, tattered Dulcet Point crewneck and black sweatpants, bulky black headphones over his ears. So instead I settle on, "You're right in front of me."

He slows as he searches, nearly getting knocked over by a family of five in a rush to get to their flight.

"Look to your left," I suggest and he does. I watch as his face mirrors my sense of relief. I feel my mouth split into a smile before I can even attempt to suppress it. Because I missed him and he's here and maybe he missed me too, but that might be a desperate extrapolation. This also might be a *thank-God-my-five-thousand-dollar-investment-actually-showed-up* face.

Neither of us hang up even though there isn't a good reason to continue the call.

"Get through security okay?" he asks.

"I packed my edibles in my gummy vitamin container. I wasn't sure it would work, but what fun is life without a risk."

"Why would you do that? You know it's legal to buy in Colorado right? Kind of known for it."

"I'm joking, Liam," I say. "I wouldn't do anything to jeopardize this for you." *Not again,* I tack on mentally.

"Oh, I should have picked up on that. There was just a champagne tasting at work and I'm a little out of it."

"Had to get drunk to put up with me?" I tease.

"God. No. Shit." The words tumble out of him and I have to bite back a laugh. Same Liam as ever. "You look great, by the way."

"It's because I'm sitting. There's a hole in the butt of these sweatpants and they are saggy as hell." He's a foot away now, eyeing the seat where my tote is resting.

"Well, I will make sure not to get stuck behind you. Or maybe I should? So other people can't see."

I lift my bag and pat the worn leather. "Are you just going to stand there or sit?"

"I'm on a very important call; I can't just hang up."

"I think we could talk like this the entire trip," I joke but the phone gives this degree of separation from reality. The absurdity forming a shield between us and what happened the last time we were standing this close together.

Our eyes lock and I quirk a brow. "Same time?"

We lower our phones in tandem and end the call. Wow. This feels so good. If it weren't for *the-last-time-I-saw-you-I-kissed-you-and-ran* shaped elephant sitting here with us it would be perfect.

When he takes a seat, it takes him a moment to settle into place, arranging his long legs into a comfortable position.

"What can I get going for you?" the bartender asks, expertly sliding a coaster in front of Liam as she talks. "Or do you need a minute with a menu?"

"Whiskey sour, thanks. And could you put her drinks on my tab." He hands over a card and the woman disappears with it before I can protest.

Finally, he looks at me again with those warm brown eyes of his and lashes that fan against his cheeks when he looks down at me. "Hey."

"Hey."

"So . . . about the other night," I start, then we both say in unison, "I'm sorry."

"Why are you—"

"I was the one who—"

We both pause and then I try again. "I think we can agree that we shouldn't have crossed that line and we're better off as friends. We didn't talk about public displays of affection before and that's my fault, so let's do that now."

Boundaries. That's what we need. A fuck ton of them.

"You're right. I shouldn't have asked."

I shake my head. "I know how it can get. Proximity and time together are some of the biggest indicators of attraction. I've read a few studies about how the more you see someone the more likely it is to develop feelings for them. You asked, but it was also my job to tell you no, and I didn't."

This has happened before, people mistaking how careful I am with them as a client for me being interested. I've never been on the other side of it before, though, and I guess I'm just as susceptible when it comes to Liam's interview questions as people are to me getting to know them.

"All right then, what are we thinking? Hugging? Hand-holding?" he asks. "PG rules?"

"We're great at those things—not that it was a bad kiss." Why the fuck did I say that? "But no kissing?" *Yeah, rough recovery, Henri. Way to NOT stick the landing on that one.*

"Emergencies. We can kiss if there's an emergency." He tugs at his collar as if the words are threatening to choke him as the bartender hands Liam his drink. Instantly, he raises it to his mouth and downs at least a quarter, his Adam's apple bobbing along the strong column of his throat. And shit he has a good neck.

The sound of ice clinking as he sets the glass on the counter rattles me back to my senses.

"And what would a kissing emergency be to you?"

"If one of my family members suspects we aren't together?"

"Great! That works. We'll just have to make sure they don't suspect anything!" I can do that. I do it all the time. "And now that we have a plan, let's do this thing."

And we can move on to not talking about kissing ever again.

17

Liam

Our flight is blissfully uneventful. Henri makes fun of me for paying attention to the flight attendant's safety demonstration. I tell her I'd hate being up there and feeling like everyone is ignoring me, so she stops and listens along with me.

When she scrolls through the movies and selects *Crazy Rich Asians*, I say that I haven't watched it before. We end up watching it together on our own screens. But really, I'm less watching the movie than I am watching her.

It's safe territory, her knees knocking against mine when she lets out a laugh that causes the couple next to us to shoot us a set of disapproving glares. Then there are the moments when I just know a part is her favorite because she reaches for my arm and squeezes.

We land and are sucked into the tide of passengers rushing to the baggage claim.

I rent a blue Subaru Crosstrek and maneuver onto the familiar streets of Denver. Beside me, Henri has turned up the music on the radio, singing along, making up lyrics as she goes. Every ten minutes or so she changes the channel.

With each mile, I feel myself growing more tense. My palms sweat against the wheel and I have to wipe my hands against my sweatpants. The city eventually gives way to winding mountain roads lined with towering pines with branches laden with snow. The sun has started to kiss the horizon, blue sky blending into a mix of pinks and purples overhead—it will be dark by the time we arrive.

It's another half hour before we reach Dulcet Point. Out of the corner of my eye, I see Henri straighten and hear her gasp as we round the final corner. It has that effect on people—a sprawling resort appearing out of seemingly nowhere.

There it is, burned into the massive wooden sign, notched into two poles the size of tree trunks: *Welcome to Dulcet Point Resort and Lodge.* The road snakes lazily past the main lodge, a massive green-roofed wooden complex that stands at the foot of the slopes. Lifts trail up the incline, disappearing into the distance and depositing vibrantly-dressed guests to their desired destination.

"Is this shit designed after a snow globe or something?" Henri's nose is all but pressed to the window, breath fogging the glass.

"I believe snow globes are traditionally designed after places like this." I have to admit I love it, sharing this part of my life with her. Her mouth is agape in pure awe, and my heart soars. I feel a few pounds lighter.

"I've always had a hard time with the basics of cause and effect, but I'm assuming you mean that if I wander into the gift shop, I'll be able to walk out with a snow globe. After purchasing it, of course. Both of us can't be shoplifters."

"Funny," I deadpan and adjust my grip on the wheel.

Henri's gaze darts to my fidgeting hands. "Anxious about your family meeting me?"

"They're going to love you. Penelope is probably already scheming how to steal you from me and become your best friend because she thinks I'm boring." Honestly, she'll fit in with them perfectly. She's hard working and driven, loud enough to make sure she's heard over the chaos.

"But does she think you're a virgin loser like your parents do?" I can tell she's joking to lighten the mood and it works.

"Nope. When she was little she used to be the first one up so she could get out on the slopes, and sometimes that meant four or five in the morning, and I'd be sneaking back in, wearing the same clothes as the night before." My shoulders lower from where they've creeped up to my ears as I recount the memory. "Then, of course, this meant I was stuck being the one who would take her out to the slopes. I liked it, to be honest. It meant I got out of some of my own training." I sigh. What I don't say is that I think she waited for me because she'd rather have me coach her instead of our dad, and I couldn't say no to that. "Just being home reminds me of all the expectations I'll never live up to. How I'm so different from them. I feel caught up in a wave, choking on water and barely breaching the surface to suck in air."

When I applied to MFA programs I got accepted to three across the country, NYU was the farthest choice. I needed space, needed to be able to breathe my own air. But I always knew it would be temporary. And here I am, back again.

And this time, I'm not leaving.

"No matter what, I'll be there," Henri promises. "And I'm a pretty damn good swimmer."

"Are you now?"

She shrugs. "I was sixteen and had a crush on a lifeguard at the country club. I'd get up early to swim laps and show off. I wanted him to see that I was serious and mature."

"Tale as old as time," I say, drinking in this new tidbit about her, itching to write it down. Each part of her that she offers is precious and I don't take it for granted. So often she's other people because that's who people want her to be.

But I just want her.

"What's with all the banners?" she asks. "Is that the competition you mentioned? This seems like a pretty big deal."

"Yeah, it's what we do on Christmas day. Rich people and a few pros pay thousands of dollars to enter into different events that are streamed live. Then, that night, they all go to the gala and talk about how, if they wanted to, they could do international competitions while drinking a shit ton of champagne," I explain. I guess I didn't convey how massive it gets. To me, it's just what we do over the holidays.

"Do you participate?"

"Not anymore. Our dad used to sign us up because it was a way to keep us active. Pen still enters because she takes every chance she can get to throw herself down a hill. I haven't for years though, and Juniper helps run the whole thing so she's ineligible. The money goes to kids who need financial support to be able to participate in winter sports."

We grew up with all the resources anyone could dream of, but for most kids, that's not the case. Sports can lead to scholarships for people and create opportunities for their futures, but equipment and lessons cost money.

June can come off as cold and harsh, but she's always had a secret soft spot for kids. She used to say that she was only helping them because she hated watching people with bad form. But now, she coaches whenever she isn't competing and helps organize the Dulcet Point Christmas Fundraiser.

"It's fun to watch. Some people dress in costumes, and there's good food too. My parents will probably want us to stop into the gala to show our faces, if you don't mind," I say.

"That all sounds good to me, but remember, you don't have to ask me to do anything. I am your perfect adoring girlfriend for the week, and anything you want or need to do, I'll be right there with you."

I eventually stop the car another mile up the road to let us through the gate that blocks off access to my parent's private driveway.

The house itself is two stories tall—a sturdy log cabin style with black shingles and three stone chimneys spearing upward, visible as we slowly rumble our way down the last hundred yards. Christmas lights fixed to the gutters gleam in the rapidly-dimming golden dusk light, now that the sun has melted against the horizon. A set of winter-weather-ready vehicles are parked out front.

"Is the house as old as the rest of this place?" Henri asks.

"Yeah, three generations. Originally, it was just a few cabins that people would rent. My grandpa was the one who made it into what it is now. My grandma was the first athlete in the family—a downhill skier. She was one of the first women to be in the Olympics for it. She'd come here every year to train, and he made sure to keep improving it so she'd come back."

"So, who's the next lucky owner?"

"I've been meaning to talk to you about—" I'm cut off by a neon pink form that launches in front of the car. I slam on the brakes and the vehicle threatens to fishtail on the ice-speckled road. "Shit!" I yell as the world blurs while I wrestle back control of the car. Panic consumes me even after we stop moving.

"I guess I don't need any coffee to keep me awake through dinner now," Henri says. Her eyes are flared wide, chest rapidly rising and falling as she sucks in air, and hands braced on either side of the car.

A thump comes from in front of us as Penelope, a wild smile tearing across her face, slams her hands against the hood of the Subaru.

I shove open my door and stride up to her. "What were you thinking?"

"I knew you wouldn't hit me." She crosses her arms defiantly over her sweatshirt-clad chest. Twin braids drape down her back and the baby hairs around her face have been flattened to her face, letting me know she's recently had a helmet on. Her brown eyes gleam with mischief.

"And what if I did?" I demand.

Penelope grins, stepping around me and closer to the car. "You'd feel really bad and owe me for the rest of your life."

"Are you sure about that? My life would be a whole lot easier if I didn't have to worry about—" I try to say *you* but the word is knocked out of me. The world tilts then goes dark and very cold as I sink and hit the ground.

Did she seriously shove me? Hell no.

I scramble, my fingers met with powdering snow. My hand thrust up into the air, breaking the surface like a zombie in a B-horror film, sending up a flurry of white directly into my eyes.

A car door slams and then Henri calls my name. "Liam!"

"Oh, he's fine," Penelope says. "He forgets that his life would also be monumentally boring without me."

"Pen. I swear to God." I shove up to my feet and, without thinking, run after my little sister. She leaps just out of reach on those deer-like legs of hers, taunting me. When I get close enough to exact my revenge, she darts away all over again.

Then Henri appears in her thin leggings and sneakers that are already damp from the calf-deep snow she's shuffling through.

"What are you doing?" I ask.

"Defending your honor." She winks. "What's the plan?"

"We need to block her off on both sides."

"You got it, baby!" she says. The term of endearment catches me off guard and I nearly trip over nothing and take another tumble into the powder.

"Yeah, *baby*, come get me." Penelope mimics a gagging motion, taunting us both.

Five minutes later, Henri and I are panting, her face is nipped red from a mix of cold and exertion, but we've closed the gap.

One chance, that's all we've got. I give Henri the slightest nod before I lunge. Penelope jumps to the side, action-movie-bullet-dodging style.

This leaves me hurtling toward Henri, arms outstretched. My hands connect with her shoulders as we go down. Down. Down. Her eyes squeeze shut, bracing for impact.

I shift to land with my hands planted on either side of her head. Her body has cut into the snow, as if she flopped down with the intention of making a snow angel, and I just stay there, hovering. A few strands of her short hair brush her cheeks and I fight back the need to brush them away.

"Hi," I whisper.

"Hi." Her chest brushes against mine as she gulps in air.

"*Baby* was a nice touch," I rasp.

Her lips twitch. "Liar."

"You're right. I like it best when you just say my name."

"Is that right, Liam Hughes?" She draws out the words as a shudder rolls through me.

Somewhere in my mind, there's a boxing match. In one corner of the ring, there's common sense, telling me to get up. And then there's the needy, desperate part of me that's telling me this is fine as long as we have an audience, as long as I can use that flimsy logic to keep the lines in place.

Guess who's winning.

Goodbye, common sense.

"We should get up," I mutter.

"Yeah."

Still, neither of us move.

"You two can eye fuck later. Dinner is going to get cold soon and you both need to change," a stern voice calls to us.

With more effort than it should take, I roll to the side. "Hey, June. I know you missed me."

Juniper is shorter than Penelope, but sharper. Her dark hair falls in soft, natural waves over her shoulders. She shouldn't go to parties because her cheek bones would pop balloons. She's colder than the mountain, but has a soft spot for the children she coaches. Out of all of us, she's the only one who's training and working on the mountain year round, and even has her own cabin. But over the holidays, she stays with the rest of us in the main house.

"Not that much," she says before disappearing back inside.

Henri and I clamber to our feet and grab our luggage. We head up the steps of the wrap-around porch and through the familiar burgundy door with its gold handle to the tight entryway that's already crowded with bodies.

"We have a mudroom for a reason. How many times do we have to go over this? You're acting like a child." June's voice rolls through the corridor, as she blocks Pen's path.

"I'm sorry, *Mom*." Not backing down, Pen puts a hand on her hip. "I was just having a little fun. You remember fun, right? You used to have it before you went and had that stick-up-your-ass surgery." She taps her chin and cocks her head.

Great.

Hey, Henri, here's my family. They are really nice people who you're going to love spending time with between them being constantly at each other's throats.

"Well, excuse me for not wanting to slide on one of your puddles and break my back." June thrusts out a hand, gesturing to the wet spots collecting on the wood.

"It's fine, Pen can get some towels and take care of it—I forgot, too. So if you're going to be mad at her, be mad at me too."

Pen has always had the most freedom, the most promise, but also has managed to maintain the most joy. Competition has always seemed like play to her, and so what if she hangs on to being young as long as possible?

"Fine. I'm going to go help Mom with the table. Can you two hurry up and change?" June starts to turn the corner, but leans back just to say, "And. Liam, try to look put together."

"I'll make an attempt." When June vanishes, I cock a brow at Pen for her to explain. It's not unusual for June to be stressed around this time of year, but this is a lot, even for her.

Pen rolls her eyes and shrugs. "She's been like this since this morning, checking when your flight will get in and trying to help Mom with everything. Don't worry, I got the *wear-something-besides-sweatpants* lecture too."

"Maybe she just wants to have a nice dinner?" Henri offers as a solution.

"*Maybe,* but we won't find out until we get changed," I say, and I have to admit, I would love to make it out of this trip without hypothermia.

We head through the living room, which is mostly decorated. Garlands of dried oranges droop over the tops of windows, and nutcrackers stand resolute on the mantle. But the three trees we pass, one at the base of the stairs and two tucked in the living room on each side of the brick fireplace, are naked.

Henri must note this because she asks, "Not a fan of ornaments?"

"They were waiting for us. None of us were able to agree on how to decorate the tree when we grew up, so now we have one for each of us. We'll probably get to it in the morning," I explain. "It's a whole thing. Mom lets guests vote on their favorite in the lodge and whoever wins gets to open presents first."

"How many times have you won? I mean, you have an eye for detail."

"Never."

"I'm sorry, but your family doesn't really seem all that aesthetically inclined."

It takes me a moment to realize that she's not directly behind me anymore and instead is lingering on the stairs. "I'm fine with going last. It's more important to them."

It's always been worth it, to sit back and watch while my sisters tear into their presents.

"That doesn't really seem like your responsibility," Henri says, as she climbs the last two steps and joins me.

"I'm the oldest. I like taking care of them." I need to.

We stop at the two rooms at the end of the hall, my room and the guest room being across from each other.

"Virgin loser," she whispers as we stand in front of the solid oak doors.

"Don't corrupt me, temptress." I make a cross with my fingers as if to ward away evil, before slipping into my room.

Once freshly clothed in jeans and a thick fisherman's sweater, I knock on Henri's door. Here's the thing, she could be wearing anything and knock the breath straight out of me, and the off-the-shoulder body-hugging black shirt and dark jeans are no exception.

"Should I change?" she asks, adjusting how her sleeves fall.

"What?" I ask, coming back to my senses.

"If this is too much or not enough"—she continues to pick at the fabric—"I can change. I just thought your family didn't seem super formal, but I didn't want to be in anything too casual the first time sitting with all of them."

"No. It's perfect." *You're perfect.*

"Great. Then, shall we?"

Mom has gone all out with dinner. Pepper-crusted roast. Creamy mashed potatoes. Caramelized carrots. A vat of stew on the side. Beyond that, she's brought out the good plates, hand-painted with little bows and wreaths.

"Oh my God." Henri moans around a bite. "Thank you so much, Mrs. Hughes, you're an amazing cook."

"Thank you, and call me Ally," Mom tells her. She's the one we inherited freckles from. They splash across her sharp cheeks and down her neck, but her hair is blonde, compared to our brunette.

"Just be happy you weren't here three years ago," Pen says.

"The pork." Juniper shivers. "So dry."

"Mom's been taking cooking classes from the chef at the restaurant," I add.

"I didn't need to be a good cook when I was younger. I was happy with bland chicken and rice or undercooked pasta from the training facility cafeteria," Mom explains. "Now I have the time and it's fun. Speaking of which, I've prepped some gingerbread dough. Just say the word and I'll pop it in the oven."

"Can I have that?" Pen asks, reaching across the table for the gravy boat.

"No. You're still training while you're here," Dad says and Pen's hand retreats back to her lap. He's a large man with weather-worn features from decades outside. Tonight he wears one of his usual flannel shirts and jeans. His phone is on the table next to his plate just in case he gets called back to the lodge for an emergency. "You can't let your diet slip just because it's a holiday. You have just a few months before the World Championships, and that new Wagner girl is improving faster than you are."

"June has some," Pen whines.

"She didn't qualify this year."

"I chose to take the year off. One of my kids needs a coach with her—she's got a good shot at the U16 Nationals," June says, tersely, as tension feathers through her jaw, making me think this has been a point of contention for a while. "And I've been busy with the fundraiser."

"It's just one meal, Peter." Mom rests a hand on Dad's arm and squeezes gently. "Remember how much we used to love the holidays? All that food and beer? It was always the best time. And we always worked it off on the slopes."

"I also remember it was hard to get back into a routine after," he grouses, then shoots a look at June. "Any time off puts you at a disadvantage."

Oh, casual shop talk at the dinner table, how I don't miss this at all.

Done with this conversation, I go for the gravy boat the same time Henri does. Our fingers brush and we both jerk back, nearly launching our glasses of water off the table. After what happened in the snow, I'm conscious of her, how I need to be more careful about touching her.

"Here," Henri says, the first of us to brush it off, handing over the gravy to Pen. "It's amazing."

Dad glares at her, and I can tell she sees him, but doesn't flinch, which is impressive. He's a man of iron resolve and has never been known to back down.

"You know you can touch each other? This isn't a convent," Penelope says. "You didn't seem to be having any trouble outside."

"Could you act normal for one second?" June saws at the slab of roast on her plate.

"Everyone's thinking it!" Penelope proclaims then leans toward Henri. "Blink twice if this is a hostage situation. If you agreed to come here before breaking up with him, you don't have to follow through with it."

"No! It's nothing like that!" I insist and reach for Henri's hand in what is possibly the least convincing way possible, because the distance between our chairs is awkwardly far.

"I've just never gone home to meet someone's parents before and it's a big deal. I'm just nervous," Henri lies, but it seems to work for now.

"Liam told us you're about to start graduate school, that's a big achievement," Mom says.

"Yes. It's a big step, but I'm excited to get into a career to help people long term. For now, I'm a bartender, and only help folks for a few hours at a time," she says.

"Where's the program?" Dad asks, eyes narrowing.

"It's in New York. You know we met because of his articles? I was kind of a fan of his before I even met him. You could say he was my celebrity crush." She scoops mashed potatoes onto her fork and takes a bite. "His writing is amazing, but of course you know that; you must have read his work." The jab is subtle but I see that it lands, the vein in Dad's forehead pulsing.

"Well it seems like you have a solid foundation that even some distance can handle." Smiling to himself, he grabs his nearly full wine glass, pushes up from his chair, and stands. "This is as good a time as any to make it official."

Couldn't he have just waited one night? My gaze darts around the room. Across from me, June straightens, attention locked on Dad. A plate clatters as Pen stabs a piece of roast and shoves it into her mouth. Mom barely conceals the upward tilt of her lips as she takes a sip of water.

"Over the next few years, I intend to slowly step down as owner of Dulcet Point. This is going to be a time that will require a lot of patience as the transition takes place for the next generation of Hughes to take over." He turns to me. "Liam, I'm so happy to welcome you home."

All eyes are on me for only a second before glass shatters.

18

Henri

ater spreads across the table in front of Juniper. Shards of her cup shimmer all around her, some managing to land on the serving plates, making the remainder of the meal inedible.

"Stay there," Ally directs.

"I'll get the broom!" Liam leaps out of his chair. I have to shake myself from my state of shock before I follow after him.

What the hell does his dad mean Liam's taking over the resort? Liam has a job that he loves and an entire life back in New York. And he's expected to do . . . what? Just drop it and come back here?

I catch up to Liam in the kitchen as he's pulling open a cabinet with cleaning supplies.

"Do you think I should grab a bag, or would that be hazardous?" He reaches in and picks up an empty dryer sheet box. "Maybe put it in this first?"

"I think you should tell me what the hell is going on," I say. I hate feeling stupid and in the dark and right now I feel both of those things.

His shoulders sag as he turns to me. "I was planning to tell you. I tried in the car, but Pen ran up out of nowhere."

"This is something you should have told me about weeks ago. I need to know these things or I'll look like I don't know you. A girlfriend wouldn't go on defending a job you aren't going to have soon. When are you quitting?" What I'm feeling right now isn't the standard fleeting irritation that comes when my clients fail to disclose important information. No, it's an ache that plunges deep into my chest.

"I was already supposed to be done, the original article we did was just to fill a spot that opened up because the person assigned to it went into labor. But then Fallon requested this follow-up article and I couldn't say no."

"I thought you trusted me?"

"I do; it's complicated. Let me help clean up and then we can talk and I can—" His mouth slams shut and he looks over my shoulder as shoes clack onto the tile behind me.

"The box is smart." Ally comes up beside me and grabs the dryer sheet box. "Sorry the little celebration got cut short. I know it was supposed to be a big secret, but I heard June talking to your father the other day about the resort. She's been so helpful, making sure everything was ready for you, so I know she must feel awful for ending dinner that way."

"Is there anything I can do to help?" I ask.

"No, we'll take care of it. But it's sweet of you to offer."

"Of course. I'm going to head upstairs and unpack and turn in early."

I can tell Liam wants to keep talking, but I need to calm down before I see him again. What's wrong with me? I'm usually great at letting this shit roll off my back, but this feels like a small betrayal.

Up in the guest room, it takes me all of five minutes to unpack the already-folded clothes into the top drawer of the dresser. I change into a matching flannel pajama set before washing my face and brushing my teeth in the small en-suite bathroom.

Back in my bedroom, my phone lights up with new texts from Iris.

Iris

> So, how's it going?

Iris

> You haven't fallen off a mountain, right? Because I really don't want to cover rent by myself.

Me

> I'm here. We're fine(ish). And it's really pretty. Like a Hallmark billionaire. Nice.

Without having a closer look at the resort, I know this is the case.

There was a time I'd travel to places like this with Kurt and Laura. That last Christmas, just before everything went to shit, we were supposed to go on a ski trip. Nothing special, something we did at least twice a year. We would spend thousands of dollars without batting an eye. I was packing when Mom called. I had been prepared to tell her to call back later, but then she told me I was needed back home, her voice choked with tears.

But that feels so distant now. Almost like that wasn't my life at all, just a story someone told me once.

Iris

> Work your sugar daddy for all it's worth (obviously I mean Spitfire)

I snort a laugh before navigating to my work email to distract myself. I find a few inquiries and three more cancellations that I draft responses for. It's a good thing I didn't blow up this thing with Liam. At this rate, nothing's predictable. I schedule the emails to be sent tomorrow morning, before moving to my personal one, that I've neglected to check for at least a week.

There are three emails from the university's registrar, all with urgent bold subject lines that scream ACTION NEEDED. Only three? They must have slowed down for the holidays. How considerate.

Before fully turning in, I wrap a robe around me and pad downstairs for water. I've had enough experience rummaging around in other people's cabinets under similar circumstances that it doesn't take me long to find the cups. I grab one with Snoopy wearing a Santa hat printed on it.

A light is on out back, and at first I think it's a motion-sensing one, but then I see the steam rising out of the fenced-in area. Stepping closer to the window, I see him.

Eyes shut, broad shoulders stretched with his arms spread wide along the lip of the hot tub. A crease cuts between his brows and tension ripples through his exposed chest—freckled like the rest of him. God. That chest. He might not be a pro-athlete anymore, but it doesn't seem like his body got the memo. Rivulets of water cling to his skin, a few rolling lazily down his body, from the cut of his jaw down his neck and—

Shit.

Brown eyes lock on me and I nearly jump back. Okay. Great. Now he's seen me lurking in the shadows, staring at him.

Sorry, Liam, I was just looking at you the way people admire Roman statues, could you just stay there looking all hot and moody while I grab a sketchbook?

He waves at me—a swift, casual flick of his fingers.

I wave back, take a breath, and head toward him. The sliding door sticks as I shove it open, and the stone path is brutally cold against the bare soles of my feet.

"Come on in, the water's fine," Liam says. He gazes at me through half-lidded eyes.

"I'm good."

"I can literally hear your teeth chattering." He stands, revealing a teal pair of swim trunks that suction to his thighs. Steam drifts off his skin. "I'll pick you up and put you in here if I need to."

Tempting as that offer is, I climb the small ladder myself. "Fine. Since when did you get bossy?"

"Since you walked out here in zero-degree weather."

I fight back a smile as I settle on the edge, feet burning at the initial shock of heat. The water hits up to my mid-thigh, and I pull the top of my robe tighter around me while the rest trails behind me. "There you go again, worrying about my well being."

"Obviously, someone has to."

"What about you? I should have asked how you were doing after what happened." Instead, I got mad at him. Not because of my work, but because I truly thought we were close enough that he'd disclose the information about him taking over the lodge.

"I'm fine."

"Historically, that's what people say when they're not fine," I say and make sure to soften my voice as I continue. "It's okay if you aren't. I'm here for the not okay bits too. That's why I'm here."

I've found that people are rarely "fine" for their own sake. More often than not, it's because they don't want to make other people uncomfortable, or feel obligated to share their emotions. And Liam is the prime example of someone who'd fold himself up as small as possible if it meant making others more comfortable.

He slaps his hand through the water, sending a spray to hit the exposed skin of my thighs, my shorts now barely covering my ass. "I wish he had held off long enough for us to at least get settled in. I really did mean to tell you, I just kept putting it off." A laugh puffs from his lips. "Jasmine was always on me to get out more so I could enjoy it all before heading back here. When I finally did get out there with you, I had the time of my life. It's not like I belonged there. You saw; I couldn't hail a cab for shit."

"Thank God for the subway. It's far cheaper too and where else can you get free mariachi performances at six in the morning?"

"You know what I mean."

I do, still I ask. "Can't you just tell him no?"

"We made the deal a long time ago. If I had been competing, we'd wait until I was ready to retire, which could have been anytime leading up to my mid-thirties. But obviously, I tapped out early. So he paid for my college, let me get out of here to experience the real world and build a work ethic, however I chose to do so, as long as I came back after I turned twenty-eight."

"So, then what? You just stop writing?"

"Because gift guides are world changing. They're just silly little articles."

I shrug off the robe and sink into the water. My shirt balloons around me, the hem of my shorts hovering at my sides. I step closer until I'm standing between his spread legs. I grip his face with my hands and tilt his jaw so he has no choice but to look at me. All thoughts about boundaries vanish as a need to tell how completely stupid he sounds consumes me.

"Those *silly little articles* helped me survive when I had no direction. They were humorous and full of heart and gave me a chance to feel like a person again when my life was in shambles. You don't have to be Tolstoy to be important—to touch lives. You touched mine before I met you. You asked me once what I did at the end of the day when I came home from being someone else? I felt like a goddamn wreck—a shell. So I'd throw on some sweats and see if you'd written something new. I read what you wrote and I was able to forget my worries and have a few moments of pure joy; you can't put a price on that."

I don't know who I'm more mad at. Liam, for seeming like he's giving up without a fight. Or the people in his life that make him want to dismiss what's important to him.

"Fuck, Henri," he says, that full bottom lip of his dragging between his teeth.

"So, what do you need? Another pep talk? Space? For me to march up to your dad and tell him he can find someone else to run everything? What about Penelope and June?"

"Pen would burn this place to the ground. June has years left of her career and she loves coaching. If she wants to keep doing that here, of course I'll support her. This is my family's legacy, my home. I made a commitment." He leans into my touch, breathing deeply. "Thank you, for being on my side. I know it's what you're here to do, but it was really nice. When you originally told me about why you did this, I thought I got it, but now I think I really do."

"I would have done it for anyone, but I liked doing it for you."

"Oh."

"Yeah. So, when you write about me . . . ?" I ask.

"I'll call you a devastating force and a threat to parents everywhere."

"Don't talk dirty to me now."

His hands move from their resting place, drifting through the water, before grazing up my thighs to land on my hips. My mouth goes dry, and when I meet his gaze I find a heat there that glues me into place.

"We shouldn't." Though the words are weak as they spill from my lips—one final feeble defense.

"Why? Because of the article? Fuck the article. The only reason I agreed to do the follow-up was because it meant I had more time with you. I have everything I need for it and I know that if I don't go for this, I'll regret it every day," he says. "Go ahead, lie to me again. Tell me that our kiss was just fine—just a blip. Tell me you don't think about it all the damn time. Because I've never stopped."

"I do." I swallow. "I think about it and don't know how to stop."

"Then why can't we have a week of this? Of us?"

He draws me closer and I let him. I float up and land so I'm seated on his lap, my thighs on either side of him. He's hard under me, his erection pressing between my legs.

"Because I don't know how," I say, placing my hands so they rest on his shoulders. It's one final excuse, because I do want this, want him, and I'm running out of ways to push him away. It will be temporary—just a few days—and, as Iris has reminded me plenty, he's not paying me to be here. *Spitfire* is.

"Are you a—" His grip loosens.

"I'm not a virgin. It's just been a really long time and I'm pretty sure I've forgotten everything. Like . . . I'm bad; I'm not worth your time. It's not going to be good, Liam. I'm only a fantasy and those aren't ever satisfying." The truth rushes out of me. For all my flirting and suggestive jabs, I'm clueless. My bravado is just an illusion. Behind it, I'm safe and powerful. It wasn't like it was even ever that good in college. My mind always went to how my body looked or drifted somewhere else entirely. More often than not, I'd pretend to come and then lay there waiting for it to be over. "It's easy to put on a show when it's for people who don't matter."

And that's it, isn't it?

I've lived behind this wall, able to control exactly what people see, making sure I live up to all of their expectations. Moving when things started feeling too real. And now I'm on the precipice, about to tip over into a phase of my life where I can't just wear a disguise and it terrifies me.

One of the hands on my waist lets go, moving to my face to tuck a strand of hair behind my ear. "I don't see how that's possible when you feel like the one thing I can hold onto right now. Just standing there, with that shirt clinging to your chest, does fucking dangerous things to me. But if you want, I can teach you how to make yourself feel good. How to use me to make yourself come."

"How selfless."

"God. No. You've got it wrong." A smirk flashes across his mouth. He leans in, nose feathering across my cheek until his lips are next to my ear. Fingers splay across my stomach, teasing, dipping just into my waistband and I squirm, desperate to relieve the blooming heat between my thighs. "In ten years, you'll remember this; you'll think of me. I'm terribly selfish when it comes to you. My favorite vice."

"Just hooking up? That's all?" I check. I can do that—just make each other feel good. And it would be nice to get past this fear of mine. One less thing to have a hold over me.

"And you still have to pretend to be wildly in love with me until Christmas. I like that." He rocks his hips and I gasp. "So, Henri, can I touch you?"

I nod frantically.

"I need your words."

"Liam, fucking touch me or I'll run out of here to take care of it myself."

"There's that mouth of yours."

His hand slips into my shorts, past my underwear. I buck forward against his shoulder as his fingers explore me, testing, stroking, not quite reaching where I need him.

"I thought you were good at this," I groan in protest, rocking my hips to help him.

"Oh, you want me to do this? Right?" With swift finesse he finds my clit—just a quick flick.

I cry out, but the sound is cut off when his mouth meets mine. My hands slip into the damp strands of his hair as his tongue slashes into my mouth.

Teeth nip at my bottom lip before he pulls away just enough to speak against my mouth. "No one can see us here, but they can hear you. And I doubt you want that. Can you be quiet for me?"

"Yes."

"Good girl." A finger drives into me and curls. "I'm going to add another soon and then you're going to ride my hand as if you were riding me. You're going to use it to get yourself off, do you understand?"

"I'll try." I try not to tense at his attention fixed on me, how I must look like a drenched rat. The glimmer of satisfaction dims. Why can't I just get out of my head?

"Relax, Henri baby." That's all it takes and I'm back in my body, feeling him pressed against me, a second finger slipping inside me. "You're safe. I've got you."

I rock my hips, tentatively at first, finding a rhythm. Using his shoulders to support my movement, I bounce. And as I do, Liam's attention snaps to my tits, trapped in wet cotton. With his free hand, he undoes the buttons, exposing my chest. My nipples are peaked against the kiss of the winter night, but the cold melts away when his tongue swirls around one, teeth scraping in a shock of delightful pain.

He worships my skin and I know I'll see the marks of his mouth painted on me in the morning.

"You ready for another?" He looks up at me from between my breasts.

"Another?" I gasp as he spreads the fingers already inside me wider.

"I know you love a challenge, and I bet your pussy is no different. Just know I'm not letting you leave until you come all over my fingers."

The third finger stretches me and I can't help but wonder if this is what taking his cock would be like. I reach for him, stroking his length through his pants as I move. He's just as turned on by his need for me as I am by the sensations shining through my veins, collecting hot in my stomach.

Every muscle in my body quivers, brimming with the need to shatter. To break.

And I do. The orgasm consumes me in a heady wave and I fall right into Liam's chest.

"Thank you," I whisper against his hot skin.

He strokes my back, soothing me in the sanctuary of his arms. "Oh, that was all you, smart girl."

We stay there until our skin is pruned and I know I can stand on my own without my legs turning into Jell-O. Liam grabs heated towels for us and we dry off the best we can without freezing before heading inside.

Up the stairs and outside our rooms we stand, dripping and in need of fresh clothes.

"Goodnight," I whisper.

"Goodnight." He steps up to me, kissing me softly as he cups my chin.

"Greedy," I murmur.

"I have a week, Henri. I'm not wasting it."

19

Liam

I t's six a.m., the air smells of burnt bacon, and someone is running
down the hall with all the grace of a baby rhino.

Even before she yells, "Get up, bitches, it's go time," it's pretty easy
to guess it's Pen. I roll over, covering my ears with a pillow.

A fist pounds at my door, rattling the hinges. "Liam!" Pen yells.

"It's too early for this!" I shout back.

She cracks open the door and leans in the frame. a steaming mug in
her hand. "Too bad, our trees have been ugly because we had to wait
for your sorry ass. Take a nap after we're done; I made coffee."

"Do you ever sleep?" I take the mug and sip the contents. It's
nothing special, just a dark roast, but after last night I'll need at least
two more cups to get through the day.

"Don't need to. That's why I'm better than you."

"Anything else?"

"I'm so glad you asked," she says and walks to my bed before sitting on the edge. "So, you know how it's impossible to get a good run in after ten with all the over-confident tourists taking on slopes that are too hard for them?"

"Yes."

"Well, I agreed to take on a café shift because a ton of the college students who usually run it are off for the week. But look outside and tell me that snow isn't begging for someone competent to snowboard on it." My eyes follow to where she's pointing out the window. It snowed at least three inches last night—perfect dry powder formed under the ideal conditions that come frequently this time of year.

Just looking at it reminds me of mornings where I clung to a thermos of black coffee as my body carried me to the slope, and that first run that shot pure adrenaline through my veins.

Pen continues, taking my silence as rejection. "It would also show Dad that you're a good, loyal worker bee. There's also the fact that I'll keep your fake relationship a secret if you do me this favor."

I jolt upright, coffee sloshing over my fingers and I hiss at the contact. Dark spots fleck the navy comforter over my legs. "What the fuck, Pen? How do you know?"

I have to hold myself back from saying that, after last night, I don't think it's really all that fake, but explaining what happened in the hot tub to my little sister is the last thing I want to do. Ever.

"The internet?" she says and then looks at me like I'm an idiot. "I saw the damn article, Liam. It was hard not too, it was everywhere. And you might not talk about your work with us, but it was pretty easy to figure it out when a journalist has the same first initial and last name. There are also pictures of you two together at the *Spitfire* party."

"So you're blackmailing me before I even get out of bed?"

"If I have to. But also it's kind of a shame. She's hot and nice." She pats my knee and all but jumps from the bed back to the door. "Now, get up. I'm not above using a spray bottle to get you out of bed."

"Fine. Fine. I'm moving." I kick off my covers. "Happy now?"

"Extremely." She nods and takes her miasma of chaos with her. "And the shift starts at seven-thirty! Thanks, you're the best."

I tug on socks and throw on a hoodie, knowing that if I don't hurry, she'll be back. Across the hall, a door creaks, and Henri steps out. Her blonde hair is fluffy from sleep, and red crease marks from her pillow are pressed into one cheek. When she yawns, she stretches her arms over her head, revealing a strip of pale skin.

Fuck. She's amazing.

The memory of her panting against my shoulder, fingers digging into me, making indentations in my flesh, floods me, and I have to rein in the memory so I don't risk walking downstairs with an erection.

"Like the view? I can do some yoga if you need to keep watching. I've got a killer downward dog, and my ass isn't bad either." Her voice is scratchy from sleep. Does she know how her humor steadies me? Keeps me from sinking into a corner and hiding away?

"I wouldn't mind. But I think we might get yelled at if we don't join everyone downstairs."

"Yeah, I wasn't expecting a complimentary wake-up call, but who am I to complain about an added luxury?"

"Pen asked me to cover a shift for her at the lodge—the cafe we have in the lobby. So after this, if you wanted to go back to bed, feel free to."

"You've been back less than a day. How'd that happen?"

"Blackmail."

"Makes the world go round. But, seriously. How?"

"I'm not joking. She knows about us." I stop as we reach the top of the steps and lower my voice. Jazz renditions of Christmas songs are playing loud enough I'm sure no one will hear us. "Yes, Pen figured us out because she knows who I am. And it made me realize how publishing that article put you at risk. Say the word and I'll write a check to cover all of your losses."

"Don't." She puts a hand up. "Not if you want to keep doing what we started last night. It would be uncomfortable for me. It would feel like you're paying me to be here."

"I get it. I just still feel like shit."

"Ease up on yourself. Let's go have fun decorating a tree."

We're the last ones in the living room. Everyone else is clutching coffee mugs, curled up under blankets. A fire blazes in the fireplace, crackling through the silence. Plates of burnt bacon and blackened toast sit on the table, untouched.

The couch dips under me as I take a seat, leaving enough room for Henri next to me, but instead, she sits on my lap, looping an arm around my neck.

"Greedy," I whisper into her ear, echoing her from the night before even as I hold her closer.

Six days. That's all I have left and damn if I won't do my best to stretch them as far as I can.

Something about that timeline seems to have flipped a switch in her too. She has an easy out at the end of this now, which is something she seems to need. A runner—that's what Jasmine called her.

"Liam, if you have time later, I'd like you to come by my office. It's the busy season now and it would be good for you to get a look at the basics of what we've got going on, especially leading up to the gala," Dad says. He's the only one, other than Pen, who manages to look alive this early. I bet he's already cleared his email inbox and put out a few fires.

This place is his life. It gives him meaning, years after his retirement from skiing. Old clippings of his wins hang in the office, as well as pictures of

Mom and him holding June and I as he waved a camera with a metal around his neck.

"We have plans; Liam was going to show me around the lodge," Henri says.

"And he's going to take my café shift," Pen chimes in.

"Well, getting your footing again will be just as helpful. Everyone respects a boss who isn't above working odd jobs," Dad relents. "And this time next year, you'll be running around non-stop like a chicken with its head chopped off, like your sister, so you better soak it in." He cocks his head to where June is pacing out front. She's pinching her brow and shaking her head as she takes a phone call.

"Next year, I'll make sure she's not so overwhelmed," I say as guilt wracks through me. I know she loves what she does, but I hate how stressed she looks.

Dad reaches over and grips my shoulder. "That's the spirit."

"But this is the last time you're going to bother him about this, Peter. I know how excited you are to have him back here, but you can wait a week." Mom comes in with two fresh mugs of coffee. Dad reaches for one but she pulls it away. "Here, Henri, I wasn't sure how you took it so I just put a splash of cream in it."

"Thank you, Ally, this is perfect," Henri says as she takes it, wrapping her hands around the mug and holding it close to her chest as she gently blows on the steaming surface.

The door opens and June comes inside. There's a rustle of a coat being hung up on a wrack before she comes around the corner.

"Finally!" Pen says.

Instead of sitting with the rest of us, June impatiently leans against the doorway. "Come on, let's get this going."

"Okay, Henri, since you're new, we have a few rules," Pen starts. "You get twenty minutes. No adjustments until after the photos are taken. Decorate the entire tree. First touch on ornaments." She pauses. "Shit, but it wouldn't be fair if Liam has a teammate."

"Does it matter? It's not like we care who opens presents first anymore."

"It's tradition, Juniper. You don't fuck with tradition. That's how you get cursed."

"Well, Penelope, that sounds made up."

Henri tenses as the girls continue to bicker, less like someone who's stressed, and more like a cat ready to pounce.

"I'm not the one who's been having shit luck lately, so maybe you should listen to me," Pen counters.

There's a second gap before June says something and Henri takes full advantage of it, "You know what would be fun? There's six of us and three trees. Nothing says we can't all team up." She turns to my parents. "Come on, have fun with us. Or do you think we'll beat you."

This woman not only jumped into my sister's petty argument at six in the morning, she has also done the one thing that would get us back on track: created a challenge. It was one thing to watch her at work over Thanksgiving, and another to be in the middle of it.

"Oh you don't know what you're asking for," Dad says.

"Sounds like you're scared to me," Henri taunts, but maintains an air of innocence all the same.

Dad claps and that's it. "Girls, you two work things out as you work together and get ready to learn what some good decorating looks like."

We all start at our respective trees, Mom and Dad to the left of the fireplace, June and Pen to the right, and Henri and I in the hall, bracing like sprinters waiting for a gun to go off. Tinsel garlands overflow past the lips of the bins that have been placed as equidistantly as possible. Due to the nature of our decorating, nothing inside is fragile. I mean, if you slammed the plastic ornaments hard enough they'd crack, but it would take effort.

The phone timer we set as the countdown blares and I run, grabbing a string of silver tinsel and darting back to Henri who meets me halfway.

"Red, gold, and green, Pen. Put that back," June instructs, frowning at the white sparkly deer in Pen's hand. They've both opted to run back and forth instead of the relay style Henri and I are opting for.

"Just let me have this one thing," Pen snaps back. "You're wasting time being picky."

Dad breezes by, moving in lethal silence, and scoops up an arm full of hand-painted ball ornaments.

In and out. That's what I need to focus on.

A smile blazes across my face, broadening each time I turn the corner into the hall and see Henri waiting for me.

"Go. Go. Go," she cheers me on. And for the first time in years, I want to win this.

Our tree starts to fill with an eclectic assortment of decorations. My goal is to go for object-shaped items not just classic orbs and bulbs—all things fun and bright. But by the final stretch, the pickings are slim and I have to dig.

June is doing the same, both of us up to our elbows in the same green tub.

There.

A red felt star with thick yarn needle work, trimmed with old thread. We've had it for as long as I can remember, and it's probably older than I am. I grip it and stand, ready to bolt back to my tree, but my arm is yanked back toward the bin and I nearly lose my footing.

"What the hell, June?" I pivot and grip my edge of the star with both hands.

"I was digging for that!"

"How was I supposed to know you had this one in mind?" I tug but June digs in her heels. "We grabbed it at the same time." Something in me snaps. Why do I always have to give something up? Why do they expect me to just let go and give them what they want when I have every right to it?

"If you had just paid attention, then you would have figured it out."

"It's just an ornament."

"If you don't care about it, just let go."

"But it matters to you?"

"*I* put in the work. *I* earned it."

Riiiiip.

The star splits down the middle, fabric giving way. June and I both rear back, each of us landing on our asses. I grunt as the air is knocked out of me. Cloudy white fluff flies into the air before landing on top of the stack of ornaments between us.

"Why couldn't you just let me have it?" June asks, despondent, looking at the limp scrap of hand-embroidered fabric in her hand.

"Is everyone okay? I heard a thud." Henri slides into the room as she skids across the smooth floor on her socks, overshooting the door just a bit. "Shit, that's gnarly. Let me go get my sewing kit."

20

Henri

I sit on the overstuffed chair in the corner of the guest room with the torn fabric star turned inside out on my lap. I didn't have the same gold thread as the original in my emergency sewing kit, but I can at least try to make the stitches mostly invisible.

Knuckles rap at my door, and I look up to find Liam standing there sheepishly, with his hands in his pockets. "Sorry."

"For what?"

He walks in and takes a seat on the edge of the bed nearest to me. "For the fact that it's been nothing but chaos since you got here."

"You want chaos? How about being hired to spend the holidays with a man because he's in love with his brother's fiancé. I took pity on the guy, but that was before I realized I was just there to cover up the fact that he and the fiancée were hooking up this entire time and didn't want to ruin Christmas." I swiftly push the needle through the felt, sped up by my mild annoyance at the memory. "This is nothing compared to that. Everyone thinks their family is weird in some way, but let's be real. The families on TV? If we were actually a part of those, we'd feel the same way. We're all just a little fucked up."

"You would be the expert with all your experience," Liam says, not knowing how true that is. "But you do have to admit, it's at least a little crazy."

I smile to myself, my fingers slowing as I reach a point on the star's points. "Yeah, a little, but it's fun. I don't really have any traditions of my own, so it's always nice to see other people's. For a week each year, I get to pretend they're mine too and I love feeling like I'm a part of those memories."

"You really do this every Christmas?"

"Christmas. Thanksgiving. Valentines. Easter—now that's a fun holiday. Brunches and egg hunts are a blast."

"Do you ever have time for yourself, Henri?"

"Are you asking as L. Hughes or Liam?" I ask, really hoping that this is just part of the interview and I can give a clean-cut answer.

"Both."

"Well, I would tell you that being with others, helping them feel close to the people they love helps me to feel fulfilled. It's a gift in and of itself to do that, make a difference. Not going to write that down?"

"My notebook is in the other room, I'll write it down later, but I tend to remember everything you say." He cocks his head. "So what would you tell me if it was just me and just you?"

Just me and just you. He makes it sound so simple.

"That I'm terrified to stop moving, of everything collapsing. When I think of taking time for myself, my mind goes to all the other things I could be doing to make my life better or the grocery budget that might be tighter, the bills that I'll just barely be able to pay. I run my own business. I rely on myself and no one else." With each word my needle moves faster. In and out. That's all I need to focus on. In and out.

"Sounds lonely."

"I'm always around people." It's a choice, so why do I feel myself growing defensive?

If I don't rely on anyone else there's no one to disappoint me.

I stab the needle through, but it slips to an odd angle and I catch my thumb. I hiss and lift my hand to find a small bead of crimson collecting on the pad of my finger. "Ouch."

I don't even see him get up, but a moment later, Liam is there, kneeling in front of me with a small plastic first aid kit cracked open next to him. He splits open an antiseptic wipe and cleans my finger before peeling off the paper tabs of a Band-Aid and wrapping it over my thumb.

As he seals the adhesive strips into place, his fingers trail down the lines of my hand, before lingering. As if he'll take any excuse to touch me.

"All good?" he asks.

"Liam." I pull out of his tender grasp, placing my hand on my lap and looking out the window at the falling snow instead of his face. "About last night."

"You don't want to keep going." I can tell that he's trying to wipe any emotion from his face, but he fails as his lips twitch downward. It's almost like he expected this from me—to let him down. I hate that.

"No, it's not that. It's just . . . we need rules. Hard lines. I like my contracts. I know what to expect, and so does everyone else. When someone steps out of line then there's a plan already in place."

"Okay," he says. Then he gets up and leaves, which I have no idea how to react to, so I just keep stitching along, working my way down the final edge.

A few seconds later he's back, notebook in hand. Taking the same spot as before, he flips to a blank page, and nods. "What are your stipulations, Henrietta?"

"Pulling out the full first name. So official."

"This is important stuff."

I take a moment to think. It's less about what I want and more about what's reasonable to expect. What will keep us in safe waters? No feelings. No wishful thinking.

"This ends the moment you drop me off at the airport." As I start to speak, his pen begins to scratch against the paper. "Six days to do whatever makes us feel good, but we stop if either of us asks. If things start to get complicated, we let each other know. You still have an article to write, and I need the money." Using the small gap I left in the fabric, I pull it right-side out and start to put the stuffing back inside.

"Right." A grin captures his mouth. "By the end of this trip, I'm going to make sure you know how to have fun, Henri. If you want to do something, we do it."

"But—" That is not what I meant.

"Don't say this is my holiday or some bullshit like that. I want to do it for *you*. If I was your boyfriend, that's what I would do—make sure you enjoyed your time here. And I'm half the act, right? It'll be less convincing if I don't do my part."

"I think we might be overestimating my ability to chill the fuck out, but then you have to agree to have fun with me—no doing shit for your dad. If you take the position, you deserve to have one last winter here without having to be the big boss worrying about everything." With the star filled, I make the final stitches and fix a knot to secure it.

"Deal." With a flourish, he adds two lines to the bottom of the page and signs his name on one, a looping *L* that devolves into illegible scribbles.

He holds out the notebook to me and I trade the now-repaired ornament for it. I sign my name at the bottom next to his and then thrust it his way. Standing, he tucks it in his back pocket then closes the gap between us. Fingers brush under my chin, tilting my gaze up to his.

"What are you doing?" I gasp as his face lowers to mine.

"Were you hoping for a handshake?" His breath feathers over my skin.

"No. This is good." Not in the middle of the night. Not in a torrent of need.

The light slashing through the window brings out streaks of gold in his brown eyes. I could stay here for hours and count all of his freckles.

"Hey," someone says and my eyes dart to the door to find June standing there, arms crossed over her chest. I slam the notebook shut. Since I saw her downstairs, she's changed into navy bib-style snow pants that fasten like overalls over a teal underlayer.

"Ever heard of knocking?" Liam groans.

"Door was wide open."

"Here." Liam grabs the star from the bed and tosses it across the room like a frisbee and June snatches it from the air with ease. "Put it on your tree. You wanted it more than me."

"Thanks. I was coming to say I overreacted."

"It was the heat of the competition. And you're stressed about the fundraiser, right?"

"Something like that." June rubs the back of her neck. "You know the Wilsons?"

"Yeah. The ones who do the dual slalom."

"Well, Mr. Wilson has a concussion and can't compete this year," she says. "His wife called this morning and is threatening to pull out unless we find someone to fill the spot. That's ten thousand dollars of entry fees we'd be losing, and it would wreck the tournament bracket that we have. Not to mention, I have some assholes who signed up for private lessons today."

"Shit."

"Yeah, whatever." She shrugs, shoving her hands deep in the pockets of her snow pants. "I'll figure it out. I need to get going before something else falls apart. Have fun at the café."

The lodge's café is situated in the lobby, facing the front doors so guests have a clear view of them when they walk in, kicking off snow and craving something to warm them from the inside out.

I've worked in cafés before, though I've always preferred bartending. The tips are great, but there's also something about talking to people and sinking into their stories, helping them voice whatever has been festering inside them. I'd take it over an asshole demanding a red-eye at five in the morning any day.

We have a line from the moment we step behind the counter, I take orders and Liam makes drinks, mostly hot chocolates and drip coffees. About thirty minutes in, we hit a lull and Liam starts making new whipped cream canisters.

"So, why don't you sign up for the free ski spot?" I ask, taking a sip of the latte I made for myself as I watch Liam make more whipped cream. I've been trying to figure out a way to ease into it, but sometimes it's better to just dive right in, especially since I don't know when we'll get another break between customers.

His attention snaps up and he fumbles with the frosted metal canister, nearly spilling the cream inside on the floor. "I don't think that's a good idea. I'm nowhere near as good as I used to be."

"No one said anything about winning the damn thing. As you explained it to me, half the people in the competition are just rich idiots, and it's for charity."

"See that hill?" Liam walks up to me and points out the window across from us to a steep incline dotted with bright blue and red poles. "I'd be going down that—weaving through those poles going head to head with the person on the other side. Normally, slalom skiing has one person making quick turns down a hill to be scored on a mix of points and time. The dual head-to-head event is done tournament style and adds a level of entertainment for those watching."

"See, you already know all the rules, and all you need to do is get to the bottom in one piece," I say. "I'm going to tell you something about hobbies: you don't have to be good at them. And if you're going to be here, it's worth trying to rediscover a part of it that you enjoy. I just want you to be happy here."

"I'll think about it, okay? Could you help me with these canisters? We need to have at least eight more ready for the lunch shift."

"All right, show me how." I don't push against his attempt to redirect the conversation, and it's nice to do something with my hands, to work.

He demonstrates as he explains the process. "Pour this liquid into a canister, to the line, and then screw on the top, pop in one of these nitrous canisters into this bit and screw it on." There's a hiss from the bottle as he finishes. "Shake the bottle and then you've got whipped cream, but you should always test it first."

He grabs an empty cup and tips the nozzle inside, pulling the trigger hard. White flecks explode out the top, sending the cup flying across the counter.

He flushes. "I might have been a little too trigger happy."

"Nah, I think it's perfect." A laugh burst out of me, the full body type that shakes me from the inside out, causing me to clutch at my stomach. "I personally love it when my whipped cream explodes in my face."

"I hit you with a bit." Liam starts to reach out but pauses at the last second, fingers hovering next to my cheek. "Can I?"

"Yeah," I say, the word coming out husky and almost unrecognizable.

I fight the shiver running through me as the pad of his finger swipes away the cream. "Got it."

Something must possess me because I lean forward and flick my tongue out to lick his finger clean. "Tastes good."

His Adam's apple bobs heavily. "You need to stop before I close this place up and carry you off to somewhere private."

"Hmmmm tempting."

His eyes go toward the entrance and his entire body sags. "Fuck. Let me take care of this next group."

"What's wrong with them?" I ask.

With my back pressed to the counter, I can't see them, but I can hear them laughing and roughhousing behind me. Throwing taunts and challenges at each other.

"Just some rich entitled assholes who treat this place like their personal playground. They've been coming here for five years now."

"I work at a bar where my main clientele are finance bros. I can handle it. And you're faster with the drinks anyway. This way, we'll get rid of them faster."

"Excuse me, could I order?" a woman says.

I turn, a bright customer service smile plastered on my face. "Hi, what can I get started for you," I say, but the last few words crumble into ash on my tongue as I take in the all-to-familiar slender curly-haired woman standing before me.

"Henrietta?"

21

Henri

T ime is the worst form of distance. You keep living life and become a different person thinking you've left the past behind, that what happened years before can't hurt you anymore.

And then, the people who were supposed to be your best friends walk into a ski lodge in Colorado laughing and having a good time, and all that distance is gone. No warning. No time to brace yourself.

I can still remember the last text I sent Laura, one that she never replied to.

I really need you right now.

"What are you doing back there?" And there she is, smiling at me like no time has passed at all. Like I hopped behind this bar like the time we were in Cabo for spring break and I convinced the bartenders to help them make a round of shots.

Kurt stands right next to her, ski goggles hanging around his neck, snow dusting his gear. His smile is as wide as ever. Blue eyes sparkling. "Don't tell us you work here now."

I've never felt embarrassed about being in the service industry before; it's the hardest I've ever worked. It's not just physically exhausting but also mentally. But right now I feel the weight of the power dynamic between us. In another life, I would be on the other side of the counter with them.

"Yeah, man, she's with me." Liam steps behind me and I relax at the reminder of his presence.

"Hey." Kurt reaches out for a bro handshake, clapping his hand against Liam's. "Good to see you, Liam. Was starting to think we wouldn't see you around this year."

Holy shit. This can't be happening. They *can't* know each other.

"We got in last night and Henri was nice enough to give me a hand this morning."

"That's a relief, I was about to call up my dad and see if he had any open positions for you, Henri. Being back there doesn't suit her," Kurt says.

Laura cocks her head. "Wow, you two are really together?"

"Yes," Liam says without hesitation.

"You've always had rich taste—gotta find a way to support your shopping addiction, right?" Kurt says.

"My girl likes nice things and I like to treat her right. Why wouldn't I give her my card?" Liam asks. "Did you want to order or not?"

"Two black coffees and three of those sweet cookie latte things," Kurt says with a wave of his hand. "You know the ones."

"Got it." Liam steps away and slots the espresso filter into the grinder.

I tap the order into the sales system as Laura playfully slaps Kurt's chest and says, "Oh my God don't be dramatic. You know the name." She leans across the counter to tell me, "He really hasn't changed. At bars he'll pretend the fruity drink is mine when he orders and then we'll swap. God, if his fragile masculinity wasn't always in the way, he'd have more fun." The casual familiarity feels like an itchy sweater against my skin. One I can't take off because that would leave me naked in public, so I just have to put up with it.

Is it not weird for them? It's not like we're college friends who never seemed to be able to make time for each other.

Kurt swipes his card, but instead of heading back to his friends he lingers by the counter. "So, what are you up to? I can't believe it's been so long. Seriously, it's hard to remember why we stopped talking."

Always fun to know that the event that felt like a meteor crashing into your world was essentially a pebble to someone else.

"I'm in New York, freelancing," I say.

Kurt nods. "I have this buddy who does that—upcharges like crazy and hardly does any work."

"Good for him. But I keep busy and I applied to grad school for next fall," I say, feeling like I have to prove something, for some reason.

"You can't be serious." Laura nearly chokes on a startled laugh. "You remember that girl who took your SATs for you? She had to wear a wig to look anything like your school ID."

"Yeah, that was really something." My cheeks flame. I feel helpless as my past and present collide. Despite the hiss of steaming milk, I know Liam can hear every word.

There's no point in denying that's exactly who I was, the same type of person Liam would call entitled. If my life had been different I would have been out there with them and Liam would hate me with the rest of them.

"People change. It doesn't seem like you know her anymore." Liam's voice is colder than I've ever heard it before. "Here's your stuff. Better get back to the slopes before they get too crowded."

"Thanks, man." Kurt smiles and grabs the carrier. "And, Henrietta, I guess this means we'll see you around? My family's coming to the charity gala this year, and I know my mom would love to see you. She still talks about how she wishes you were around to go shopping with."

"It would be great to catch up," I say.

Yup, a night with a room full of people I never thought I'd see again? Perfect. And if Kurt's behavior is any indication, they'll pretend nothing happened, because of course they have some new scandal to fixate on.

"Are you okay?" Liam asks when they're out of earshot.

Those three words snap something in me. I feel stretched thin. The backs of my eyes burn.

"I'm going to go to the bathroom really quick." I make quick work of the apron ties around my waist and toss it onto the hook.

"Henri, wait," he starts but a woman and child come up to the counter.

"Go ahead. Ask the man about the hot chocolate like we practiced," I hear the woman say as I walk past.

It occurs to me ten minutes into searching for a bathroom, that I have no idea where it is. I've found myself on the second floor, walking past game rooms and a restaurant. I reach a set of double doors and pull them open.

A breath leaves from my lungs as I stare at wall to wall bookshelves, only broken up by a large window facing the ski runs. I lose myself, running my fingers over cracked spines of books that would otherwise feel out of place together, but here make sense. Romance, horror, classics, history.

Hinges creek and I drop my hand, as if trying to not get caught.

"I was planning on bringing you up here later, but it seems like you found it on your own. This is my favorite room in this place." Liam walks to me, feet sinking into the plush crimson carpet. "When I got injured, I would just stay up here and read all day."

"Sorry, I got sidetracked, I didn't mean to disappear."

"It's fine. You looked like you needed a minute, especially after you went the complete opposite direction of the bathrooms." There's a lick of humor in his tone that subsides into concern. "How are you really?"

"Just surprised. I haven't seen them in a long time, and I wasn't expecting to run into them here."

"You know them."

"So do you," I counter.

"Not the way you do."

"They were my best friends for pretty much my entire life—elementary school through the first few years of college. I was just like them, Liam. If things were different I would have been on the other side of that counter and you would hate me the way you hate them," I say, even as it kills me a little. I don't want it to be true, but it is.

"Good thing you were back behind the counter with me."

"You don't get it!" My voice cracks as I yell.

"Then explain it to me," he pleads. "I want to understand."

"They left. They knew me for almost my entire life and the moment I needed them they were gone. And it wasn't just them, either. The reason they pushed me away was because it came out that my dad had this secret life. My own dad didn't choose me, Liam." I dodge around the truth: my dad chose money over my mom and I. Not just that, he put us at risk for it. "There's nothing about me worth sticking around for."

"Well that's a fucking lie," he bites out, voice dangerously low.

"Says who?"

His eyes flash with frustration as he slaps a hand to his chest and clutches at the fabric of his shirt. "Me. I know you!"

"Maybe I'm just that good at faking it. What if that's who I really am and I'm just hiding it?" I fear it so much. So I run and I play pretend and I let Iris in as much as possible, but keep the heavy things to myself.

"I can tell when you're faking it."

"How?" I demand.

"Do you make dirty jokes with all your clients?"

"No. But it's not like that matters."

He reaches in his back pocket and pulls out the green notebook of his. "I know gifts make you uncomfortable, and that you make some of the best drinks in Manhattan. I know that you aren't like them because they would just throw away old clothes when they're damaged, but you treat them like pieces of art to be cared for. You care so deeply about strangers and leave people better than how you found them." He stops reading and looks up at me. Clever fingers reach out and brush hair behind my ear, the touch cool against my blazing skin. "You fought for the life you have now and that's something to be proud of. Fuck those assholes for making you feel like you're anything like them. I know because I—"

I don't want to hear the rest, so I seal my mouth against his. At first he's stiff, but then his lips work against mine, meeting the rhythm of my urgency.

I need to shut him up so he'll stop saying all these nice things about me that will make me care about him. Because no matter how good they feel to hear, that doesn't change the fact that, at the end of this, I'll be leaving him like I do with everyone else.

And I already know that Liam Hughes will be incredibly hard to walk away from. I don't need to make it worse.

Hands in his hair. Him kneeling between my thighs. Yes, that's what I need. More of it. No thoughts. Just his body and mine.

I'm trying to drown in him and he pulls away.

"Henri, really I—"

I cover his mouth with my hand. "No. No more being sweet and kind and saying all the right shit. That's my job and I never mean what I say. This is supposed to be fun and feelings aren't fun. They're messy and sticky and complicate shit. So stop being nice to me and make good on the contract you have in your slutty little notebook and make me come." I lower my hand and wait, promising myself that if he tries to confess something I'll run out of the room, pack my bags, and buy the next ticket out of Colorado.

"Is that what you want Henri? To use me?" One hand abandons my leg to roam up under my shirt until he cups me over my thin lace bra, thumb teasing my nipple into a stiff peak.

"Yes." And it damn near comes out of me as a whimper.

"Then use me. But I'm not going to stop being nice to you." He kisses me, just a peck that has me following his lips for more. "I'm going to be so damn nice to you."

"A nice man would get the door. We need to lock it," I tell him, even as I attempt to shove down the swarm of butterflies that have chosen that exact moment to burst to life in my stomach. No one invited you, you damn insects.

"I locked it on my way in. Didn't need anyone barging in on you," he explains.

"No other reason?"

"A library is a great place to learn something new."

"What's next in the curriculum?" My voice comes out thin and airy as goose bumps spill across my skin.

"Tell me, what are you anxious about? You haven't been with any-one since college. What do you want out of this?"

"I want to know how to not look like a fucking idiot," I tell him through a self-effacing laugh.

"I'm going to tell you a secret," he says, his voice a low rumble as he plants kisses, trailing from the base of my neck, up my jaw. "Sex is messy and awkward." *Kiss.* "But good sex takes good communication." *Kiss.* "Telling your partner what feels good, what hurts. If you like it when it hurts." *Kiss.* "Helps you build trust and be comfortable." *Kiss.* "So tell me, what do you want to do?"

My back arches, straining to press closer to him. "I want to suck you off. I want to know how to make you come just with my mouth and hands." The request spills out of me and in response Liam groans against my skin. A hum of need sings through me.

"One condition."

"Yes."

"You get to taste me, only if I get to taste you."

Protests burst from me. "You don't have to. I haven't shaved or really done anything. I was meaning to pick up a razor, but we've been so busy."

"Like I give a fuck about that." His hands fly to the button on my jeans, starting to peel them off. "Henri, do you know how hungry I am for this pussy? How last night I licked the remnants of you off my fingers and it wasn't nearly enough."

Denim drags down my skin only to be caught around my ankles. He frees my feet from my boots to slide the pants off the rest of the way.

I'm squirming now, thighs pressed tight against the building, aching need.

Using two fingers, he pushes my blue cotton thong to the side. I don't exactly have sexy underwear, and right now, I wish I did.

Slowly, he spreads me wide, my wetness soaking his fingers. "So fucking pretty."

Leaning in, the pad of this tongue swipes over me before pausing to flick over my clit. My whole body jerks and I moan so loudly that my eyes snap to the door. I slap a hand over my mouth just in time to trap the desperate whimper that comes when his tongue plunges into me, fucking me like he's starving.

"I don't think I'll be able to stay quiet," I pant out.

"I think we can find a solution to that." His fingers hook into the sides of my underwear. He takes them off and balls them up in his fist. "Open wide."

I do and he shoves the damp fabric into my mouth. The taste of my own arousal coats my tongue. I thought it would make me feel gross, but there's a part of me that loves this, giving up some control, being told what to do.

"If I need to stop, tell me. You can tap me twice." He demonstrates, patting my thigh. "Or take out the panties and say so. Nod if you understand."

I nod.

"That's my smart girl."

The praise rolls through me in a burst of exhilaration and anticipation for what he'll do to me next.

He licks up the sensitive skin of my thighs and I have to fight the urge to squeeze my legs closed. When his mouth finds my clit this time, he sucks at me. I grasp at his hair and he moans, the vibrations shooting straight into my core. I cry into the underwear in my mouth, the sound muffled and making me far more comfortable now that I know it's far less likely that we'll be heard.

A finger dips into my entrance, winding me tighter. My hips buck to meet him and he pins me into place, the rough fabric of the chair beneath me scraping against my skin. I've never felt like this, and it's so fucking freeing.

Between his mouth and fingers, he works me tighter than a violin string. He pulls back and simply blows on my swollen clit and I come, collapsing back against the chair.

"How was that?" Liam asks. His lips glisten from my wetness, hair stuck at odd angles, eyes glassy. With a thumb on my bottom lip and index finger under my jaw, he tips my jaw open and removes my underwear so I can speak.

"For someone I scandalized so easily, I never thought you'd be so good at that."

"I wasn't scandalized. A part of me wanted to do this since the day we met, it just wasn't all that appropriate to do under those circumstances."

He caresses the soft skin of my stomach. "I mean, *fuck*. You don't know what you do to me."

My gaze falls to the very evidence of what I do to him straining against his pants. "I think I have a pretty good idea, and I can help with that if you tell me how."

He rises to his feet and steps back to give me room. I shuck off my shirt and he hisses a breath, attention pinned on me. Slowly, I slide from the chair and crawl. I like the effect I have on him and I want to draw it out.

When I reach him, I graze my fingers over the dusting of hair on his lower stomach, his muscles rippling and tensing as I do so. I lower my hand, pausing at the button but not undoing it. His hips jerk as I palm him through his jeans.

He's big. *Shit.* Maybe this was a bad idea. I'm going to fucking choke and look so gross and dumb. Nope. It's going to be fine. It's Liam and it's not like we're together.

We're just friends. Friends who, for a short period of time, are helping each other out. In a week, it won't matter.

I steel myself, sucking in a lung full of air. With shaky fingers I fumble with the button.

After a few seconds of struggling, Liam grips my fingers and pulls them away. "Same rules. If this is too much, we stop."

"I just need you to talk me through it." I flush. "Step by step. Tell me what to do."

"Here." He presses his thumb over the seam of my lips. I open up and let him in my mouth. I can taste myself on him as the pad of his thumb presses against the flat of my tongue. "Now suck. Yes," he grunts, jaw tensing. "Just like that. Breath through your nose."

I tease him with my tongue and it seems to break something in him.

"If I wait any longer, I'm going to come at the sight of you like that." He pulls his hand from me. "I need you to take out my dick," he instructs and I start with the damn button again. Once loosened, his pants slip down toned thighs. "Please," he whimpers as his fingers sink into my hair, not gripping, just resting there as if to guide me if needed.

With a tug on his boxer briefs, his cock springs out in front of me. A bead of pre-cum glistens on the swollen head.

"Now what?" I ask.

"Start slow, just the tip."

I close my lips around him and his body twitches. Looking up expectantly, I find his eyes locked on me and blazing with a startling intensity, his chest heaving.

"God. You look so fucking good on your knees with my cock in your mouth." He pants. "Use your tongue, swirl it around for me, baby."

I do as he instructs and grow more confident with each sound that escapes him. I take more of him, bobbing up and down as he curses under his breath.

Okay, maybe this isn't that hard. I just need to show a little enthusiasm.

I go faster.

And then I gag, a heaving retch escaping me. I pull back, sputtering for air. Fuck. *Way to kill the mood, Henri. He fucking rocked your world and you sound like a cat with a hair ball in it's throat.*

"Sorry. Sorry," I say.

"Nothing to be sorry about. You don't know your limits, yet." The hand in my hair smooths up my neck to catch my chin. "It's hot how much you want me. Use one hand." He grips the base of his cock. "Here. But do me a favor, spit on it first."

"You want me to . . . what?"

"I want you to get my dick wet; it helps with the friction. Now spit," he commands.

"Okay," I say hesitantly, rising back on my knees. Saliva pools in my mouth and I bend so I'm over his cock and spit.

"There you go. Now try again."

First, I wrap a hand around his base and twist. Then my mouth joins. I suck and swirl my tongue as Liam babbles encouragement, his thighs shaking.

"If you don't want me to come in your mouth, you need to let go, Henri."

But I don't. I go faster.

His cock jolts, his abs clench, and hot salty cum spurts down my throat. I swallow it down.

"Fuck. How are you real?" Liam gasps.

And for the first time in a long time, I truly feel like I am real. Not just a figment of someone's imagination. A real person who wants and needs and is fucking hypnotized by how this man I can't let myself get too attached to is looking at me.

22

Liam

Want to try something new for your first date? Take them to get the worst coffee you know of. That's what Jane (name changed for anonymity) does for the more than fifty men she goes out with each year. But Jane isn't exactly looking for a second date. No, these men are ones who seek her out for her services: to have a date for an event.

Why bad coffee? Well, we all think we know the person we are, but when coffee grounds coat your tongue and you're fighting off gagging in front of the barista who made it, that's a whole different story.

And that's how she gets her dates to talk: bad coffee. The thing is, you want to tell her everything because she makes it so damn easy. She sits and listens and for the first time in your life you feel not just listened to but understood.

You want to return the favor. You want to know her. But she won't let you. She won't let you care about her. You try and you try and you try and—

"The words are just pouring out of you, aren't they?" Dad asks. His lips wear an amused tilt from where he's standing on the other end of the table looking down at me.

I lift my hands from the keys and place them in my lap, knowing that I'll have to delete some of what I've just written. I came to the lodge this morning to write, setting myself up at one of a collection of tables set around the central hearth in the lobby, because I need to make significant headway on this article if I'm going to submit it in time for it to go live on New Years. I sure as hell am not able to be productive when I'm in the house with Henri. She's so fucking deep in my head and I can't get past what happened yesterday in the library. But every time I get close, she shoves me away.

It's the smart thing—the right thing. Doesn't mean I have to like it.

"Yeah, they do that sometimes. When I'm really into it, I work for five hours straight."

"That can't be good on the bladder." He places a hand on the back of the chair across from me. "May I?"

"Go ahead." I nod.

"I know your mother doesn't want me talking about this, but you and I haven't really had a chance to chat, just the two of us." His fingers knit together, hands resting on the dark stained wood separating us.

"You've been busy and we'll have time later. I know I'm not at the top of the priority list right now—there's the fundraiser and all the other holiday madness."

"Your sister is working so hard to put that together." He heaves a sigh. "I'm just so worried she's going to overexert herself, and I can't stop thinking about if she gets injured. She's got a decade left before retirement and a coaching career that will follow that. Keep an eye out for her will you?"

"I will," I promise.

"It's so good to know that I can count on you again. And you know, I don't want you to stop your writing thing. You can do a newsletter about the lodge. A monthly thing and you can have complete control over it—no pesky editors to tell you what to do."

"Sounds like a great idea, Dad." I try to sound enthusiastic at the idea of a newsletter that would be created only to be deleted the moment it hits people's email inboxes. But at least he's trying?

His phone chimes with a text and he pulls it out to check. "Duty calls. Only ever a few moments of peace during this season. Go home, spend time with that New York girl of yours. Maybe you can pull a Christmas miracle and convince her to move here." He puts his phone down and digs out his keychain—a vintage style we sell in the gift shop—and slips a key from the loop. "Speaking of which."

He tosses it at me and I manage to catch it before it thuds against the table. Unfurling my hands, I find a gold key resting between my palms.

"Dad, this is the key to the cabin." There are plenty of cabins on the property, though online we call them luxury chateaus, fitted with fun additions like personal saunas and game rooms. But this cabin, like the main house, is something just for family.

"Didn't think you were going to live with your parents, did you? I thought it would be the perfect place. Spend a few days there and catalog any maintenance issues we need to take care of before all your stuff arrives," he suggests before his phone chimes again, this time with a call that he picks up as he walks away.

I put in another ten minutes of attempting to work on the article, get maybe fifty more okay-ish words in, and decide to call it a day.

Outside the lodge, I'm about to text Henri to tell her I'm on the way back, but there she is, walking toward me. Well not me—she doesn't see me—but in my general direction. She smiles at something Pen says, and I notice Mom is with them and they all have skis propped over their shoulders. I guess that's what she got up to when I was working.

I take the moment to just watch, etching the image of her into my head.

Then she sees me. God she sees me and I'm surprised the snow doesn't melt around her with how she brightens like the damn sun breaking free from a cloud.

"Liam!" Pen yells, her voice threatening to shatter my eardrums as she waves.

I jog up to meet them and kiss Henri, holding her cold cheeks in my hands.

"Good time on the slopes?" I ask.

But Henri isn't the one who replies, Pen is. "Someone had to take her."

"I was going to," I protest.

"But you only go on the kiddie slopes and the toddlers pass you." Pen scrunches her nose.

I turn to Henri. "I really was going to take you. I can again later if you want."

"I believe you. That could be fun."

"She really was a natural," Mom says. "Productive morning?"

"I got a bit done. Hard to stay on track knowing she's around." My arm slips to hug Henri's side. "Dad gave me the key to the cabin; he suggested we take a few days there."

Mom puts a hand over her heart. "Oh, you have to. You had the best times there as kids."

"If you call getting up at five in the morning for bootcamp good times," Pen mutters.

"What are you signing us up for, Liam?" Henri teases.

"My dad would take us up there for a week each year and put us through a bit of a training camp. There's a solid run there and it's private so we never had to worry about anyone else getting in the way," I explain.

"You know, normal family bonding," Pen adds.

"Who wants to be normal?" Henri asks. "Count me in, especially if that means I get a few days alone with you."

"You best head into town to stock up on groceries," Mom suggests. "And if you leave this evening, I can make sure to have my gingerbread ready so we can make the houses before you leave. How does that sound?"

"Great, Ally," Henri says.

"Amazing, well I better get that started." Mom leaves us, heading to store her skis.

"Can we keep her?" Pen asks, leaning into Henri so their shoulders smoosh together. "I know you guys aren't really together, but please? I like her too much."

Henri lets out a strangled laugh as an unreadable expression flashes across her face. "Could be fun."

"Don't be weird, she's not a kitten you found in a box by the tavern," I admonish.

Pen turns to Henri. "Even if you don't like him, we can still talk and hang out. I'm objectively more fun, so honestly, it's the better deal."

A soft sad smile tugs at Henri's lips. "Only if you promise to pretend to hate me when I break up with him. Like make me your worst enemy."

"God, why?" Pen jerks back.

Henri reaches behind me and I feel her fingers against my back pocket and she works my notebook and pen free. I have to try particularly hard not to think about the lingering feel of her hand on my ass. She places them in my hand and nods. I flip to a blank page and only then does she start. "Because Liam is going to tell everyone I broke his heart—I did the worst thing we can think of. I get to walk away as the villain and no one doubts that it was real. That way, there's no going back."

At her final words, her gaze snags against mine. I don't know what to say to that.

"Well that's shitty." Pen shrugs. "But I can play along."

The three of us head to our family's storage area where we store our gear. It looks like a small locker room, and protein bars and electrolyte drinks are always available on one table, just in case we need the boost. Next to them is a typed-up training plan with Pen's name on it. A hand darts out to swipe it before I can read more than the first few lines, but I'd know Dad's style anywhere.

"You don't need to listen to him, you know?" I say to Pen. "He's not your coach anymore."

"I do. But it's easier to let him have his way, and it's nice to get a different perspective. It's only for two weeks." I can't tell if she means it or if she's trying to brush me off. "And according to this, I have a massage right now, which sounds really nice. You two have fun preparing for your fuck fest," she hollers the last bit as she runs for the door.

"Pen!"

"Who knows, anything could happen in the cabin! Oh, they moved the condoms to aisle three!" She ducks out as she makes herself laugh.

I shake my head. "I don't even want to think about why she knows that."

"I'm hoping she forgets about us, about me," Henri says, still wearing that odd expression.

"You aren't going to stay in touch?" I join her where she's sitting on a bench along one wall.

She lays her head on my shoulder and grabs my hand, running the tips of her fingers over the creases in my knuckles. "I like her, but it's a bad idea. It's always the hardest when I like the family."

"You like my family?"

She nods. "Yeah."

"So, tell me, how will you break my heart?" I try to make it sound like a joke, but the ache in my chest gets in the way.

"I pick a fight with you." She drops my hand, shifting away so she can look at me. Her eyes well with emotion. "I tell you it's me or the lodge. You choose the lodge because it's your family legacy and I'm being selfish, not even willing to try and figure out how we can have both."

"That is shitty." She helps people only to be remembered as a bad person. "I don't want my family to see you like that. Let it be my fault. Let them think I'm the asshole."

"You wanted to know my process, right? This is the way it is." She pulls away. "Let's go get those groceries."

23

Henri

I can tell the conversation about our fabricated break up must bother Liam because he's mostly quiet on the drive into town, turning up the radio as we navigate the winding roads down the mountain. But at least the conversation's out of the way, and he knows what to expect when I leave.

While we shop, deciding on what we want to cook and eat on our little getaway provides a new, safer topic of discussion. Liam's mom texts him to pick up candies for the gingerbread houses and any other decorations we can think of, extending our trip. I don't mind. I like just lazily spending time with him.

We do in fact go to aisle three and grab condoms because a cabin fuck fest doesn't sound too bad. Okay, fine, *I* go to the aisle and grab the condoms, toss them into the nearly-full basket from five feet away, and nearly give Liam a heart attack as his head whips to where an older man with glasses is walking by.

"That's my principal," he hisses.

I cock a brow. "Does he have kids?"

"Yes, six."

"I was going to say he knows what condoms are, but now I'm not so sure."

A smile splits his mouth as he buries his red face in his hands.

I have to leave. I know it. He knows it. But right now, this is good.

We finish our shopping and load up the Subaru when we're done. The trunk closes with a solid thunk. Instead of going back up the mountain, we head to the town square, a collection of mismatched colored shops with snow-dusted awnings. Light posts trimmed with garland are posted in front of small brick buildings with hand-painted windows illustrating winter wonderland scenes. Trees strung with warm-hued string lights are tucked into every available corner, and the mountain watches over the town, appearing a purplish blue in its majesty.

We walk slowly as Liam peppers me with questions that I guess are inspired by his attempt to write this morning. Still, he doesn't pull out his notebook, he just listens. I like that a lot—more than I should. It makes me think my words might be something worth holding onto.

"How do you do it? Convince people you're in love?" he asks as he steps over an ice patch on the sidewalk and waits for me to do the same.

"It helps that, for the most part, the people I help are decent. I don't think like myself, and I'm not really myself in these contexts. I'm the woman they need me to be, so I think about being that woman. What does she see in them? What part of them is lovable? I cling to that. I remind myself that they're determined or passionate about their work or are so funny they could actually be a stand-up comic, but I'd never tell a man that because we really don't need more men out there in the world trying to be funny." I look at Liam and wait for him to ask what I cling to for him.

It's easy, just resting there on the tip of my tongue. He's curious in this intensely genuine way. He cares more for the people around him than for himself. For years, I knew him by the words he put on the page, but the real deal is so much better.

Instead he says, "Not everyone can do that."

"You can. You can interview the shit out of people—make them comfortable with being heard. Or at least that's what you did with me."

You saw me. Intentionally. Willingly. And what a gift it is to have someone want to understand you.

A familiar voice comes from down the alley just ahead of us, shattering the moment. "Like I told you when we talked over the phone, I'll come back down for the second load."

"Is that . . . ?" I ask.

"June." Liam nods and we both head toward the alley. There, Juniper is standing, hands on her hips, next to her SUV. The car's trunk is open, revealing that every surface is loaded with clear tubs holding deep crimson linens with threads of gold shimmering through the weave.

Across from her, a gray-haired man with a cane says, "Come back tomorrow morning. We close at three today, but by the time you're back, it will be late."

"I don't have time in the morning. I have other vendors to work with and I went out of my way to come here because your driver is unable to fulfill the request we make every year. Maybe you could leave the extra linens with one of the other shop owners?" Juniper says, the edge in her tone a tell-tale sign that she's close to snapping.

"What's the problem?" Liam asks.

"His grandson took a last minute trip to Steamboat and can't help deliver the rentals for the gala that we use every year. I need to get them to the staff today so we can start to steam them and prep the ballroom, but my car will only carry so many boxes." Juniper gestures behind her.

"We have some room in our car. I'll take whatever's left," Liam says, more to the shop owner than to his sister. "Does that work?"

"Just pull around here when you're ready," the shop owner says before ducking back inside.

"June, is it just the linens? What else can we help with?" Liam reaches to touch her shoulder but she shrugs away from him.

"Nothing. I've got it. Once this is done I'll just have to remake the stupid ski bracket because I haven't found a replacement and I can't use a software for it because I need to appease the rich idiots and give them the illusion of winning."

"Next year, I'll be here already and you can catch me up on things so I can fix them. That way you can focus on more important stuff. This can be my problem."

"Yeah, you and dad have made that very clear, but this isn't for you to swoop in and fix at the eleventh hour. If it's a problem, it's my problem."

"June," Liam starts.

"No," Juniper bites out as she fishes for her keys. With them in hand she slams the car doors closed and takes a deep breath. When she speaks again, most of the fire has left her voice. "Thanks for your help, Liam, but I'm fine."

Liam and I step to the side so we aren't in the way as the SUV zips out of the alley and onto the street.

"I hope someone gets her to the spa soon cause all that stress can't be healthy," I mutter. Suspicion prickles at the back of my mind. Something is clearly off between these two. Unfortunately, though, I'm not a mind reader and don't want to assume anything yet.

"Yeah, that's what I'm worried about. She's doing too much and is going to make herself sick, or get hurt."

"I mean there is one way you could ease some of that stress."

"Henri." He sighs.

"Liam." I raise a brow, crossing my arms over my chest.

"Maybe. I just need her to cool down before I suggest another way to take the spotlight from her. For now, let's bring the car around and take care of this."

As it turns out, there are only three tubs left. Any more and we probably wouldn't have been able to haul the rest. Liam chats a little with the shop owner while the man starts to close up his business, no doubt making a connection that will be useful in years to come.

It's a funny thing, seeing the threads of Liam's future—one that I won't be in. Next year, these two will likely talk about similar things while I'll be somewhere else entirely. My phone chiming in my pocket saves me from the wash of melancholy thoughts.

A tiny bell chimes overhead as I push out of the shop to take the call. Speakers positioned around the square spill out a crackling jazz arrangement of "I'll Be Home for Christmas" into the brisk air.

"Hey, did your present arrive? It should be in today. I'm not telling you what it is, but keep a look out so Ms. Cooper doesn't snag it," I tell Iris. Though our apartment is pretty great, Ms. Cooper in 3C has a tendency to grab extra mail "on accident." She'll return it if you ask, but it's always easiest to get there first.

"Not yet, but I'll stay vigilant. Last time I had to retrieve a package, she held me hostage with cookies and cats for two hours. So, how is it? I haven't heard from you since you got there," Iris says.

I tug my hat down further on my ears as the wind cuts by. "You can just say you missed me."

"No, I'm just nosey. So, have you boned yet?"

"Iris," I hiss.

"What do you prefer? Boinking? Bedroom rodeo? Cave diving?"

"I might prefer to stuff cotton in my ears if you continue." I roll my eyes and kick at a snow drift that's swallowed a section of the curb.

"Fine. But I'm not hearing a 'no' come out of your mouth."

"That's umm . . . Because."

"No fucking way. I wasn't serious!" She sounds as if I've told her I just won the lottery. Honestly, I kind of have. Empathetic, caring, hot men like Liam aren't exactly falling from the sky.

"Yes, you were."

"Okay, fine. But that's because I'm a romantic and you're perpetually repressed and avoidant."

"I'm not . . ." Yeah, fine she's right. "That doesn't matter."

"I can't wait for you to have ridiculously cute freckled babies."

"Hold the fuck up," I say. "One, we've done nothing that would lead to baby making, just like everything else. Two, this is just a temporary arrangement."

"Yeah, we'll see how temporary it is when you're both back in the city and don't have that stupid article as an excuse for you to not be together officially anymore." And I know if I could see her, she'd be waggling her brows at me.

"Iris." My traitorous voice cracks. "He's staying here. That's the only reason he and I got physical at all. This is just fun."

"God, this is just like you." Which is probably the last thing I expect her to say.

"What the hell is that supposed to mean?" I demand.

"You push him away when you think he'll be around and only let yourself have something with him when you know it's going to end. I'm happy to move around with you, stick by you, but it's frustrating to see you just shove good things away because you're scared. I know about the admissions emails you get, Henri."

"You know?"

"Of course I know. You're always on your damn email and our apartment is really fucking small. I've tried to be encouraging, but it's hard when you're not just lying to me, but it feels like you're lying to yourself too."

"Great. Thanks for telling me how *you* feel about me being fucking terrified of one of the biggest commitments of my life." The truth tears out of me.

"Anytime," she bites out.

I press the red end call button so hard that I'm surprised I don't crack my screen. While I'm thinking of it, I check the tracking info for the gift. The email says it's out for delivery, and even though I'm pissed at Iris, I forward her the tracking number.

I'm about to close my email when, of course, a new damn admissions reminder pops up at the top. I toss my phone into the nearest snow bank, but the light swish it makes on impact is vastly unsatisfying. I want to kick something, and due to the fact my options are the lamppost next to me and more snow, I'm shit out of luck.

Instead, I just stare up at the grey sky as heavy, snow-laden clouds swiftly block out the remaining blue. "I'll Be Home for Christmas" ends and gives way to "Have Yourself a Merry Little Christmas."

A bell chimes behind me and shoes crunch in the snow before stopping next to me and I know it's Liam without looking.

"You know, I hate this bit of the song," I say to the sky, fighting the stinging at the back of my eyes. "Fuck the fates. Why do they get to allow anything? You can plan all you want, but one winter storm or little mishap and your fucked during the holidays. It's not fair."

"Any particular reason you've been possessed by the spirit Ebenezer Scrooge in the last ten minutes since I saw you?" Liam asks as he crouches down, hand dipping into the snow to retrieve my phone. He wipes the screen, pulling his sleeve up over his hand and rubbing the glass with his palm. Once done, he inspects it and jerks back. "Henri, did you see this?" He tilts the screen so I can see the email.

"Yup. I've had my admissions letter waiting for weeks now. I get one of those emails every day," I explain, over hiding shit. What does it matter?

"Okay."

"That's it? No lecture? No *you're being a stupid coward, Henri*?" I demand, throwing my hands in the air, even though it's not him I'm mad at. I'm not even mad at Iris—she's not to blame. Hell, she's followed me everywhere.

I'm mad at myself. Why can't I just go for it? I know I want that life in New York, I feel it deep in my chest. And yet, I can't take this final step. Pathetic and scared.

"Seems like you've got all that covered already. Though, I suggest not throwing your phone in the snow. I mean they claim these are waterproof now, but I'm pretty sure that's a lie." He holds out my phone to me and I grab it, but he doesn't let go. As his grip remains firm, he drags me to him until I'm wrapped in his arms.

I bury my face into the thick cable knit of his sweater and say to his chest, "I'm really scared. What if I've put in all this work and I'm not enough? Or if I do get in and go through all of it and my life is fucking terrible and I just have to live with the fact that I feel cheated by all of it?"

A hand ghosts over my hair to comfortingly clutch the nape of my neck. "You are enough. A school doesn't get to determine that. And I can't promise that it will all work out, but those fates you're so mad at? Sometimes they do let things just work out. But you don't know if you don't try." He scoffs a laugh, a quick rise and fall of his chest against me. "I know I'm a fucking hypocrite for saying any of this shit, but you're better than I am, Henri. I've never had to worry about a damn thing. I always knew I'd end up running this place; I've never had to risk anything."

"Do something terrifying with me, Liam?" I ask. "Take a risk?"

"I'll make a deal with you."

"Another one?"

"Well, you hate gifts and favors, so equivalent deals seem to be the only way to convince you to do anything."

"Money," I joke so I don't have to acknowledge the hum of pleasure that rolls through me that comes from being understood.

"But only if you feel like you've earned it." He lowers his head and whispers, "I know you like to work for the things that make you feel good."

"Oh fuck off." I bury myself in his sweater again as my cheeks flame.

He laughs again. "I'll sign up for that ski team if you open your email."

"I'll open it once the competition is over."

"After I submit the sign-up form."

"Fine," I relent, not feeling like arguing anymore today. "Just let me stay here a little longer."

Wrapped up in you, where it's safe.

24

Henri

Do you have any tequila?" I ask as I stare at the red *Check Admissions Status* button in front of me. My laptop rests on the kitchen island opposite Liam who is typing on his across from me as he finishes filling out the forms Juniper sent his way once he agreed to sign on for the ski event. "I think I need a shot." My gaze darts over the kitchen, searching to no avail.

And I didn't see any alcohol around when we were putting up the groceries either.

"It's three in the afternoon." Liam quirks a brow.

"We're on vacation. It doesn't count."

"We can steal some champagne once this is done," he says and finally looks up from his screen. "I'm ready if you are."

"Can you just press it?" I start to shove my laptop his way, but he stops me.

"You can do it. It's just a button."

A button that will determine the course of the rest of my life. When the hell did we give technology so much power? Take me back to the days when we got thick-ass acceptance letters so I could at least manage my expectations before tearing open a seal.

There's a quick *click* from Liam's keyboard. "See? Easy."

With a deep inhale, I screw my eyes shut and jam my finger into the trackpad. Cracking an eye open, I groan. "You've got to be fucking kidding me. I have to log in again. I just did that shit."

Liam rounds the counter and looks over my shoulder at my screen, resting his chin on my shoulder as he does. "I guess your fate is highly sensitive information that needs to be protected at all costs."

It's really hard to glare at someone who's pressed against your back, but still, I make a valiant effort.

His arms band around me. "Fine. Even I have to admit that's just fucking cruel."

I type in my login information again and click.

Henrietta Elm,

We are pleased to welcome you into the Master's of Counselling, Mental Health Concentration.

I scan the rest of the page until I reach the bottom. "In addition to standard need-based aid, the Psychology department has decided to offer you one of the available assistantship positions, wherein tuition and fees will be waived." Holy shit. I never planned for anything beyond the basic need-based aid. "I did it! I fucking did it!" I spin in Liam's arms, grab his face, and plant a kiss on him, unable to contain the pure relief washing over me.

"Yeah, you did," Liam says when I pull away.

"I'm going to need to pay my deposit and register for classes. I need to tell my mom and *fuck,* I need to call Iris and tell her that she was right, but also, we need to celebrate. And—"

Liam stops me with a finger on my lips. "No, what you need to do is stop and be proud of yourself. Everything else can wait."

He's right. I can finally relax as I take the next step toward the stability I crave. And it's terrifying. There will be classmates I see every week, people who will get to truly know me. But because of the smiling man here with me, I'm finally not overwhelmed at the thought of it.

Because I'm Henrietta Fucking Elm. I work my ass off and make stupid dirty jokes and like clothes more than most people and I have really big feelings for Liam Hughes that I can't say out loud.

It hits me like a knife piercing through my heart. This is supposed to be just sex. I *need* it to be just sex and good memories.

My smile fades against his finger.

"What?" he asks, brows pinching in concern.

I shake the thoughts from my head. "Nothing. I'm just happy that I get to be here with you."

This time when I kiss him I don't pull back. I wrap my arms around his neck and hold on to what we have left. He deepens the kiss, his hot tongue swiping into my mouth. I rock into him and I swallow the groan that rumbles through him as he hoists me up, hands digging into my ass as he carries me and starts to walk.

"Where are we going?" I ask

"Bedroom," he rasps

"You're carrying me up the stairs? You tend to have a hard time with those."

"Fuck you."

"I thought that was already the plan," I say as the easy humor dissolves the ache in my chest.

He doesn't let me go. He carries me up the stairs and into his room, dropping me onto the mattress so I fall with my legs dangling off the sides. I tear off my shirt and chuck it to the side.

But he just stays there, hovering over me. Hazel eyes devouring every inch of me and that fist around my heart is back squeezing with all its might. I need it gone.

Come on, Henri. You know better. You don't get the guy. You don't want the guy. You hang out with them, you listen, you stand with them, and then you fade into a memory. You leave because when people get too close, when you've already given parts of yourself to them, they vanish.

That's how it always goes.

Liam isn't—can't be—any different.

"Liam, please. I want you to fuck me."

He stops again. *Damn it.*

"Are you sure?"

Can't he be a little bit of an asshole just once? Would that be too much to ask?

"No, I publicly humiliated you with a box of condoms so we could blow them up like balloons," I say, but then see the tender look in his eyes. "Yes, I'm sure. I can't think of a better way to celebrate."

"Okay." He kisses me quickly and pushes off the bed.

Opening a drawer in his nightstand, he grabs the box. With a yank, he pulls at the top and the thin cardboard tears, sending a cascade of metallic packaging onto the floor.

A laugh whooshes out of me as I roll off the bed and help him shove the condoms into the drawer, both of us on our hands and knees, wrappers crinkling as we grab them.

"The last one," I say as I grab the final one from the thin carpet. Liam tries to take it from me, but I pull away. "I want to."

He nods and gets to his feet. In one swift movement, he pulls off his shirt before working his pants and boxers off. He's bare, towering over me, cock at eye level and so fucking hard. I reach out and stroke him, relishing the feel of his length in my fist. The muscles of his stomach clench and he leans back, bracing himself on the nightstand.

"Shit," he hisses, eyes on me.

I tear the condom wrapper open with my teeth, something I've read about men doing in books, but I like the power that comes from being the one to do it. Slowly, I roll it over him. The moment my hands are off him, I'm lifted into the air, arms like steel around my waist, his cock pressing against my stomach. I bounce as I land on the mattress and a giggle erupts out of me.

And I'll be damned if I let my catastrophizing brain ruin this.

"I'm going to start like this. I want to see every expression you make when I'm inside you," Liam mutters. His breath is hot on the skin of my stomach as he pries off my pants and underwear. He replaces the fabric covering my pussy with hand, rubbing his fingers over my clit as I squirm. "You ready, baby?"

"Yes," I gasp.

He lines himself up with my entrance and pushes in slowly. God it's so different than when he fucked me with his fingers. So full. I reach up, needing to grasp something, my fingers find his back, clinging to him. With a final snap of his hips he's fully seated inside me.

"Taking me so well, like I knew you would," he praises, starting to roll his body against mine. I clench around him and that spurs him on.

"Tell me what to do," I say.

"Right now, you're going to lie there and take everything I give you, and then, if I survive your pussy long enough, I'm going to pull you on top of me and you're going to ride me until you have everything you need." As he speaks, he thrusts. Slow at first, but rapidly turning frenzied. His eyes pinch shut and something riding the line between utter anguish and pleasure consumes his face.

I claw at his back and my legs wrap around him as I'm pressed into the bed. Behind us, the headboard pounds against the wall.

When he pulls fully out of me, I whimper at the feeling of emptiness, but then I'm flipped around, straddling him.

Need takes hold in the place of nerves and I position myself over him. He grips my hips as I sink onto him.

Without me having to ask he starts to talk me through it, anticipating my over-active brain before I have time to panic. "Perfect. Now roll your hips." He gulps and groans as I rock tentatively. "Use me, Henri. Chase what feels good. I'll tell you if I need you to change something." He takes one of my hands and places it on his chest, where I'm met with his thundering heartbeat. "Brace yourself against me. You won't hurt me if you put some weight there."

I rock forward and back, testing what works and swallow a moan. "It's so much more, like this." Not just him inside me but the stimulation on my clit pressing against him that sends bursts of pleasure streaming through me.

I move faster, taking exactly what I need, embracing the heady rush that blocks everything else out. Just feeling him and me—all that matters.

He shifts, sitting up, arms around me as his mouth crushes against mine. But I don't stop moving—I can't, as he groans against my lips and I drink in the sound. His pleasure is a euphoric catalyst. The simple knowledge of what I'm doing to him is the final push. My body quivers as I orgasm, legs locked around him.

With few final jerking thrusts against me, he comes too.

We collapse against the soft flannel sheets of his bed, limbs limp but still touching.

Minutes drift by like lazily floating clouds. We clean up and take turns in the bathroom, but return to bed. Liam trails fingers down my side, as if tracing an outline of me, and I lie against his chest, counting freckles.

"Has it hit you yet?" he asks.

"I don't know if I'll ever believe it's real until I'm in the classroom."

"It's all working out." His chest rises in a sharp inhale that's not quite a laugh. "Honestly, I didn't think it would. This article almost didn't get off the ground."

"I thought they were pushing for you to do it?"

"They were, but when I talked to Fallon about the budget, she was only able to cover the flat fee and none of the incidentals, so I've been paying for everything else. The flights, the rental, the dates we went on."

I shove away from him, crawling back off the bed. "You what?"

"Shit." The realization of what he's admitted seems to cut through the blissful post-sex haze that lulled him into revealing the truth as he jerks upright, eyes going wide in a mix of shock and terror. "It's not a big deal. You needed this."

I scramble for my clothes. When I can't find my underwear, I just grab my pants from where they've landed halfway under the bed and yank them on. I need to get out of here *now*. "I told you how I felt about you paying for shit. How that makes me feel, especially now that we're sleeping together."

Shirt. Where the hell is my shirt?

"If you were actually dating me then I'd pay for all of this anyway. It's not like I'm paying for anything extra."

"You don't get to decide that type of shit for me. I thought you were all about communication. Or is that something you only preach about when I'm naked?"

"Henri," he says and I can hear the pain in his voice even as I refuse to look at him. I kick his pants aside and find my top. "Please just let me explain."

"No. You said to tell you when to stop. Stop. I'll finish this out for the article because that's what I agreed to, but don't you dare think what's between us will continue." I pull the shirt over my head as I storm out. I don't know where I'm going, but I can't be here in this house alone with Liam for another second.

Heat scorches the back of my throat as my eyes start to sting.

I'm on the last step of the stairs when the front door flies open. Ally is there, blocking my exit, arms full of aluminum food containers.

"Oh, Henri, could you give me a hand?" she asks.

Rushing to her, I catch one of the containers just as it starts to fall. "What are these for?"

"The gingerbread houses. I've texted the girls—they should be in soon. Peter is stuck in the office, but the five of us will have fun."

I help her carry everything to the kitchen and arrange the containers on the island where Liam and my laptops are still open.

"Were you headed somewhere?" she asks as we start to gather the icing and bags of candy we picked up from the store. "Your shirt is inside out." She reaches over and plucks the label sticking out behind my neck.

I flush. "Oh. I didn't notice. I guess I was just in a rush to get out this morning."

She gives me a knowing smile, but spares me an ounce of dignity by not saying she knows exactly why I'm so disheveled. "Could you hold this open for me?" She grabs a piping bag from a drawer and hands it over. I grab it as she scoops icing inside and continues to talk. "You know, I didn't know what to think at first when he said he was bringing someone home. He's very private about his life in New York. But seeing you both these last few days has been the biggest relief."

An uncomfortable pressure presses against the inside of my ribs as she talks, but I manage a smile. "It's not easy trusting someone with a person you love, but he'll be here with you soon."

"Mom, don't bother her about this stuff." Liam walks into the room and his gaze flicks to me for the briefest moment before he reaches for a bag of candy.

Ally swats his hand away. "Wait until after we're finished and you can have the leftovers."

It's another fifteen minutes before Penelope and Juniper arrive. We all gather around the dining room table set with the pieces of the houses in front of us—a base, four walls, and two slabs for the roof. Each of us has our own technique. Juniper is meticulously decorating the sides with icicle-like designs. Overeager Penelope constructed the house first so all of her icing adornments droop as she places them, though that doesn't seem to deter her. I do my best not to look at what Liam is doing, but I catch the small snowflake details he adds to his.

Do I want gumdrops lining the top of the roof? The color could be fun.

"Here." Liam pushes the bowl of gumdrops toward me.

"Thanks, but I'm going for these." I grab the peppermints next to me instead.

"Sorry, you looked like you wanted these." I hate that he can read me, that I let him behind my walls and I can't just get him to unknow me.

"You could have asked instead of assuming you know what's best for me." I nudge the peppermint into place and grimace.

"Well, they're here if you change your mind," he says, voice gruff.

"Don't worry. I won't." When I press the next candy into place I use too much pressure and the cookie structure cracks, a jagged split through the roof. "Shit." When I go for my icing bag, it's out.

"Take mine."

"I'm good. I think I'll leave it like this. It adds character."

"Well that's stupid," Penelope says, which earns her a look from everyone at the table. "What? She should take the icing. The crack is ugly."

June cocks a brow. "Pen, I don't think you have any room to talk, your house looks like a toddler made it."

"It's maximalist and fun. At least mine doesn't look like it was designed by someone who's favorite color is millennial beige," Penelope shoots back before looking between Liam and I. "Henri, just take mine so whatever you're fighting about doesn't ruin this for us."

"We're not fighting," Liam and I say in near-perfect unison.

"Sure," Pen says as she picks up a sifter of powdered sugar to dust her monstrosity of a house to give it the appearance of snow. "Because normal people are passive aggressive over candy. Yup, makes perfect sense."

I take Liam's icing. "We're fine."

The rest of the house building goes without incident, but everyone gives us distance once we're done. Upstairs, I pack for our trip to the cabin.

"I can go alone," Liam says, closing the door behind him.

"Because that would read as a united front," I say, sarcasm dripping from my voice as I shove a sweater into my bag. "And this way we won't have another incident around your family."

"All right, if you think that's what's best." His lips press into a firm line. "I'll pack up the groceries and get them secured on the snowmobiles."

25

Liam

It's a twenty-minute ride on snowmobiles to the secluded cabin. The silence between Henri and I is cut through by the whirring of the engine as we ride over the snow. When we arrive, we find The steps to the porch are covered with snow and there's no sign of the driveway that's accessible during late spring and summer.

We don't speak as we head inside, carrying in our supplies. The moment I put down my load, I flip on the lights and head to the thermostat to crank up the heat. As is, even inside, my breath is hanging in the air.

"It should be good within the next hour or so, but until then we should just keep on our coats. I can make some soup for dinner so we can have something to warm up," I explain.

"That would be great," Henri says, pulling her hat lower over her pink ears.

She claims one of the three bedrooms and unpacks as I turn on the stove and get to work. The chicken noodle soup comes together quickly and I ladle out bowls for the both of us. The cabin has internet, but the TV we have isn't set up with streaming services, just a dusty DVD player that I put *Home Alone* into and press play, because I can't handle another minute of this excruciating quiet.

Even if I try to talk to her now, I doubt she'll listen. I just wanted to take care of her. That's it. Especially since I was the one who put her in a precarious position to begin with.

By the time the credits roll, the heat still hasn't kicked in, at least the house is well insulated so it's not as cold as outside, but it's still brutal. Yeah, the plan for a grand romantic getaway is going great. We'll freeze to death being frustrated with each other.

"I'm going to head to bed," Henri says, speaking for the first time since the muttered *thank you* she gave when I handed her the soup bowl she's now carrying into the kitchen.

"Do you need extra blankets?" I ask.

"I found a sleeping bag in the closet. I should be good." The message is clear: *I don't need you. Fuck off.*

I wake up to my teeth clacking together. It's a damn miracle that I could sleep at all, but after a long day, my body must have just shut down. I flex my hands to find them stiff and numb. Checking the small clock next to the bed, I find that it's two in the morning.

Great. Still hours until the sun is up.

I toss back and forth for another few minutes before gathering my blankets and heading to the living room to build a fire. There's plenty of wood and there's a chance we might need to use it all. At this point it would be best to head back the moment it's light out—there's no point torturing ourselves in these conditions.

My hands are clumsy as I put the logs and kindling into position. Thank God Dad got past his aversion to commercial firestarters, otherwise I'm not sure I'd get the flames to come to life.

Once I'm sure the fire won't choke out the moment I walk away, I go back down the hall to where Henri is sleeping. She selected the room June and Pen would share and it looks like she collected all the blankets from both beds. Only her nose pokes out but the mass of fabric shakes as she shivers.

I go to her and peel back a layer. "Henri, come on."

"So cold," she mutters. Her eyes crack open, but they're gauzy with sleep.

"I know. Come here, let me get you warmed up."

She nods slowly and tries to move but she's trapped herself in the sleeping bag. After her second failed attempt to locate the zipper, I free her from the sleeping bag and scoop her up. I know the only reason she nuzzles against me and claws at my shirt is the combination of cold and sleep, but that doesn't stop me from liking it.

In the living room, the fire is crackling and I sigh in relief as the warmth licks at my skin. I lower the bundled up Henri on the blankets and pillows I've arranged before joining her on the ground.

Not giving her time to protest, I wrap a blanket around her and pull her to my chest.

"I'm still mad at you," she mumbles even as she relaxes against me.

I stroke her hair, fighting the urge to kiss the top of her head. "Then be mad at me and be warm. Be mad at me, but be safe while you do it."

"Fine." The word drifts out of her as her eyes flutter closed.

For the first time since we got to the damn cabin, I finally feel warm. Henri shifts in her sleep, one of her legs draping over me so she's all but laying on me. I squeeze her tighter and it's not lost on me that this might be the last chance I get to have her this close.

A sudden jolt of friction spurs me into consciousness, and my eyes fly open. The fire has burned to embers, it wasn't the smartest idea to leave it going unattended while we slept, but it was the only option we had. Gold light streams through the window, pooling around the nest where Henri and I fell asleep. Where she's now rocking against my leg, whimpers escaping her as she dreams. Her hands clutch at my shirt and with each movement her thigh rubs against my dick.

"Liam," she says, my name barely recognizable in her sleep-slurred speech.

Henri, dreaming of me? At least she doesn't hate me in her sleep, but I don't think I'll earn any brownie points with awake Henri if I let this keep going.

I groan as I extricate myself from her grip, but fuck she's holding on tight to my shirt. Maybe if I just wriggle out of it? I pull the free arm that isn't under her out and start to shimmy out of the fabric.

Almost there. I just need to get my head through.

"Why are you stripping?" Henri asks and my head whips in her direction. Thing is, I can't exactly see her with the face full of wool I'm stuck in.

"Because you looked comfortable," I say.

"And that's the universal signal for taking off your shirt?"

"It is when you have a death grip on it." At my words, she must realize that her fingers are still digging into the fabric, so she lets go and rolls away.

Thrusting my bare arm into its sleeve, I wriggle back into the sweater. When my head pops through the top hole, I find Henri sitting a solid foot away from me.

"Sleep all right?" I ask, then, because I can't help myself, add, "Good dreams?"

She swallows and looks at her hands as she flushes the prettiest shade of pink. "Yeah. Dreams were . . . great. Umm . . . thanks for getting me and doing this." She waves at the fireplace.

"We can leave after breakfast. I'm not going to force you to cuddle up to me to survive another night of this."

We both throw on an extra layer before silently working together in the kitchen, the air fills with the crackling of the thick slabs of bacon on the cast iron and the burble of coffee. As I'm dumping frozen hashbrowns in the pan, Henri jerks upright from where she's seated on a stool at the breakfast bar.

"Did you hear that?" she asks.

"What?"

"Listen."

I do and there it is. A low rumble and hum that resonates through the entire cabin. Putting down the mug she's been using to warm her hands, Henri gets up and darts to one of the floor vents, putting her hand over it.

"We have heat!" And she does an honest to God fist pump as an expression of pure glee brightens her face. With a whoop she rushes at me. I barely register what she's doing to have enough time to put my spatula to the side before she pulls me into a hug. "I promise to never fantasize about any time period without modern amenities ever again."

"Noted." Do I hug her back? Or if I stand here like a scarecrow and hope she will forget she's upset and keep holding on.

The oil in the pan pops and Henri looks up at me before stepping away, crossing her arms as if it's an active effort to keep them from me. "Sorry."

"All good. I bet the inventor of modern heating would appreciate your enthusiasm. So, what are you thinking?"

"You still have a ski competition to train for."

"Yeah, I guess I do. You could come, or there's some stuff to do around here? Pen and June leave their old skates here so you could skate on the pond out back, or there's a solid stack of movies. My only request is that you don't watch *Home Alone 2* without me."

"I'd never."

I help Henri find the old skates before heading out to the mountain. The cabin is at the base and without a lift, I have to climb uphill. The skins attached to the base of my skis allow me to propel myself up without sliding backward, and it's far better than hiking up the way Dad used to make us for training.

At the top, I look down and visualize the turns I'll have to make since there are no gates set up. But even a decade later the route is seared into my mind. With a fortifying breath, I push myself down the untouched snow.

It feels like flying, gliding on an endless cloud as powder kicks up around me. I shift my weight into the first turn, and *shit*. I know how it's supposed to feel. I know what my body is supposed to do, well I *knew* what it was supposed to feel like when I was sixteen and my body hadn't finished growing.

"Fuck!" I yell loud enough that birds burst up into the sky as I pull to a jerky stop.

A familiar irritation crawls against my skin. This is why I quit in the first place, because I'd beat myself up for every small thing and I hated it. I hated competing and feeling like even though I was surrounded by people I had so much in common with, I couldn't trust them. Hated that winning became more important than joy.

"All you need to do is get to the bottom in one piece." Henri's voice breaks through the fog of the past.

"Let this be fun," I tell myself. I have all this fresh powder. A run all to myself.

No one is watching. No one is rooting for or against me.

Fun.

And for the next two hours, that's what I let it be. This mountain is where I grew up. It's a part of me and I make peace with it, reclaiming a joy that has been missing for years as I cut a path around imaginary poles. Slowly, my body listens as I speed down, faster than the wind, feeling in total command.

This doesn't have to be for anyone else but myself.

By the time I unclip myself from my skis, I'm absolutely beat. I'm guaranteed to be sore as hell tomorrow, but I'm also excited to do this all again.

I kick snow off my boots and unzip my jacket as I head inside, a wild smile on my face.

"Henri," I call out, excited to tell her how right she was. I bet she'll listen to that. "What are you feeling for lunch?"

But there's no response. I guess she's still out ice skating. It's not like there's much else to do here. As I head toward the back door, I find the red hat I got her resting on the bench that also conceals a storage area. I grab it and my old skates, shaking my head. She'd freeze to death without me.

There's been a light snowfall but I follow the trail she's cut through the snow to the circle of ancient trees that wrap around the small lake. I pause and listen, expecting to hear the scraping of skates on the ice, but nothing. She could be just sitting to the side resting.

"Liam, please tell me that's you!" she attempts to yell, her voice hoarse and quivering in terror.

I drop everything and run the rest of the way, crossing the treeline to find her, legs wobbling, standing maybe ten feet from the edge. Under her, there's a white fissure in the ice. When her wide, fright-filled eyes find me, she moves and the ice cracks.

No. No. No. This can't be real.

"Henri, just stop and listen to me." I hold my arms out the way I would if I were to encounter a frightened animal.

"My legs. They're going to give out. I've been stuck like this for half an hour. I called for you and you weren't there." Her chin wobbles.

"I'm here now. It's going to be fine." It's hard to stay calm even as my heart thunders. *Stupid.* I was so stupid not to check and see she knew what to look for on the ice. I should have come to check it. I shouldn't have let her come out alone. "Do what I do." I crouch down and slip onto my stomach at the edge, dispersing my weight as much as possible. After a second of hesitation she starts to do the same. A crack sounds and she flinches. "Just like that. Keep going."

I didn't realize I was holding my breath until it gusts out of me the moment she's on her stomach. Not safe yet, but one step closer to being so. "Now, slide toward me." I start to scoot forward, so my torso is on the ice and my lower half is firmly on the ground. I want to go further, but adding more weight on the ice would just increase the risk of us both being pulled under.

Inch by torturous inch she comes closer, pausing each time the ice creaks and groans under her.

"So close. Just another foot and I can pull you the rest of the way. You're so brave." I don't stop talking, urging her to me and trying to distract her and myself from the fact that the ice is thinnest here at the edge. Behind her the fissures have spiderwebbed and it's an effort to keep my gaze from wandering.

So close.

Come on, Henri. Keep moving.

I'll do anything if she can just get back to me.

Three inches. Two. One.

A splitting crack rips through the air. Ice severs.

I lunge.

"Henri!"

26

Henri

Liam's body curls around me as we tumble into the snow. A sound halfway between a sob and a laugh launches out of my shaking body.

"I'm here. I'm here and I've got you. You're safe," he soothes the both of us. A hand strokes my hair and pins me against his heaving chest. "Let's get inside."

He carries me the short distance back. Just as we reach the tree line, I look at the pond and all the thick floating chunks of ice bobbing along the surface. I was so sure I was going to die there on the ice. That Liam would come out and there would just be a hole where I disappeared, my body blue and stiff. I stood as still as I could, praying for him to come.

I'm so stiff that when we get inside Liam has to help me unlace the skates. They're damp because even though he hauled me to safety, my legs took a solid dip into the unforgiving frigid water. The fabric of my thick rainbow-striped pants clings to my skin, making it feel like a thousand little needles have been speared into my flesh.

"I thought the heat was working," I get through the chattering of my teeth.

"Fuck, it is," he grits out. "We need to get you warmed up. Can you walk?"

I shake my head and he carries me again, this time toward the bedroom. "I can't feel my legs," I admit as another sob wracks through me. Hot tears come, spilling from my eyes. "I was so scared. I waited for you and thought you'd never come."

I screamed his name until my throat went raw. Even now it's tight and I'm not sure if I'll be able to speak tomorrow.

"I'll always come for you. Always." He nudges the door open with a knee and places me on the foot of my bed. Pausing he swipes away my tears with his thumb. "I've got you now." Making quick work of my socks, he peels them off and tosses them to the side, each making a wet plop against the wood floor. "I'm going to help you with your pants next, okay?"

"Nothing you haven't seen before," I joke.

"Yeah, but that doesn't mean I have the right to see it again."

"Your help would be appreciated since they are essentially glued to me right now."

It's a team effort to work them off. Me, lifting my hips and holding myself into place. Liam, tugging so hard that when they do come free he stumbles back, having to catch his balance.

"Arms up," he instructs and helps me out of my shirt. "Shit," he hisses at the sight of the red splotches on pale skin. "Get in the bed."

I do so as he exits the room and I can't stop shivering. If I thought last night was bad, this is a whole new level. I feel the cold all the way to my bones, to the point that it almost feels like heat.

Liam comes back holding a pair of his boxers and a hoodie. "Here put these on. I'll be right back."

As I change I can't help but appreciate that clean laundry scent that seems to cling to his clothes extra long. This time when he returns he's holding a glass with . . .

"Is that whiskey?" I ask.

"Bourbon, but yeah. Warm you up from the inside out." He hands it over. I expect him to leave for good, but he pulls off his shirt. "Body heat," he explains. "I know you want nothing to do with me right now, and the only reason you were calling for me was because you didn't have other options, but this is the best way to get you warmed up. It's just like last night."

"Yeah, last night." Well, thinking of that sure does send heat rippling through me. It felt like a dream, him carrying me and holding me close. Then, when I did fall asleep, I dreamt of him—of us—having a repeat of what happened in the library. He woke me up and I was all tangled around him with an ache between my thighs.

The moment he left to go skiing, I laid back down on those blankets and had to get myself off before I could think of anything else.

The bed dips as he slips in next to me and lifts me onto his lap, arms around my waist. Okay, yeah, I really need this bourbon. I take a hearty sip and then another. It doesn't take long for a nice fuzzy feeling to fill me. I relax back, my head against Liam's shoulder. The adrenaline from nearly falling through the ice has evaporated and my bones feel heavy. My eyelids droop and I hear the clink of ice as I fall asleep.

I'm back on the ice.

Kurt. Laura. Dad. They're all there standing staring at me. I shout, or at least try to, but no sound comes out. They see me. I know they do, gazes locked on my shaking body. I reach out, pleading. They turn their backs to me and walk away, leaving me to the fate of a frozen tomb, knowing that I wasn't worth saving.

This time the ice splinters, water welcoming me into its greedy embrace. The sky goes dark, my limbs numb.

A shadow crosses above and a form breaks through the surface.

Liam.

He reaches out for me when no one else did. Pulling me out. Saving me.

"Yeah, I'm right here, baby. Not going anywhere." Somewhere else, somewhere more real, hands rub heat into my skin.

I crack my lids open. He's here. Real and warm. "What?"

He flushes. "I didn't mean to wake you up, you were just starting to shiver again and said my name."

I burrow closer. "Hand me the bourbon?"

"Here." His hands leave me and it's an effort to not whimper in protest since he's literally just fulfilling my request. "Can I just explain about the money? You don't need to like me after this. I want you to know why. Please."

"I guess after you saved me, I can at least listen," I say.

"I felt like shit after I learned that I put you in a bad spot, jeopardizing everything you worked for. It felt like my responsibility to fix everything, and I still think it was. Back then I hardly even knew you; I would have done the same for anyone in that position. I'm not going to apologize for that. But I am sorry, though, that I wasn't transparent about my methods. I like knowing that you're taken care of. Fuck, I like being the one to take care of you." His arms tighten protectively around me. "And, God, seeing you out there on the ice . . . I don't think I've ever been so scared in my life."

My throat tightens and I tense. "I'm bad at this. I don't know how to let people in, Liam. It's hard to let people look after me because what if one day they stop and I'm reliant on them? I've begged for people to show up for me before, people I trusted, and they blocked me out." Fresh tears roll down my cheeks, falling into the last dregs of my bourbon. "This feels so good but that just means it's going to hurt when it's gone. When *you're* gone. Finding reasons to shove you away is easier than being close enough to feel my heart ripped out."

These years I haven't walked around wanting to be close to someone, to be chosen. I've shrunk my life down as small as possible, and tricked myself into thinking that's what's best. It's an effort to make enough room in my world for him, but one that might be worth it.

"I don't want to go. Henri, you don't have to break both of our hearts. There's school breaks and planes and summers. We can make this work if we want to. If you need me, I'll be there," he promises and I believe him.

I believe that he'll come for me the same way he did when I was on the ice. But that doesn't change reality.

I shake my head. "Let's not be careless with each other. I don't want to resent you. I want to have all these memories with you and know that they're good, because what happens when you have to choose between me and your family's business, this legacy? It's not going to be simple."

His breath hitches. "But for now?"

"I can commit to right now. I can swear I'm yours until the moment I'm on that damn airplane." No more running. I will only have this with him once and I'm not going to be a coward about it. It's going to hurt, but I'd rather have that pain than not have him at all.

"Then you're mine. Right here. Right now."

Twisting in his arms, I plant a kiss on the corner of his mouth. He captures the nape of my neck, fingers threading through my hair. Somehow, I manage to reach out and find the nightstand to set down the glass in my hand. He drags me up his lap and I moan as he hardens under me.

"Fuck. I had a dream like this last night," I tell him as nips at the skin at the juncture of my neck.

"Yeah, I had that impression."

"What?"

"Why else do you think I was trying to escape?" He laughs. "I'm all for getting you off but I want to make sure you're awake and consenting."

"And if I want you to right now?"

His brows raise. "Are you sure you're up to it?"

I lock my hips against his. "Seems like a good way to raise my core temperature."

"Shit, woman, you're a fucking menace," he says with a grunt, flipping us over so I'm on my back and he's hovering over me.

My legs wrap around him as his smiling mouth claims my lips. Reaching down, I palm him through his pants. This. All of this is mine, and I'm not going to back down.

He breaks away, giving me a clear view of how his irises have blown wide enough to swallow the hazel of his eyes. "Do you trust me?"

I answer without having to think. "Yes."

"Let me take control." His hand dips under the hem of his sweater that I'm wearing, stroking the soft skin there. "You don't need to think. You can turn off that brilliant brain of yours and just let me show you how fucking obsessed I am with you."

"I thought that's exactly what you were already doing." I cock a brow.

"My way would mean you can't touch me. Or see me."

"Show me."

He gets up, giving me a full view of the erection tenting his sweatpants as he goes into the hall. When he returns, there's a bundle of scarves in his hands.

"What do you say if you need to tap out?" he asks.

"Stop."

"Good girl." With those words, he grabs my ankle.

I yelp as my body is dragged to the center of the bed. He yanks the boxers from my body, leaving me in only the sweater as he gets to work. The brown scarf he winds around me then secures to a bedpost is soft, but tight enough that I won't slip free if I tug against it.

"Open those legs for me, baby," he instructs and I obey.

Fuck there it is again, that thrill that comes with not having to make decisions and just giving up control.

With both legs spread wide he crawls over me, pausing for a moment to swipe his tongue over my slit. I buck, but my legs stay where they are.

"I've been imagining what you'd look like all tied up for me since the day I showed you around my office and you rubbed your ass all over me." The back of his hand trails up my thigh, sending a spray of goose bumps up my flesh and causing my nipples to tighten. "Perfect. Arms up."

"The sweater," I say even as I hold up my arms and he secures my wrists together over my head.

"My sweater is staying on while I fuck you." He leans in, pressing a kiss against my cheek. "Gotta keep you warm. Now, close those eyes for me and relax."

The final scarf is folded so it covers my face and I'm in complete darkness.

He gets off me and my body protests, arching to find him, to call him back to me. The crinkle of a wrapper cuts through the air.

"You brought the condoms?" I laugh.

"Of course I did. I wasn't going to get here unprepared in case, well, in case this happened." He chuckles.

I hear him walk toward where I think the end of the bed is. Everything in me tunes into him and this moment. Anticipation builds alongside my increasing heart rate.

The bed moves. Fuck. What is he going to do? Is he going to fuck me? Eat me out?

His mouth connects to my clit, sucking. I moan, pulling against my restraints. He laps at me hungrily before fucking me with his tongue and I scream his name. Not seeing him and not knowing what he'll do next adds a dose of adrenaline that heightens every sensation swirling through me. I've never gotten this close to coming so fast.

And then he's gone, pulling away.

"Fuck you," I bite out. "Edging me after this morning."

"Call it payback."

He thinks he's so clever. And he just might be, having me like this to play with as he likes.

There's another shift, then his thigh brushes over mine and his dick teases along my pussy as he coats himself. He thrusts into me in one go and I curse for all I'm worth. He's relentless, picking up a brutal, punishing pace that causes the iron bed frame to rattle against the wall.

"Maybe I'll just keep you like this forever. Splayed out for me whenever I want. Tell me that doesn't sound good."

But my brain has officially melted and I can't think of any other word besides his name. It bursts out of me over and over again as my body tenses. The orgasm causes stars to explode in the darkness of my covered eyes. All I am is blinding pleasure as he fucks me through it.

He pulls out and I sag into the mattress. His legs straddle me, knees landing near my waist and there's a sound? Fuck, what is that?

Cold flashes across my chest as he flips up the sweater.

"These tits." His fingers work over my nipples, pinching and rolling them between thumb and forefinger in a way that zaps down to my clit. "I'm going to use them to make myself come. Okay, baby?"

"Yes, fuck. Do it."

Large hands cup my breasts and press them together. His hard cock pushes against them and works into the tight gap. He groans as he thrusts, still toying with my nipples, as he chases his own pleasure. I can't think of anything hotter than how he is obsessed with every inch of my body.

It can't be more than a minute before he groans and a gush of warm liquid covers me.

"You have no idea how good you look, Henri."

"There's one way to show me."

I have to blink against the light as the scarf is removed. Then Liam runs a finger through the cum coating my breasts and stomach. He lifts it to my mouth and I lick it clean.

"All warmed up?" he asks with a smirk.

"Nice and toasty." I lick my lips.

He unties me from the bed and cleans me up with a warm towel. We end up agreeing to stay at the cabin the amount of time we originally intended to, and will be heading back on Christmas Eve. We go to bed together again that night and the heater struggles against the low temperature, but with Liam pressed against me it's not bad at all.

The next day, I join him on the slope, cheering him on as he slowly regains his confidence on the run. After, I work the tension from his stiff muscles with a massage that ends with us both naked and ravenous.

I can't push past the feeling that this all feels like a dream. Like we're trapped in a snow globe while the rest of the world continues to move around us.

After a slow morning, we call Jasmine and Iris on Christmas Eve. The intention was just to call Iris and apologize, but she heard Liam and then it turned into a FaceTime call. We caught up on what we've been up to while they tell us about the New Years masquerade party they've been planning with Marty and Alexi.

"Speaking of work, this one has kept me so distracted that I haven't finished the article," Liam says, kissing my cheek as he gets up off the couch.

I wrap myself tighter in the blanket. "Um, Jasmine, could we have a moment?" I ask.

"Sure thing." She nods. "I need to pick up dinner anyway. My girlfriend is craving a good slice."

This has me raising my brows as Jasmine maneuvers off screen and the muffled sound of a door comes from the other side of the call. "Girlfriend?"

Iris bites her lip. "You know I haven't been a girlfriend for a long time."

"I know. I'm really happy for you and really sorry for being an ass when all you ever do is help and accommodate me," I say.

"Oh, bitch, you're not the only one with commitment issues here. We've been enabling the fuck out of each other. I just let you think you're the mastermind."

"You're so brave admitting that miles away."

She sticks her tongue out. "So, are you going to open the email or just live in limbo?"

"I did."

"And."

"I . . ." I let my face fall for a moment and can practically see her trying to find people to cover her shifts so she can fly out here and comfort me. "Got in with an assistantship!"

"Rude. You had me worried there for a second. I wish I could throw a pillow at you."

"Payback and you'll have plenty of time for pillow throwing when I'm back."

"And the deal with Liam? I mean besides the fact that you have the most severe case of sex hair I've ever seen."

"We're using all the time we have left here, and I'm trying to pretend I'm going to be fine at the end of this," I admit.

"I'll have a bottle of wine ready when you get back and a full day where we can watch *Sex and the City* and I promise to listen to all of your fashion commentary like I understand it."

"But for now. I'm happy."

"And thoroughly dicked down, thank God." On the screen we both wear goofy smiles.

That night, Liam and I pack up the snowmobiles and head back to the house. Juniper and Peter are out working, but we spend the night with Ally and Penelope, who gives us a smirk the moment we get inside.

All of this is actually happening. The house with the big windows, giving us a clear view of the snow falling outside, and too many hastily decorated trees. The laughs that bubble out of us as Liam tries to drink hot chocolate and gets whipped cream on his nose as *A Christmas Carol* plays in the background.

And after, when we pad up the stairs and Liam pulls me into his childhood bedroom. With its walls lined with medals and newspaper clippings, I know for the first time in years, I'll get to wake up and spend Christmas with someone I love.

27

Liam

Usually, I mind when Pen knocks on all of our doors at five in the morning on Christmas, but usually, I don't have Henri curled around me. I can't complain about taking advantage of all the time that we have left.

"It's still dark out," she mumbles.

"She's just trying to be the first family on the entire property to open presents." I brush a hair off her face as she gazes up at me. "Can I ask for one thing today?"

"To pull me aside whenever you please and have your way with me? How did you read my mind?" She smirks and stretches before rolling onto me, her body trapping mine.

I laugh. "I love that mind of yours. That could be part of the wish."

"A Christmas wish? Let's hear it then, Liam Hughes."

"Today, you are my girlfriend. Nothing more, nothing less. We don't talk about tomorrow or flights or anything that's going to happen. We have this Christmas together."

"All right, *boyfriend*. I think I can agree to that." She kisses me softly, taking her time with it, pressing her smile against my matching one before breaking away to say, "I've never had a boyfriend, not a real one."

"Then I have my work cut out for me being your first." *And best,* I can't help but think.

I flip her over and kiss her some more between her fits of laughter until Pen pounds on the door, again.

By the time Henri and I straighten our clothes and untangle ourselves from each other, everyone else is already downstairs seated around the tree armed with mugs of coffee for what's destined to be a long day. The events of the fundraiser start at eight with the competitions and entertainment going until dark, when the gala will start for guests who purchased the exorbitantly-priced tables.

There's some magic in how everyone turns into the childhood version of themselves when presents are involved. The air fills with the crinkling and tearing of wrapping paper. Mom attempts to capture it all on her phone while Dad and June shove the scraps into the waiting massive black bag.

"Here," I say as I hand a box to Henri. I wrapped it before we flew out so the edges are scuffed white and the bow slides off as she takes it from me.

To my relief, she takes it without question. Instead of ripping the paper, she picks at the tape and removes it in one piece. Her hand flies to her mouth and tears clutter her eyes when the box pops open. I've been waiting for this moment since I talked to Fallon about the gift.

Henri reaches in and gingerly takes out the magazine in the plastic sleeve.

"It's from the first-ever print run of *Spitfire*," I explain. "Fallon signed the note from the editor's page."

"I can't believe you got a hold of this," she says.

I shove a hand through my hair. "To be honest, it wasn't too hard since they had boxes in storage considering they didn't sell all that well."

"It's perfect." She punctuates her words with a quick kiss.

"Oh, June, isn't that the magazine you like?" Mom asks, peering over Henri's shoulder.

"You're thinking of a different one," June rushes to say.

"No it's definitely that one," Pen chimes in, a smirk curling her lips as her gaze darts between June and I.

Does that mean she's read my articles? No that's not possible. There's no way she knows it's me if she has.

"They have good human interest pieces and fun quizzes and stuff." June flushes. "I grab them when I'm stuck in line at the store and buy them because print is dying. It's good for the economy."

Henri looks at me. "I couldn't agree more. The writers are incredibly talented." I don't know who else hears because Pen opens her next present and lets out an eardrum shattering whoop when she finds a blanket that has a pattern that looks an awful lot like Pedro Pascal's face pasted over and over again. "Speaking of." Henri grabs a small box from behind the tree and gives it to me.

Inside, I find three new notebooks, the exact type I like because of how well they fit in my pockets, and a touristy *I Love New York* pen.

"You have to keep writing if you want to fill them up. If you don't use them, you'll hurt my feelings," she says.

"There's no way I'll let that happen. Thank you." I grab her in a hug. "For believing in me."

Once all gifts are open, everyone moves to get ready, bundling up to face their responsibilities for the day. The lodge is already buzzing with activity when we all arrive.

With the intensity of a high school theater director with the casting list for the school's spring musical, June posts the tournament bracket for the dual slalom at eight a.m. by the reception desk. It's not made public earlier because in the years when it wasn't posted the day of, there were some mysterious incidents between competitors.

Henri and I hang back while the first wave of competitors fight to get to the front. Only one or two think to take a picture and slip away.

The sound system cracks. "All competitors for the adult women's half-pipe please report to the registration tent if you have not done so already. We will start in thirty minutes."

"Pen's in that one, right?" Henri asks. I smile, which causes her brows to furrow. "What?"

"Nothing. It's just that you called her Pen," I say, then cock my head toward the emptying area next to the bulletin board. "Let's go check who's going to kick my ass."

There are thirty-two competitors and sixteen match-ups—eight men's pairings and eight women's. I trace my finger along the page, finding my name at the bottom. Points are given as a collective, so even if one member of a team gets eliminated in the first round, the team still has a chance of placing, even if it's unlikely.

"Okay, not bad. Mr. Bakshi is good, but I have a chance of winning." I nod.

"Nice!" Someone slaps me on my shoulder and I snap my head up to find Kurt next to me. "Looks like if you don't immediately fail, it's you and me, man."

"What a fun coincidence." God. I just know June did this on purpose.

"Guess this is my chance to see how I stack up against a pro."

"Don't be stupid, Kurt. Liam is only a substitute. If you beat him, that doesn't mean a thing." Laura gives me a pitying smile. "Good to see you on more than the bunny hill after so long."

Another announcement blares over the speakers for the half-pipe.

Henri tugs at my sleeve, taking a step toward the exit, as she talks to her old friends. "Always so fun to run into you both. But we need to go get good spots to watch the half-pipe." We push outside and she looks me dead in the eye. "I take back everything I said. I need you to crush him and his ego."

"Oh, baby, I'm planning on it." I can't fucking wait to cut that asshole down to size.

We get to the half-pipe run with time to spare, allowing us to get front row seats to Pen dominating the competition. She wears her helmet and jacket, broadcasting her sponsorship deals, and gives cheeky thumbs-ups to the cameras. A pair of commentators hunch over their mics, detailing the series of gravity stunts that cause the crowd to burst into cheers.

I snort at the end the first of her two runs, the higher of which will be used as her official score.

"What? Don't tell me that was bad," Henri says, eyes wide.

"She just treated it as a practice run. Watch the next one, she'll add at least one full rotation to each of her moves," I tell her.

Sure enough, that's exactly what happens.

Pen runs up to us after a brief interview with a feral grin on her face.

"You were toying with them," I say as I pull her into a firm hug. "You bailed on that first 1080 on purpose." She'd done two and a half of the three full rotations before cutting it short and failing the trick.

She winks. "Gotta keep them guessing."

"Show off."

"Had to set the Hughes family standard high. Don't lose and embarrass me later; I'll be watching."

"Rude."

"I judge because I love you," she says, skipping away. "I'm going to go touch up my hair so I look good wearing my gold medal."

There's no point in commenting on how there's five more athletes who need to take their turn, because inevitably she does win. Henri screams and cheers with me, but the moment the ceremony is over, I go to change in my gear for my race.

The door to the family locker area swings open as I'm clicking the closures of my boots into place. When I look up, I blink, not expecting to see my dad there. His black coat is emblazoned with the resort's mountain logo with his name embroidered underneath.

"Came to give me a pep talk?" I ask wearily, as years of discussions flood my mind.

"Just a quick reminder that when you're on that mountain, you're representing us as a family. We have fifty thousand people watching the livestream. That's fifty thousand people who will see if the future owner of Dulcet Point is worth his salt as a skier or not. Understood?" he asks.

A moment is all it takes to feel sixteen again, waiting for a way out of a role I was expected to fill from birth, always ready to give a quick "Yes, sir." But I don't want to feel that way, especially not now when it will set the tone for my future here, working with him.

"You're not my coach anymore. You're not Pen or June's either. But you are our dad, so I would appreciate it if you would just go out there and act like it." I stand. I'm taller than him now, not a kid looking up to a hero. "I'm going to go out there and enjoy the snow, the same way we encourage all of our guests to."

I walk past him, not waiting for a reply. Still, one comes as my hand lands on the door handle.

"Good luck out there, kid. I am proud of you, no matter what."

I give him a sharp, curt nod and head to face my opponent.

Mr. Bakshi and I are locked into automatic gates at the top of the 180-meter incline, hands gripping our poles, ready to launch ourselves forward the moment we're released.

Beep. Beep. Beep.

The gates fly open and Mr. Bakshi flies out. I'm off by a second, but that could make all the difference in the world. I tuck myself, hands forward, elbows in, trying to pick up speed as the poles come at me. My vision sharpens. I go wide on the first turn, but make up for it on the second, swatting away the red pole as I pass it.

The wind whistles in my ears over the roar of blood and adrenaline pumping through me. Mr. Bakshi clears the third to last poles just before me and I push even harder. I can't lose this. I won't.

We're neck and neck at the final stretch toward the finish line, so I stop looking at him and focus on the only thing I can control.

Myself.

28

Henri

"Go Liam!" I scream his name as he rushes toward the line so loudly that multiple people look my way. Watching him on the initial drop sent my heart racing, and that was before I noticed he had fallen behind. But he closed the gap and it was glorious to watch.

He commanded so much power, his body pushing to reach its full potential. I can only imagine what it was like to watch him when he was younger.

Liam crosses the finish line, the blades of his skis swooshing across the snow. Just like that, I'm racing to him, feet pounding on the packed snow, because today I'm his girlfriend, and I want to share every ounce of joy I have with him.

"Folks, give us one minute to replay the footage and determine the winner for this final matchup of our first round," an announcer says.

Security and cameras stand in the way for a moment, but June is there with a clipboard and tells them to let me pass. Liam's just clicked out of his skis when I barrel into him and kiss him hard, my arms flying around his neck. It takes him a moment to clutch me to him and match his intensity.

"What's all this excitement for? We don't know if I won," Liam says, breathless, as his mouth pulls away, giving me a clear view of the unbridled grin on his face as his arms still press me against him.

"I don't care if you win. You were so . . . so . . ." I fumble for the right word. "Beautiful out there. And it seemed like you had a good time. I want to celebrate that."

"Thank you for pushing me to do this." He shakes his head, hair slick against his face, eyes glossy with wonder. "I forgot how close to flying you get when you're moving that fast down a hill. Fuck. I feel it vibrating through me."

The announcer's voice returns. "Moving on to the next match up is Dulcet Point's very own, Liam Hughes!"

The crowd erupts around us, but Liam doesn't seem to notice, his attention fully on me. "Since you don't care about me winning, does this mean I don't get a victory kiss?" He cocks a brow and smirks.

"Oh shut up." I wipe that smug expression right off his face as my lips meet his for everyone to see, garnering a new wave of cheers and a flurry of whistles from the crowd.

Liam and I watch the first round of the women's matchups. Both Mrs. Wilson, Liam's teammate, and Laura, make it on to the next round. He lingers for one of the men's rounds, but has to get to the lift to prepare for his race against Kurt.

"I'm going to kick his ass," he tells me before leaving. And there's something deeply sexy about this confident side of him that sends currents of warmth rolling through me.

I make sure to reclaim my spot at the front to get a clear view of the action. My excitement almost, *almost*, makes me forget the cold. With gloved hands, I pull down the brown beanie to cover the tips of my ears.

I couldn't find the red one Liam gifted me, but I'm sure it's just mixed up somewhere in my clothes.

"Cute hat," Laura says as she saunters up beside me.

"Thanks. I watched your race; you killed it." She did. It was obvious from the moment she and her opponent burst out of the gates that Laura was the clear winner.

"We'll see how the rest goes. There's some absolute monsters in the competition." She huffs and rolls her eyes as the countdown beeps, marking the start of the next race. "Kurt won't shut up about going up against them."

"He's not going to. Liam is going to take him out," I tell her with absolute confidence.

"Maybe. Either way, we should all get a drink later and chat. I miss having you around. Like, seriously, it's not the same. Is your number the same? I could text you and we could make plans," she says, all so easily.

"You're kidding me, right?"

Her brows pinch. "What? I thought—"

"I'm fine with talking to you, but we're not friends, Laura. You can't just jump back into my life now that I have everything figured out and I won't be a burden to you," I say.

"God. It's not like it was simple for us, Henri. Of course I wanted to be there for you, but our parents told us talking to you might link them to your dad and we'd all be in trouble," she says so genuinely that I can't stop the shocked laugh that tumbles out of me.

"You only believe that because you wanted to. We were nineteen, our texts wouldn't mean shit. It's not like we were working at the company. It might be a simple thing that seems like it's in the past now, but I lived it and it's a part of me. I'm proud of the person I've become and everything I've learned," I tell her and mean every word. I didn't have any control over what happened to me; I could never have predicted it. But I survived it and am strong for it. I can always count on myself and have learned how to know when I can truly count on those around me. "I'm happy you seem to have a good life and I hope that continues, but I don't need you in mine. Not anymore."

I leave her and go search for a cup of apple cider before finding a spot on the opposite side of the hill just as Liam gets into position. I cheer him on until my throat burns.

"And look at the way he throws his helmet and just storms off," I say, scrolling to the saved recording on my phone to the end of his race with Kurt. Liam beat him by a solid three-second margin.

After, he won his match in the quarterfinals but lost in the semifinals against a guy he told me he competed against when he was younger. Mrs. Wilson ended up losing her second race, so they didn't end up placing as a team.

We hung around for the rest of the races, the winner of the tournament being a pair of international title holders from Sweden, before heading to the house and taking advantage of it being empty. Now, showered and thoroughly satiated, we're rewatching the event on my phone as we sit on the couch. Outside, the sun is sinking low.

"Wow. He's so red. I can't believe I didn't notice," Liam says, taking the phone from my hands. "We better avoid him tonight at the gala."

"Or at least wait until he's had a drink or two. He's always been a happy drunk."

"What do you mean you don't have a dress? You planned this whole damn thing and don't have something to wear to the party?" Pen's voice reverberates through the house as the front door slams open.

"I'll just wear the one from last year. It's not a big deal," June counters as she comes into view through the doorway, making a beeline for the stairs. "We're wasting time arguing. I have an hour before I need to be back at the lodge to do final checks. You're lucky I agreed to come over for this long."

"It will be obvious in the pictures and it will look sloppy since you're in charge of all this," Pen points out.

June stops mid-stride and huffs, obviously irritated that her younger sister has made a valid point. "And where exactly am I supposed to get a dress?"

"We could swap," I offer. "We look about the same size, so it could work."

"Oh my gosh, yes. Henri, please come up and get ready with us." Pen beams.

I look to Liam to see if it's okay. I want to spend as much time as I can with him, but it would be fun to have a little girl time. He untangles his arms from me and cocks his head to the door. "Go. There's a fashion emergency you need to solve."

The dress I brought has been hanging in the closet since the night I arrived to keep it from wrinkling. June gasps when she tries it on, the black A-line silhouette hugging her in all the right places before flaring into a paneled chiffon skirt that she grips as she spins, staring at herself in the mirror. It's strapless, which puts her toned back and arms on display.

"Okay, fuck you for looking so good," Pen says, then looks at me. "Do you have a second magic dress in there for me?"

"Unfortunately, no. But I can help you pick one if you let me raid your closet," I tell her, unable to stop grinning. Clothes have this power to make us feel like our best selves.

I help Pen pick out a coquettish emerald green dress with puff sleeves and lace trim detailing that looks right out of the seventies before changing into the black off-the-shoulder dress that June was going to wear.

We all crowd into June's room, decorated with delicate shabby chic florals, but is fairly sparse and impeccably clean. Pen blasts songs I haven't heard since middle school, and she and I sing along as I work to give June a blow out, taking breaks to use the massive round brush like a microphone. I'll admit, it's far better than getting ready alone.

Thirty minutes in, Pen has to give up on looking over June's shoulder at the vanity as she attempts to apply fake eyelashes and disappears into a bathroom to finish the job.

I'm finishing up the top layer of June's thick brown hair when the end of the brush hits the back of the wooden chair June is sitting on and tumbles to the ground.

I kneel down to grab the hairbrush from where it's rolled under the bed, damned round barrel. My fingers connect with the familiar glossy pages of a magazine and pull it toward me, close enough that I can see, but so it's still concealed under the bed. *Spitfire.*

I look further and there's a whole stack.

Holy shit.

"Did it really go that far? If you can't get it I bet my Mom has one we can borrow," June says and I nearly bump my head at that sudden sound of her voice.

"Got it." I crawl out and grab a magazine with me. "And I found this. You have an entire stack of them down there." I give her a look that I hope conveys that I will see right through any bullshit she tries to spin.

"Fine. I have them to read Liam's articles, all right? Just don't tell him. He's weird about that. He never tells us anything about it anymore. Hell, he hardly talks about New York at all," she admits. "I wouldn't know he even wrote for Spitfire except for the fact that I was stuck in line at the grocery store and flipped through the Halloween issue from last year. There was this article on how men remain willfully ignorant about the true commentary of *American Psycho* so they can make being a capitalist asshole their entire personality."

"Oh, I loved that one. It's how I learned that the movie was written and directed by women. Fuck, he wrote about how his sister told him that after she made him watch it."

She smiles. "Yeah. That's how I knew it was him. He hated that movie, too, or, well, anything with gore. I'm glad he got something out of it."

"I think it would mean a lot for him to know you like his work."

"What's the point? It's not like he'll suddenly change his mind and get his old job back. Both he and my father are stuck on this idea of Liam running the company. And I . . . well, I'll be right here with him." A sadness creeps across her face. "You could talk to him, explain—"

I hold up a hand to cut her off and stop her from spilling whatever secrets that have been eating at her. "You should have that conversation with him. It will mean more if you do. If you've read *Spitfire*, you know who I am to him, right?"

"Yeah, that your relationship is fake, or whatever. It wasn't the magazine, though. Pen can't keep a secret for shit." She releases a throaty laugh and rolls her eyes. "But I have a feeling whatever's there between you two is special."

"Don't get your hopes up. It's only until tomorrow."

"Then let's make sure tonight is the best it can be. Come finish my hair so you can get ready. I can't wait to see what stupid face he makes when you walk down the stairs."

I giggle at the thought, but when I do make it downstairs, there he is, looking at me like I put the stars in the sky. My heart skips a beat and it takes everything in me to not rush down the final steps, since that would almost certainly lead me to tripping and shattering the illusion of my graceful descent.

Bundled in coats, we all pile into June's SUV and head to the party since there's no way in hell we're trekking there in heels.

"Liam can you please DD? June needs to enjoy this tonight. I'm going to make sure she drinks enough that she takes her shoes off and gets on the dance floor," Pen hisses in a whisper when we exit the car.

"Yeah, of course. Make sure she relaxes a bit," he says, kissing his little sister on the cheek.

I've spent holidays with different families each year, and never before have I wished so much to spend more time with any of them. It takes a massive effort to not let my mind slip into imagining what it would be like to return year after year, allowing memories to build upon themselves until I know Dulcet Point like a second home.

"All good?" Liam asks, and my face must betray the ache in my chest.

I nod. "I'm just very lucky to be here with you."

He offers me a hand and I take it as we head inside. "Speaking of dancing, you owe me one tonight."

"You dance?"

"I have two younger sisters who both freaked out about not knowing how to dance before homecoming. June was the worst; she's such a perfectionist. I really hope that when I start she'll be able to take a real break." His gaze follows her.

Beyond the four of us, the only people in the ballroom are staff members making final adjustments. The decor is truly breathtaking. The dark wood of the lodge gives a homey feel to the formal affair. Matching with the deep hues of the red and green, the theme is distinctly classic. The massive tree in the corner is adorned with bows and is dripping in pearls that match the luxurious poinsettia table displays.

Guests arrive a short while later, the winners of each event, marked with medals hanging around their necks, garnering congratulations from all who pass. Once the room is packed, June is handed a microphone and thanks everyone for their contributions, highlighting the accomplishments of the young athletes who have been given life-changing resources due to this program before saying she looks forward to what they will achieve in the coming year and reminding the crowd it wouldn't be possible without them.

Champagne flows like water and cheer burns bright. Liam never leaves my side, hand resting firmly on my hip as we wander through the masses. We land in a circle with his parents, and a few other silver-haired men who I vaguely recognize, as well as Kurt, Laura, and their families. It reminds me of how the holidays used to be with Mom and Dad. I do my best not to tense and run out of the room. I belong here, just like they do.

"Liam brought home his girlfriend this year," Ally says. "This is Henri."

"Hello." I give a nod as a few members of our circle introduce themselves.

"Oh, Henrietta dear," Martha, Kurt's mother, bursts from the ring to give me a tight embrace, my nose flooding with the spiced vanilla perfume she must have bathed in. "It's been too long." She looks back at the group. "You know I always thought I'd be the one introducing her. I always thought her and Kurt would end up together."

"Is that so?" Peter asks with a cocked brow.

"Yes. They all grew up together—were so close. Henri was actually supposed to join us all on our first trip here, but there were a few complications," Martha tells them.

The muscles in my body start to seize and my gaze darts to an exit.

"She's the one who convinced Liam to hop into the slalom at the last minute. She's an absolute force to be reckoned with," Ally says, something bright flickering through her eyes, giving me a look at the fierce athlete she once was.

"So, you're to thank for me losing?" Kurt says, brows raising as a sly grin peals across his mouth. "Isn't it ironic?"

"Why would that be ironic?" Peter asks, even as a few members of the group smile, catching on.

"Because her father is the reason that this place almost went under a few years back, and now she's here, helping raise money for charity?" Kurt's tone is all innocent curiosity.

My stomach bottoms out. I tug free from Liam's grip, all eyes on me as a shaky, nervous giggle bursts from me. I mumble something about getting water or air or food—I can't quite tell what I default to because my mind turns to static, with one objective.

Get out. Now.

I dodge past caterers and finely-dressed guests to the closest door. I shove them open and step into the night. The balcony looks out over the lodge, and laughter floats up from below from guests who didn't come to the gala and are celebrating with beer and burgers.

Shit. This is what I get for not checking where I was headed. I could hide out here until the party is over, huddling in a corner trying not to freeze to death. Jumping could work—it's not too far. I go to the railing and check. If I just make sure to aim for the snow instead of the hard stone, I could make it out without any broken legs.

The door opens behind me and I spin to face whoever's decided to interrupt my impromptu escape.

"I wouldn't," Liam says. His expression is placid and unreadable. Does he hate me? I don't know what else Kurt shared. But I wouldn't blame Liam if he hated me. My dad put all of this at risk—Liam's family's legacy on this beautiful mountain. The legacy he's giving up his life in New York to pursue.

"What?"

"Jump. It's farther than it looks and the snow isn't deep enough to cushion you all that much."

"Thanks for the advice. Any alternative getaway routes you think I should consider?"

"I'll walk you out if you want to leave. If Pen and June need a driver they can call me when they want to leave." He holds out a hand, but I shrink away.

"That's it? Or are you trying to save yourself from being seen with me?" I demand.

"Fuck. Henri." He sighs and rubs the back of his neck. "You want to know what happened when you walked away?"

"Not particularly."

His gaze holds on me as he takes a step toward me. "I told Kurt and that shit-eating smirk of his that I already knew and that he was an ass for trying to get a rise out of us by exposing that in front of everyone just because he felt like he needed to compensate for his own inadequacies."

"How long have you known?" Somehow, my pulse finds a way to thrum faster.

"Since the night after our first interview. I asked Jasmine for your last name and looked you up."

"Why didn't you say anything?"

His body quivers with a rumbling unamused laugh. "Because I was pretty sure telling you that your dad's actions nearly led to my family's business closing was a sure way to make you uncomfortable."

"And you don't hate me for it?" I need to hear it.

"Did you personally tell him what to do? Did you benefit from it at all?" He closes the gap between us and cups my face with both hands.

"No, at least not knowingly."

"And that's my answer. I don't blame you." The pad of his thumb swipes over my cheek. "I can't imagine what you went through, but I don't blame you, not at all. How could I when you're so fucking perfect?"

Warmth surges from deep within me, chasing away the cold. This is the moment I've always been utterly terrified of, when all the pieces of my soul are laid bare for someone to see and I wait for them to turn away, disgusted at what they've found. But Liam, oh Liam, he's seen the shards and handled them with a reverence I can't comprehend.

"Fuck." My vision swims with tears. As they fall, he kisses them away until I have no more left to shed. Only then does he pull me to his chest, the stiff fabric of his suit jacket rubbing against my cheek.

"I get to say this, because tonight you're mine." He holds me tighter as if he's scared I'll run again. "I love you. All of you. I am better because I got to know you. You might hate fate, but I have no other explanation for how we ended up in that cab together on Thanksgiving and everything that came after."

I don't—can't—say it back, even though I know I feel the same way. But saying those words feel too much like goodbye. So I just rest there, listening to the heart of a man who loves me.

After a few long moments, we head back inside, but only because that's the only way to the exit. We're done being around other people tonight. Done sharing each other with the world.

With only a few hours left of solitude, we use them to our advantage.

He carries me into his bed and unwraps me like a present. Every touch lingers, every moment drawn out as far as we can take it. We know that this is it—the end that was always going to come.

We both stay up until midnight, breaths catching as one day rolls into the next. Sleep comes uneasily and I wake to a flurry of blankets being kicked off the bed. There's no time for talking or holding a single moment in the palms of our hands because we've overslept by thirty minutes and have to rush to make my flight.

There's a part of me that wants to say fuck it, let me reschedule, but that would only be drawing out the inevitable. The drive goes too fast and in what feels like a blink of an eye we're pulling into the packed departures line.

"I could go to the garage and park, help you get your luggage in," Liam offers with a hopeful gleam in his eye.

"It's just one bag," I remind him. "I don't need help."

"I know."

He parks along the curb and helps me with my bag. Then we just stand there, looking but not touching, both of us seeming to understand that one final kiss would ruin us. But it doesn't last as long as I wish it would because one of the airport attendants ushers him back into his car so another vehicle can unload.

I inch through security, barely holding it together, promising myself once I find my gate then I can duck into a bathroom and cry my guts out until my stomach is sore. It's a slog, but I get to the packed seating area in one piece before looking back in the direction I came from for a bathroom.

When I look up, I see a man without a bag, running straight at me, brown hair sticking up haphazardly.

I don't have a moment to collect my thoughts before he stops in front of me.

"You're going to Albuquerque?" I ask, tilting my head to read the paper ticket in Liam's hand.

"What?" His face scrunches, then he sees where I'm looking. "Oh, this? I just asked for the cheapest flight out. At the desk."

"You bought that here? I didn't know you could still do that."

"Yes. I parked the damn car and got a ticket so I could get past security. Because, Henri, baby, fuck. I don't want this to end. We can make it work. I *want* to make this work."

"Please, Liam. Don't make this harder than it needs to be." My throat tightens and fuck I would really love to be locked in a bathroom stall right now so I can let the waterworks flow without people seeing my splotchy red face.

"I can't let you go." He swallows. "How is the ending so hard when I knew what it would be from the start?"

"Because the journey to get there was so damn good. Let's not make this worse, though. Let me get on the plane." My hand clenches around the handle of my suitcase until my knuckles go white. "In three years, when I graduate, I'll come out here and look for jobs. Because by then I'll probably be sick and tired of New York. Who wants to stay in one place that long anyway, right? And maybe we're just friends, or maybe we just pick up where we left off. I don't know because as much as I want to be able to, I can't control that, and I have to trust that if the fates allow, this will all work out."

"You're trusting the fates with this?"

"Just this one time, and they better know how damn important it is." And then I kiss him one last time. Too brief. Too public. But I'll need this final taste of him to get me through. "And don't you dare say goodbye."

He stays until I have to board the plane, and even then, I wait until all other passengers have gone.

"Thank you," I whisper, my forehead pressed against his. "For giving me a Christmas that felt like mine, instead of someone else's. I'll never forget it."

I end up drinking so much cheap wine that I'm cut off by the flight attendants within the first hour and then I fall asleep for the remaining hours only to wake up with a hangover when we land.

I all but crawl into the back of my Uber at LaGuardia. Tucked in the corner of the leather seats, I pull out my phone and call the only person I want to talk to, really hoping that she hasn't gone to bed early.

"Hey, honey, we're just about to be seated for dinner—we have a late reservation. Can I call you back?" Mom answers on the second ring.

"Mom," I croak.

"Daniel, why don't you go sit. I'll meet you inside." There's a pause and then she says, "I'm right here. What do you need?"

"There's this boy . . ." And finally, I cry.

29

Liam

The first set of boxes arrives two days after Christmas. Between unpacking and Dad putting me straight to work with the onboarding processes all Dulcet Point management go through, I keep myself busy enough that I go back to the cabin, with its finicky heating system, so tired I'm able to get some sleep. Still, my dreams are full of Henri.

It doesn't help that I still have to finish up the article. I write and rewrite it three times before downing a bottle of red wine and just let it all out. What does it matter? It's not like I have anything to hide since the truth of what transpired between Henri and I won't put my job in jeopardy.

I submit it sometime close to two a.m., and the next morning I get an email from Fallon asking me if I'm sure this is the version that I want to print. Without hesitating, I tell her yes.

The morning of New Year's Eve, Dad asks me to check the invoices from the party vendors and note if we need to update anything with last-minute costs. Our New Year's party isn't as grand as what we do for Christmas.

It's more casual and involves substantially more hard liquor, which I won't complain about.

I try for the third time to type in the password to access the system, and again the tiny red script tells me it's incorrect. I growl with frustration. I don't know what the hell I'm doing and if I can't get this one simple thing right, how the hell am I supposed to run this damn place.

I slam my hand on the keyboard, the keys clacking and crunching.

"Wow, it seems like you're having fun in here," June muses as she pokes her head inside. She's been constantly checking in on me since I started and her mood hasn't improved the way I thought it would after Christmas. I've been meaning to set aside some time to talk, but I've been too busy.

"Thanks for the commentary," I grumble.

"What's the issue?" She walks over to me and looks at the sticky note I wrote the login info on. "Oh, I see. Scoot over."

I roll my chair to the side, allowing her access to the computer. She types in the user ID and password, presses enter, and steps away as I'm finally given access.

"How?"

"We change the passwords every month. There was a security breach a year back and ever since we've taken extra measures. It's less about stuff like this and more that we have a billionaire or three that love bringing their mistresses here," she explains.

"You should be doing this, not me."

"I know. But you had the chance to let me and insisted on carrying on some damn tradition." Which is not what I expected her to say.

"What the fuck are you talking about?"

"Don't act stupid. Dad said he'd talk to you about my offer and I didn't hear anything about it until Christmas dinner when he made his announcement. You could have at least given me a heads-up," she says, crossing her arms defiantly over her chest.

"Offer. I never got an offer, June. I'm completely in the dark here."

"I told Dad that if you wanted to stay in New York I would take your spot. I know how everything works; I've been around the staff for ages and can tell you everyone's names. I'm comfortable with the software you can't even log into. I put in the time and you don't even want this." She seethes, her cool exterior melting into heated anger. "This is all I have, all I'm good at." She gestures wildly at me. "You can write and do all this other shit. Why couldn't you be happy with that."

"I am. I was," I correct through my cloud of confusion. "Dad never talked to me. Why the hell didn't you bring this up before?" Is this why she's been so grumpy for the last week?

"I don't know? Because I didn't want to seem like some whiny brat who ruined Christmas because she didn't get what she wanted."

"June, you were still being an ass," Pen says, walking into the room to join us. Well, actually, she walks past us to the small balcony to lift up a small potted plant and grab a bag of what's unmistakably weed. "Fuck, yeah, I was hoping I hadn't used this already."

"Can't you just go into town and grab that?" June asks.

"Dispensary is closed for the day. This isn't too old—should be fine. Give me a second and I can roll a joint. Seems like you both need to partake now that you're coming to terms with the fact that Dad is a manipulative ass," she explains, holding the small bag to the light to inspect her finding. "Why do you think I worked so hard to get a sponsorship and leave this place?"

"He cares," I say, feebly defending the man. I've done it over and over, trying to understand him, justifying his actions. I don't want to anymore. Not with him playing with our lives like this.

"He does, but that doesn't mean he's good at showing it the right way. So, are you going to let June take over as heir apparent and stop torturing us with your moping or what?" Pen asks.

"You knew?" I ask.

"Yeah, but it's not like either of you would listen when you both act like I'm a kid."

"Whatever, we learned our lesson. Now will you roll the damn joint, Pen," June grumbles.

Pen does and we sit out back as the herbal smoke wafts up into the mid-morning air, reminiscing on all the things Dad would do. Siblings can be a fucking headache, but who else can you share your collective trauma with while laughing like total idiots.

"Liam, is that weed?" Dad's voice booms as he charges through the office.

"Yeah, you want some?" Pen offers.

"It's the middle of the work day and you're all high. I expected you to take responsibility, not to lounge around. This isn't some free ride," he demands, the vein in his forehead pulsing.

"Seems like June expected you and I to have a chat you conveniently forgot about," I tell him through my blissful haze.

"She still has years of competing left."

"If she wants to compete," I counter, "that's her choice, not yours. And it's my choice right now to say I quit. The job is June's, just like it was supposed to be this entire time. If you want this business to succeed, you need her." June reaches out and squeezes my hand. "I'm going to spend the morning with my sisters; it's been a while since we've hung out."

"Fine. Juniper, I expect you in my office first thing tomorrow to discuss this," he snaps and turns on a heel. The office door slams and June launches herself at me in a hug, squealing in a way I doubt she'd do if she wasn't sky high.

A few hours later, when I've sobered up and stuffed my stomach full of fries, I head back to the cabin, which of course is freezing since the maintenance folks won't get out here until next week. I could stay in the house, but I've put myself in this state of self-isolation.

I end up going out back to check the ice to see if it's good to skate on. It's not, but I sit on the edge, looking out across the glassy frozen surface, wondering what's next.

I have no job. No plans. My future is wide open.

Playing with the snow at my side, I build a small snowman. As I grab for another clump, I find a bit of red fabric. No, not fabric, yarn.

I dig until I pull out Henri's hat. I must have dropped it out here when I helped her off the ice and forgotten about it.

With it clutched in my hands, I run inside.

Maybe it's fate. Or maybe I'm done going with the flow and am finally ready to fight for what I want.

30

Henri

C ome on, we're going to be late!" Iris calls from our living room.

"Just a second. I need to find my hat." I toss clothes from my trip to Colorado aside, searching for the beanie Liam gifted me. It has to be in here somewhere, but I've looked through the pile strewn across the floor at least a dozen times since I got home a few days ago. "Where the hell did it go?"

My call with Mom on the car ride home was longer than I thought it would be, even with traffic. I told Mom about Liam, and about all the feelings cluttering my chest. The truth of everything I was carrying alone spilled out of me in a tidal wave I couldn't contain. Mom gave me a firm reminder that she was in fact my parent and I'm not a burden if I need to help. I know that if I heard that a month ago, I wouldn't listen, but now I'm leaning into being helped.

When I arrived at home, Iris was waiting for me with wine and, as promised, *Sex and The City* ready on the TV. I told her I needed just one day to feel like shit. She laughed in my face before telling me that I'd need longer than that. I wasn't just grieving the end of a relationship, but a future I had wished for before it was cut short. And in some way, wallowing and letting endless tears leak out of me was a show of respect for everything I felt with Liam.

After the crying sessions, she and Jasmine made sure to take me out to celebrate getting into my graduate program. They watched over my shoulder at the bar as I submitted the smaller- than- predicted payment I had to make to cover my fees. We cheersed our drinks, toasting to all the good things to come.

Now, I toss a sweater at the wall, but it floats to the floor harmlessly before it can land. God. I should just leave. Marty and Alexi are already at the venue setting up for their exclusive New Years party that people beg to be invited to and travel across the country to attend each year, and I promised we'd be there early to help.

It's just a hat, I try to tell myself.

But it's not.

It's walking through the Christmas market because he knew I wanted to without having to ask and then seeing that my ears were cold. It's insisting that I deserve to have something nice that I didn't feel like I had to earn. Evidence that Liam was in my life.

I slam my fist into the carpeted floor over and over.

My bedroom door creaks and Iris steps inside. "What is it?"

"I lost my hat," I blubber pathetically and my eyes start to sting.

Iris, patient as ever, sits on the floor with me, my head resting on her shoulder until I can compose myself to leave.

As it turns out, the chandelier-lit ballroom is nearly completely decorated as a regency era day dream. I'm fairly certain that they've chosen this theme so they can play out some sort of Mr. Darcy and Mr. Bingley forbidden romance. We arrive in time to help with a handful of floral arrangements and "test" the signature cocktails. Marty and Alexi are already in their custom outfits and hand Iris and I garment bags with our own period accurate silk gowns with high empire waistlines .

I've also been given a shimmering mask, which is required of all the guests.

It's nice to dress up and get out after holing up in Iris and my apartment for the last week.

But my optimism only lasts through the first few hours. Surrounded by people trying and failing to waltz to the string quartet positioned at the far end of the hall, I truly hope that I'll be able to push past the weight after midnight, and step into a new reality, however unlikely that is.

I make my way to the decadent buffet table with Croquembouche towers, macrons, bowls of fruit, crab puffs, and pretty much any other thing you could be craving. With a plate in hand, I work to stab at melon balls.

"Henri, I was hoping to run into you. The check for your services will be sent after the holiday," says a woman in a lavender dress. Her shiny black hair is secured back in a sleek chignon. It's not until she lowers her pearlescent mask that I recognize her.

"Fallon, I didn't expect to see you here," I say, giving up on the cantaloupe that slips off my toothpick.

"Marty and Alexi throw the best parties and I never miss them. God, last year it was celestial themed and there were enough beaded Staud dresses to last a lifetime."

"If I could get my hands on one, I'd make every excuse to wear it."

She chimes a laugh and starts to load her plate with pineapple. "Fair enough. I just wanted to thank you for helping Liam with that final article. I know it was last minute, but the final product was amazing. It's been live less than twenty-four hours and we're on track to break records for digital, though the ending was a bit unexpected. But you lived it, so I guess it wasn't much of a surprise to you."

"I wouldn't know. I still haven't read it."

"I think it would be worth your time to see the outcome of your time together. As always, he was deeply honest with his words in a way few people are. It's truly sad to see him go."

"He is something special."

"Tell him hello for me," she says with a wave before vanishing into the crowd.

"Yeah, I'll hold onto that for three years," I mutter.

The party swells around me, more guests pouring in the closer we get to midnight. By eleven, everyone is happily drunk. I dance with Iris and Jasmine and even manage to steal Marty and Alexi for a few minutes before they're pulled away by adoring guests.

But as midnight draws closer and people start to pair off, I start to wish I was somewhere else. Eventually, I give into the feeling. It's nice to know there will be another over-the-top party next year, and that I'm really not missing anything by ducking out early.

When I reach the elevator, there's a couple already there, making out against the wall, only bothering to pry themselves apart long enough to slip inside. It's a pretty easy decision to wait on the next one instead of becoming a voyeur.

As I wait, curiosity itches at me, Fallon's words weaving through my mind. In a moment of weakness, or desperation, I pull out my phone and type in *Spitfire*'s website.

There at the top, is Liam's article. The image used is a stock photo with the woman's face blurred out. The headline reads: *Always the Holiday Date, Never the Girlfriend.*

I tap on it before I can talk myself out of reading.

It might be easy to think someone who hires a date is pathetic. But I think they're more honest than most of us are. They know what they need. Support. Someone who is unequivocally in their corner.

And that's what Jane (name changed) specializes in. As a professional date, she gets to know her clients, what they need and fear, but most importantly what they seek to prove to others. She shows up for people in the ways they wish they could show up for themselves.

Reader: I have never met someone who cares so much about every person she meets, and over Christmas I was lucky enough for her to care about me.

When the elevator door dings open, I walk inside out of habit, barely pausing to press the button for the first floor.

My vision swims as I continue to read. Liam details our adventures through New York and our trip to Dulcet Point. To my surprise, he includes everything—our falling out and reconciliation after the office party, the way he moped around in my absence, only leaving out the intimate details of our relationship

Would I do it again? Hopefully I don't need to. But I think what Jane showed me and her other clients is what it feels like to be understood, setting the bar high for a future real partner.

The final line steals the breath right from my lungs.

Reader: One last thing. I'd be lying if I didn't tell you this. I think I fell in love with her, and I don't think I need to do it again with anyone else, because she's it for me.

I'm wiping my eyes when the elevator opens again, so at first I think it's a cruel trick of the light when I see the brown-haired man standing before me wearing a gray wool coat. A flash of red is gripped in a fist at his side.

"Henri." The way he says my name, like he never thought he'd get to say it again, clears up any doubt.

"What are you doing here?" I ask, hesitant to get my hopes up for nothing even as my heart keens at the sight of him. My eyes dance across the freckles on his slender nose, up to his shaggy hair, consuming all I can of him while I still have a chance to. Those final moments at the airport weren't nearly enough.

"You left your hat." He holds up the hand that's clutching it like a lifeline.

"I did." This isn't real. He came back for me. No one does that. But this is Liam, defying my every expectation and shattering my reality in the best ways.

He shakes his head. "And I let you go, when I shouldn't have."

"The resort?"

"I quit. It's June's problem now, like she wants it to be. I'm back, and I don't want to wait three years. I don't want to keep just accepting whatever is thrown at me. I'm making a fucking choice and that choice is you, Henri," he says and swallows. "If you'll have me."

Outside, the entirety of the city starts to chant as they count down to midnight.

10, 9, 8 . . .

"Yes." I rush to him.

7, 6, 5 . . .

"I want you here. I want everything with you," I say.

4, 3 . . .

My hands find his cold-nipped red face as his land on my back, fabric swishing under his fingers. Home. This is what home feels like. The place where I belong is here in his arms.

2, 1 . . .

And we kiss from one year into the next, knowing that there will be endless moments like this to come.

Acknowledgements

This story was a long time coming, going from holiday novella to romcom to what is now. It was the breath of fresh air that I needed from more moody contemporary pieces. As always I want to give the biggest shout out to Miah and Vai, they truly are friends I found because fate allowed me to. When I took on finishing this book, I was on a time crunch and both of these amazing women have helped me brainstorm and polish this story. Brooke has been a part of so many of my early projects, seeing them in their ugliest WTF is going on here forms. Her honesty and excitement keeps me going. My editor, Caitlin was one of the first people I talked to about this book, before I pushed the release and swore I'd write a fantasy instead. But here we are! She took so much care in pushing my ideas and nurturing Liam and Henri's love story.

And thank you, reader. It means so much that you picked up this story and gave it, and me, a chance.

About the Author

Marja is an author originally from Northern New Mexico, and though she doesn't live there now, she'll always claim the mountains as her home. She writes big stories built on a foundation of essential, small moments. If she's not writing or reading she's desperately wishing to nap in the sun.

For inquiries contact Marja at mjgrahamromanceauthor@gmail.com or on Instagram @mjgraham.author